A WAFFLE DEATH

A WAFFLE DEATH

AUNTIE CLEM'S BAKERY
BOOK TWENTY

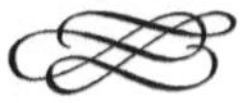

P.D. WORKMAN

 PD WORKMAN

ISBN: 9781774684832 (KDP Paperback)
ISBN: 9781774684849 (KDP Hardcover)
ISBN: 9781774684856 (Large Print)
ISBN: 9781774684863 (Lulu Paperback)
ISBN: 9781774684825 (ePub)
ISBN: 9781774685969 (Accessible Audio)

ALSO BY P.D. WORKMAN

FIND MORE BOOKS AT PDWORKMAN.COM

Auntie Clem's Bakery

Culinary & Pet Cozy Mysteries

Gluten-Free Murder

Dairy-Free Death

Allergen-Free Assignation

Witch-Free Halloween (Halloween Short)

Dog-Free Dinner (Christmas Short)

Stirring Up Murder

Brewing Death

Coup de Glace

Sour Cherry Turnover

Apple-achian Treasure

Vegan Baked Alaska

Muffins Masks Murder

Tai Chi and Chai Tea

Santa Shortbread

Cold as Ice Cream

Changing Fortune Cookies

Hot on the Trail Mix

Fateful Plateful

Cut Out Cookie

On the Slab Pie

Wedding Cake Crush

A Waffle Death

Murder Meringue Pie (Coming Soon)

Recipes from Auntie Clem's Bakery

Parks Pat Mysteries

Police Procedural Set in Canada

Out with the Sunset

Long Climb to the Top

Dark Water Under the Bridge

Immersed in the View

Skimming Over the Lake

Hazard of the Hills

Knows the Hills

Spanning the Creek

Sanctuary in the Stream

Stand Alone Suspense Novels

Looking Over Your Shoulder

Lion Within

Pursued by the Past

In the Tick of Time

Loose the Dogs

AND MORE AT PDWORKMAN.COM

*For those who stand firm
when something waffle happens*

CHAPTER 1

The warm morning sunshine spilled into the bakery and glinted off the glass of the display case at the front of Auntie Clem's Bakery. Erin studied it to make sure that everything was in order. And of course, it was. She and Vic had been doing this long enough to know how to arrange everything quickly and efficiently before opening the store in the morning. The baked goods she loved filled the case: muffins with fat blueberries bursting out of the tops, breads sprinkled with sugar, cinnamon rolls glinting with icing. The smells of yeast and spices perfumed the air. Erin walked through the front of the shop to turn the sign to Open and unlock the door. A few morning customers were already waiting outside with their piping hot coffees, ready to pick up a morning muffin or the baked goods they would require for the day or the week.

"Good morning!" Erin greeted cheerfully.

It was still early for the rest of the townspeople, so she didn't get enthusiastic smiles in response. A few muted greetings. People would be more cheerful once they finished waking up.

Vic stood behind the counter, her long blond hair pinned back in a bun and hidden by her baker's cap. Erin's young transgender employee always succeeded in looking more polished five minutes after rolling out of bed than Erin felt after an hour of preening and

1

trying to pin her dark hair back so that no locks would escape. She never even reached the door without a few strands managing to spring free.

"What can I get y'all today?" Vic asked the ladies.

Mary Lou moved forward and made a few selections. Her baking for the week. Erin knew that things were tight for the Coxes. Mary Lou struggled to make ends meet. Her husband, Roger, had lost their life savings and house in a bad investment a few years previous and, since then, the family had experienced a number of serious setbacks. Roger had been hospitalized for most of the past year but was back home again, which was an extra burden on Mary Lou financially, as well as physically and emotionally. She had one teenage son still at home to help with Roger's care, and health care workers that checked in a couple of times a day, but the lion's share of making sure that he was kept calm and happy and didn't wander still fell to her.

Erin wanted to offer Mary Lou more of the day-old baking they gave to needy families for free, but knew that she couldn't say anything about it in front of the other ladies. Mary Lou knew she could come to the back of the store to pick up day-old privately, but she was a proud woman and would not accept Erin's "charity" unless Erin managed to frame it as a favor to her, something that she couldn't get away with very often.

Mary Lou smoothed her wrinkle-free pantsuit over her hips as she waited for Vic to package up her order and put it through at the till. Erin slipped behind Vic to take up her position behind the counter to help the next customer. She smiled at Mary Lou.

"How is everyone in your home today? Everyone okay?"

Mary Lou gave a brief nod. "Yes, fine, thank you, Erin. And you? Have you recovered from your…" Mary Lou trailed off and didn't say "kidnapping" or "abduction." She probably would have preferred something more generic, like "incident," but she just let the sentence hang. Erin could fill it in as she liked.

"Oh, yes," Erin told her cheerfully. "I'm just fine. Thanks to Joshua, I'm perfectly well."

She kept a smile on her face, not letting Mary Lou see any cracks. Mary Lou didn't need anything else on her plate to worry about. Her son, Joshua, was the one who had rescued Erin—or at least found her so that the police could rescue her—and Erin knew that she couldn't say too much about what he had done. Mary Lou wanted to keep him safe. She didn't want him running around into dangerous situations, rescuing people. Let the police do the footwork. Joshua needed to be in school, earning his high school diploma, rather than pursuing a career as an investigative journalist before he was even an adult.

But Joshua had other ideas about the matter. He would, Erin hoped, go back to school in the fall with Bella Prost and the other teens. Bella was one of Erin's part-time employees and for months had been gently encouraging Joshua to return to school. Erin hoped she succeeded.

Mary Lou didn't need anything else to worry about, least of all the increased anxiety and nightmares that had plagued Erin since her abduction. It wasn't like she'd been the best sleeper before. It was a struggle to get the sleep that she needed to get to the bakery in the small hours of the morning in order to have the fresh breads and muffins ready to go when they opened.

"Now that the wedding is over, you can go back to normal," Vic told Erin. "No more wedding cake. Until the next one." She smiled cheekily. Melissa's wedding cake had been a one-off, a favor for a friend. Erin had not planned on taking on more. But Vic thought it would make a good addition to the bakery's offerings if Erin were willing to take them on.

Erin hadn't decided yet. There had been too much else going on at the same time as decorating Melissa's cake. She hadn't yet sorted out her feelings and separated the negative emotions about certain other events from that of preparing Melissa's beautiful wedding cake, which had ended up being crushed. At least Vic's creativity had saved the day so that they had still been able to pull off the fairy-tale wedding reception that Melissa had dreamed of.

"Did you get a thank you card yet?" Lottie Sturm asked the others in the bakery. "I haven't gotten a thank you for my wedding gift yet. When I was a young person, there were certain expectations…"

Erin actually had received a very nice thank you card from Melissa the week before, but she wasn't about to announce the fact to

Lottie, as it would just encourage her complaints that Melissa hadn't sent her a card yet. Erin imagined that Melissa had sent notes to those who had helped with the reception before those who had given her a gift. It had been a big reception, so there would be a lot of cards to send out. Melissa was probably attacking the process in small batches. Lottie would receive hers in the mail in the next few days.

"It isn't like it was a *real* wedding," Cindy Prost contributed. Of course she would say something like that. Cindy was Bella's mother, and her natural disposition was the opposite of her daughter's cheerful, helpful attitude. Cindy was as negative as Bella was positive.

"Of course it was a real wedding," Vic objected. "How can you say that?"

"Well, there was no groom at the reception, was there?" Cindy pointed out the obvious. Davis, Melissa's new husband, was a guest of the Tennessee penal system and would not be going to any community events in the next few years.

"But they still got married," Erin said, removing the bread and buns Lottie pointed to from the display case. "Davis doesn't have to attend the reception for the marriage to be legal."

"I'm not talking about *legal*." Cindy wrinkled her nose. "And it isn't like any of us witnessed the actual marriage, *if* there even was one. All you have is her own word on that."

"Why would she pretend to be getting married?"

"Because she wants certain benefits of being married." Lottie tittered. "But without all of the responsibilities of a wife."

Erin opened her mouth to ask what benefits Lottie was talking about, then closed it again. As far as the church ladies were concerned, any extracurricular activities outside of marriage were a sin so, as far as Lottie was concerned, Melissa had to be married to Davis for her friendly visits to the prison to progress to conjugal visits. As far as Erin knew, Melissa probably believed this too, but they had never discussed it. Why would they? Such a thing was none of Erin's business.

But it was, apparently, the business of the rest of the members of Melissa's congregation in Bald Eagle Falls. Lottie and Cindy immediately fell into a spirited debate about whether Melissa was really married in the eyes of God if she wasn't living with Davis and keeping house for him. There was more to marriage than just "visiting" with Davis at the prison.

Erin looked at Mary Lou to see what her opinion of the discussion was, but her mind appeared to be somewhere else. Erin wasn't sure she had heard a word of Lottie's and Cindy's discussion. Erin wished that she could have blocked it out herself. She didn't look at Vic. All she would need was Vic rolling her eyes expressively, and she would not be able to keep a straight face and would have to excuse herself to the kitchen to check on a batch of cookies.

"Did you hear about the waffle contest?" Erin asked in an effort to distract the ladies from the discussion about Melissa's intimate affairs.

Lottie stopped talking and looked at Erin. There was silence in the bakery.

"What waffle contest?" Vic answered obligingly, even though she knew very well what waffle contest Erin was asking about.

"Yes, what contest?" Lottie asked. She didn't actually look at all interested.

"There is a waffle recipe contest being run by The Kitchen Crew commercial bakeware company. The grand prize is a restaurant-sized waffle maker that makes twenty Belgian waffles in one go."

"Twenty waffles?"

"Yes, it has the molds for twenty waffles. You fill them all with batter, close the lid, and wait five minutes for them to cook. Open the lid, and presto—twenty perfectly cooked waffles."

"Are you planning to open a waffle house?" Cindy asked dryly. "Don't you have enough to keep you going with the ownership of the bakery?"

"I think waffles would be a great offering for Auntie Clem's. Fresh or frozen. Wouldn't you rather buy waffles made right here in the bakery than those frozen ones at the grocery?" Vic asked. "Sometimes those have been sitting in the grocer's freezer for months, and they're just mass-produced and churned out. Nothing like a handcrafted waffle made from one of Erin's special recipes."

Cindy looked as if she didn't know whether to agree or to find something nasty to say about Erin's recipes. If she didn't want to get thrown out of the bakery, she should probably keep her mouth shut.

"Have you already submitted a recipe to this contest?" she asked Erin stiffly. "I suppose you already have a dozen waffle recipes ready to go when you win that big waffle iron."

"Not yet." Erin handed Lottie's order to Vic to ring up on the register. "You're only allowed to enter one recipe into the contest, and I'm still trying to design the *perfect* gluten-free waffle recipe. It has to be just right if I want to have any hope of winning the waffle iron."

"It's never going to be exactly like a normal waffle." Cindy was not afraid to rain on Erin's parade. She never complained about the gluten-free baked goods she bought from Erin every week. They were delicious, and no one would ever have guessed they were gluten-free unless they were told so. But Cindy was right; they would never have the exact same flavor and consistency as a traditional Belgian waffle. A lot of kitchen chemistry and experimentation went into getting the recipe for each of the baked goods that Erin sold *just right*. So that they were not only as good as the regular gluten goods offered at the grocery store, but much better.

"I'm thinking of a pumpkin-based recipe," Erin told them, ignoring Cindy's jab and pretending she had asked in a nice way what Erin had in mind for the contest. "Pumpkin and spices, nutmeg and cinnamon. Nice and light and crisp, but with a hearty, rich flavor. Something that will remind people of Thanksgiving and Christmas and all of the good feelings surrounding those holidays and could be used for sweet or savory toppings."

"Mmm. I love pumpkin spice," Lottie confessed. "*Anything* pumpkin spice." She beamed at Erin as if she were a child who had just pulled off a perfect math score. "Great idea!"

"That sounds really good," Vic agreed. "Drizzled with a little syrup and topped with whipped cream…"

Someone else moaned in agreement. Erin smiled, pleased. Not everyone liked pumpkin spice or the idea of waffles that could be savory or sweet, so she was happy to hear the approvals of her plan.

"I hope you win," Lottie said. "Then you can start including those waffles in your regular offerings."

"What about chocolate chip waffles?" Cindy suggested. "Or blueberry."

"If she had that big waffle iron, she could make any kind you liked." Lottie licked her lips. "Blueberry or raspberry, cinnamon swirl, chocolate chip, *white* chocolate chip…"

"M&M," Lottie took up the list of candies that could be added to the batter.

"M&M?" Cindy repeated, sounding shocked.

"If you can put them in cookies, why not in waffles? Or gumdrops!"

CHAPTER 2

The ladies finished their purchases and left, still discussing what additives were or were not appropriate for waffles.

When the early morning rush was finished and they were tidying up and preparing cookies and pizza pretzels, Vic looked over at Erin. "So, you don't have any concerns about entering this waffle contest?"

"Concerns?" Erin shook her head. "No, what kind of concerns? It's a big company, I'm sure it's legit. And they say you retain the ownership of your recipe. So many of these contests are actually scams to get your recipes. You transfer rights to them whether you win or not. With this contest… the worst that could happen is that I develop a really good waffle recipe and don't win the prize."

"No, I was thinking more along the lines of… the other contests we've been involved with the last couple of years."

There was the Fall Fair contest where Erin had entered a gluten-free stack cake. She had won the contest, which had been very exciting. The cruise that she had won, however, had been another story. Things had gone off the rails surprisingly quickly—if a boat could be said to go off the rails.

And then there was the CO2 contest she had judged, where entrants used CO2 to make fizzy drinks or ice cream. She should have known when she found Beryl in the walk-in freezer at the restaurant that things were not going to end well.

Erin grimaced back at Vic. "Well, I wasn't thinking about any of that stuff. I'm sure that… everything will be just fine. Nothing will go wrong this time."

~

Erin's sweetheart, Terry Piper or, as Vic liked to call him, "Officer Handsome," stopped by during the afternoon lull to refill his water bottle and get a gluten-free doggie biscuit for his furry partner, K9. He sat down for a moment while Erin went into the kitchen to fill the bottle, and smiled at her when she returned, a dimple appearing on his cheek. Boyishly handsome with a five o'clock shadow and a dimple. Erin's heart did a flip when she looked at him. She handed him the water bottle, looking away and hoping he wouldn't see her blush. It was rather silly that she should have such a physical reaction to his good looks when they were living together and the magic should have worn off. After all of the challenges that they had been through, they were like a comfortable old married couple.

Sometimes.

But there were still those sparks.

When she looked back at Terry, his eyes were dancing, and she knew he was thinking the same thing. He scratched K9's ears and looked to see if he was finished eating his cookie.

"Well, buddy, I guess we'd better hit the pavement again."

K9 got to his feet and shook himself off as if he were wet. Then he was ready for them to be on their way again.

~

Erin looked at the clock on the wall, frowning. It was nearly time to close, and she had expected Naomi to stop by with a couple of platters. Erin had taken treats over to The Book Nook for their book club meeting, and Naomi had said that she would return the platters when they were done. She was usually very good about it, but The Book

Nook closed earlier than Auntie Clem's Bakery on Tuesdays, and Erin was expecting her to have returned them by now.

"What's up?" Vic asked, noticing Erin's look at the clock.

"I think I'll just pop over to The Book Nook to see if I can get those platters back."

"They're probably closed by now."

"Maybe. I'll just see. If they are, I guess I'll get them back tomorrow."

Vic nodded. The bakery was not busy; she could certainly handle things by herself for the five minutes it would take Erin to duck into The Book Nook and retrieve the platters. Even if she stopped to talk to Naomi for a few minutes.

Erin didn't bother to take off her apron. It would only be a minute and she wouldn't spill anything on it at the bookstore.

It was hot and muggy outside. The bright sun reflected off the colorful storefronts and awnings of Main Street, dazzling Erin. She wasn't sure she would ever get used to Tennessee summers. She should be able to handle them; after all, she had been born in Tennessee, but she had spent most of her years in Maine and other places in the north and had apparently lost any tolerance for the southern sun. She was sweating by the time she got into The Book Nook, which didn't seem like it should be possible. The bells over the door jingled as she walked in, just like they did at Auntie Clem's Bakery. A friendly little sound that announced the possibility of a sale. Erin looked around for Naomi but didn't see her immediately.

That wasn't unusual. With all of the shelves blocking her line of sight, Naomi could be a few feet away from her and Erin wouldn't know it. Especially if she were crouching down to shelve a book. Erin walked farther into the store, looking around, peeking between book-shelves, expecting to see the store owner at any moment. The front door had been unlocked, so Naomi couldn't have closed and gone home already.

"Naomi?"

Erin stood on her tiptoes and spun in a slow circle. "Are you here?"

She was probably taking a bag of trash out to the dumpster

behind the building. Erin held herself still and waited. Naomi would only be gone from the store for a minute or two.

The seconds ticked by. Erin looked at her phone several times, but that didn't help the time go any faster. She walked through the employee-only area in the back and pushed the crash bar on the back door to open it. She looked around, but Naomi wasn't in the parking lot. Neither was her car. Had she really left and forgotten to lock the front door? Maybe there had been an emergency and she had been too distracted, forgetting everything she had to do before leaving. It was understandable. Things like that happened sometimes.

As Erin walked back toward the front door, trying to decide the right thing to do, she saw that the door to the stairs was cracked open. What if Naomi had fallen and broken her leg, or worse? What if she was lying hurt or unconscious in the basement in need of rescue? Erin opened the door farther. The hinges creaked noisily, making her wince and put her shoulders up as if to brace herself against what was coming next.

"Naomi? Naomi, are you down there?"

She thought she could hear someone moving around, but there was no answer.

"Naomi?"

Was she hurt and unable to answer? Or maybe she was moving around the basement stockroom with earbuds in and couldn't hear Erin. Erin waited a few more seconds, each one ticking by with several beats of her thumping heart. She stepped down to the first step.

"Naomi?" she called again, as if being one step closer would make all the difference.

There were noises. The shuffling of shoes or books? Or someone lying on the floor writhing in distress? Erin tilted her head, trying to see into the basement before she was all the way down the stairs, but it was impossible to see through the walls and shelving units.

Erin tiptoed. She wasn't sure why; she had called out to Naomi already and wanted her to hear her. She didn't like intruding on Naomi's "employees only" space. A stair creaked, and she winced. But she was down to the bottom of the stairs in a few more seconds. She looked around. She could say that she was looking for her platters. Or for Naomi. But she felt like she was trespassing. She hesitated, deciding whether to complete her search or just run upstairs and pretend that she hadn't ever been down there.

But she was just there to make sure that Naomi was okay and to figure out what to do about locking the store up for her. It was the neighborly thing to do when you discovered that another store owner had accidentally left the place unlocked.

Erin didn't call out again, but made a swift circuit. She could go through the stockroom once and then go upstairs, knowing she had checked everything out and done the right thing.

It was creepy. She loved libraries and bookstores, but the basement of The Book Nook seemed hollow and ominous. She was sure Naomi wasn't down there. She wasn't listening to her headphones and just hadn't been able to hear Erin calling her. She wasn't restocking shelves or unpacking a box of new books. There was no one there. Maybe she had misheard the sounds. She'd always had a vivid imagination.

There was a hint of cologne in the air, a smell that a man she had once known had worn. It sent a shiver over her. One of Naomi's employees must wear the same scent. She didn't know the part-timers very well, just Naomi herself.

Erin rounded the corner of the shelves and saw a crumpled form at the end of the aisle.

CHAPTER 3

$\mathcal{E}$rin ran forward. It was only a few strides sprinting, and she knew it wasn't Naomi by the time she got there. The shape was bigger and bulkier than Naomi. The shiny black shoes on the legs lying akimbo were men's shoes, not ladies'.

"Are you okay?" Erin asked breathlessly. The words came out as barely a whisper, even though she had meant to be loud and authoritative. She could take charge, give the person some medical assistance, and everything would be okay. It was just someone who had tripped or fainted—easily fixed.

The figure didn't move, even when Erin reached down and shook him by the arm.

"Sir? Are you all right?" she whispered.

He wasn't all right. Something was very wrong with him. There was no resistance in the muscles and joints. No resistance to her shaking. She pulled him up slightly to look at his face and assess what kind of medical help he needed.

She saw the hilt of a knife sticking out of his chest, but ignored it, looking at his still, gray face. This was bad. Worse than she could have imagined.

Erin felt for a pulse on his neck, breathing loudly through her mouth. She had a sense of urgency and, at the same time, felt like she was pushing her way through concrete. She felt for her phone and eventually found it in one of her apron pockets. She pushed the button to wake it up. They would need a stretcher or gurney of some kind to get him out of there. They needed to be prepared for a trauma, and she wasn't sure if anyone in Bald Eagle Falls had the required training. There was only one ambulance in town, assuming it hadn't been called out somewhere. Was it stocked with blood? Enough to get this man to the city for treatment before he bled out?

She couldn't seem to get her fingers to push the right buttons on the screen to initiate a phone call. Eventually, there was a series of beeps and Call Failed popped up on the screen. Erin tried Terry's phone number instead of the emergency dispatcher's number. At least she would be able to get through to him. He would sort things out and ensure everything was taken care of.

Despite her best efforts, she wasn't able to avoid looking at the hilt of the knife. She remembered Jack Ward, a knife hilt sticking out of his back, talking and complaining to her about getting stabbed. He had miraculously survived until they could get him to the hospital and surgery. He recovered from the stab wounds faster than Terry had recovered from his head injury. Maybe this victim would be lucky too. Maybe he could still be saved if she could get help.

She looked at her phone, but the call to Terry had also failed.

She didn't want to touch the man. Her flesh crawled and she could hardly bring herself to look at him, but she forced herself to put a finger to his neck, looking for his carotid pulse. Or maybe she would be able to feel him breathing. But she couldn't find any sign of life.

That didn't mean he couldn't be saved. She'd seen things on crime TV that were unbelievable. People that police thought were murder victims when they arrived at a scene but who had survived to name their attacker and recover and live for years. She didn't know how long or what their quality of life was, but just the fact that they had survived when the cops thought they were dead was miraculous.

She took a deep breath and let it out. She tapped Terry's name once more on her phone, and it again failed. The basement was blocking her signal—too much concrete. Or maybe there was radon or something that interfered with the signal. But she wasn't going to be able to get through while she remained downstairs.

Erin abandoned the man crumpled on the floor and hurried up the stairs. She was back at Auntie Clem's in a minute, the phone to her ear, breathing heavily. It shouldn't have taken so much out of her to go up the stairs and back to the bakery. It must have been the adrenaline. She couldn't be that out of shape.

"Erin?" Vic looked at her with wide eyes. "What's wrong? What happened?"

Erin imagined she must be pale and wide-eyed. Or Vic had been startled by her dashing back into Auntie Clem's as if she were being chased. She waved a hand at Vic to indicate that she would explain when she could, waiting for Terry to pick up the phone.

"Erin," Terry's voice was calm and pleasant, "are you off already?"

"Need help—someone in the basement of The Book Nook. Hurt. Stabbed." Erin's sentences were short because of her breathing. And maybe because she was having trouble putting coherent sentences together. It seemed like it took way too many words to explain what was happening. And the longer she took explaining, the longer it was going to take for help to arrive.

"What?" Terry's voice was now urgent. But he didn't make her repeat herself or calm down and take longer to explain. "I'll be over there right away. Are you there now?"

"No. Auntie Clem's. No signal."

"Stay put until someone comes to get you."

"Okay."

He hung up. She knew he had to hang up on her to call the dispatcher and get an ambulance and the rest of the police department over to The Book Nook, but she still felt hurt that he had disconnected without even saying goodbye. Or that she had done a good job and he was proud of her.

There would be questions.

She knew there were going to be a lot of questions.

CHAPTER 4

Bald Eagle Falls was a small town. It didn't take long before Erin heard the sirens. The sounds grew louder and louder until they were piercing. Then Terry was there. He pulled his car in front of The Book Nook. The red and blue lights danced across the front wall of the bookstore. Terry didn't come to Auntie Clem's first, but waited for Stayner to arrive. Stayner left his cruiser and walked over to join Terry. Terry moved cautiously into The Book Nook with his gun drawn, K9 at his side, and Stayner just behind him and to the other side. They were graceful, like dancers or synchronized swimmers. Or like an air show with planes moving in tandem. Their movements were neat and precise. Then they were out of her view, and she could only imagine them proceeding through the store and down the stairs to the basement.

They were back out before Erin expected them to be. Terry had put his gun back in its holster. There was no one else in The Book Nook, of course. No one he had to protect himself or his partner from. He entered the store, looking at Erin with concern.

"Erin, what—" He stopped short, the words dying away as he stared at her. Erin looked at Vic, then followed Terry's eyes and looked down at her apron, which was smeared with red. She wiped at it but, of course, it didn't come out. She might have some chance if she soaked it in cold water right away. And being white, it could be bleached.

"Tell me that's cherry pie filling," Terry choked out.

That brought back unwelcome memories. Erin shook her head. "No. Not pie filling."

But he'd seen the body. He knew.

"Sit down," Terry told her. "Take off the apron and give it to me first. Then sit down." He motioned to one of the chairs at the front of the bakery, which they used for the ladies' tea on Sundays.

Erin fumbled behind her back for the string to pull it loose, but her fingers were numb and clumsy. She looked back toward The Book Nook. Stayner must be the one preserving the scene. The sheriff would want a look at it, and then they would collect what evidence they could and call the city about getting the body transported to their morgue. Hopefully, that wouldn't take more than a few hours, because bodies that sat out in the Tennessee summer heat quickly began to break down, which wouldn't be nice. Erin could smell it already.

Terry reached for her and, putting a hand on her waist to still her, reached around her to pull the string and help her to remove the apron.

"What did you see down there? Tell me slowly."

The same thing that *he* had seen down there, Erin imagined. She tried to keep her thoughts slow and orderly.

"I thought Naomi would be there, but she wasn't. I went downstairs. The door was open and I thought she must be downstairs in the stock room. I needed to pick up my platters. She always returns them when she says she is going to."

"From the book club treats?"

Erin nodded. "Yes. Right. I went over looking for them. And Naomi wasn't there. I went downstairs to look for her, but then…"

Terry waited. Erin waited for him to fill it in himself. She didn't want to have to describe the body or the scene. He had seen it for himself.

He didn't say anything. Erin made a little gesture of impatience.

"Well, *you* saw it."

"You need to tell me what you saw."

"I saw his shoes, and then his legs, and then his whole body. I tried to call the dispatcher. I tried to call you. The call wouldn't go through."

"So then, what did you do?"

"I tried…" She grimaced, squinching her eyes closed. "Tried to take his pulse, see if he was still alive. Couldn't get a pulse, so I left him and came back here to call you."

"How long between when you found the body and you called me?"

"I don't know. Thirty seconds."

He frowned. "Longer than that."

Erin didn't know how he could be so confident about that. But he was probably right. She had probably misjudged the amount of time during those adrenaline-filled minutes.

"Maybe a minute."

"And you couldn't find a pulse."

"No."

"So he couldn't have gotten up and walked away."

Erin stared at him. "No."

"There was no one down there, Erin."

Erin shook her head in disbelief. "What are you talking about? I saw him. I wasn't just hallucinating. I touched him. He was there. And he *was* dead."

"You don't think… that it could have been a prank of some kind? Someone who was trying to scare or fool you?"

"No. I think I've seen enough—" Erin broke off. She didn't want to talk about how many dead bodies she had seen since coming to Bald Eagle Falls. That was sort of a sensitive topic, and she didn't want to think about it. "I know the difference between someone dead and someone who is just playing a prank."

Though she had argued with herself that maybe he could still be revived, Erin doubted that was true. That was just her brain looking for a way out of the situation she found herself in. She was just trying to rationalize. The man had been dead. There could be no doubt of that fact.

"Was he..." Terry looked uncomfortable. He sat in the chair across from her and put his hand over hers. "When you touched him, you couldn't find a pulse."

"No."

"What did the body feel like?"

"I don't want to think about that!"

"I need to know. How warm or cool it was. How stiff. Any details you can tell me to help get this sorted out."

"He was warm. His skin didn't feel... it felt normal. Not stiff."

"So, if he was dead, he hadn't been that way very long."

"He was dead!"

He just continued to look at her, waiting for her to consider his statement.

"Yes. He hadn't been that way for very long," Erin agreed. "I thought that if I got help... they might still be able to do something for him. Like they did for Jack."

"Jack?" Terry looked blank. "What does Jack have to do with this? Jack Ward?"

"Because he was stabbed. Like Jack. I was hoping that... if they treated him... they could save him, like Jack."

"But Jack was conscious when you found him. He wasn't dead."

"I know. But... he had the knife in him. Buried to the hilt."

"Jack did? Or the body in The Book Nook."

"Both. That's why... I thought maybe if they repaired the damage, they could get his heart going, and he would be okay. I mean..." Erin looked away from Terry, knowing that her thoughts had not been logical, "I know that's crazy. I know there's no one in Bald Eagle Falls who could do that, and it would take too long to get him to the city. But that's just what my brain was doing... trying to find a way that he might still be okay. I know that... they wouldn't actually be able to do anything for him."

Terry nodded sympathetically. "I understand. Tell me about this knife. Where was he stabbed? What kind of a knife was it?"

"It was in his chest. I don't know what kind..." Erin tried to picture it again in her mind. She had not taken much in, but she had stared at the knife handle for long enough that she should be able to give him some description. "I think… similar to the one that Jack was stabbed with. It wasn't a folding knife, like a pocketknife. Or a kitchen knife. But… something meant for fighting."

"A combat knife."

"I guess so, yes."

"Can you describe the handle?"

"Black… with indentations on it, for grip, you know? Shaped for your hand?"

Terry nodded, writing it down. "Okay. And can you describe the man?"

Erin didn't want to. She wanted to forget what she had seen. She didn't want to talk about it and cement it into her memory. She wanted to forget she had ever seen his face. She shook her head and covered her eyes with both hands.

"I'm sorry, Erin." Terry squeezed her hand. "I'm sorry that you saw this and that it happened to you. But I need to get as many details as possible about what happened and who this man was. Without a body, it's pretty hard to identify him, but maybe if there is a missing person report, we'll be able to figure it out. For that, I need a physical description."

She shook her head again, hands still over her eyes. "He was… a man, white, brown eyes and hair. Going a little bit gray, I guess. Forties, I think, but looked older… dressed in a t-shirt."

"Hair was long or short?"

"Short… thinning a bit in front, longer in the back, down to his collar or a little below it."

"I know height and weight would be pretty difficult to describe when you only saw him lying on the floor…"

"A little overweight. He was a— he was a little heavy in the face, if you know what I mean? Bags under his eyes, a bit jowly, sagging." She touched her throat, then shrugged. "Past his prime."

"It wouldn't be easy to move him."

Erin knew he wasn't trying to criticize her or say that he doubted her story, but the statement still angered her.

"Are you saying that he wasn't there? Or that I must not be telling you everything? That I helped to move him?"

"No. None of that. We're just trying to figure out what happened."

"I'm telling you what I saw."

"You saw a man who had been stabbed to death lying in The Book Nook basement. And five minutes later, when we got here, he was gone."

"I don't know the second part. But if *you* say so."

She could play the doubt game too. Maybe he was the one who was lying or mistaken about what he had found at the bookstore. Erin rubbed her forehead and folded her hands on the table. She didn't understand how any of this could be happening.

"Maybe you don't think that I found anyone there at all. Maybe you think it was just a hallucination or I am looking for attention."

"No. I don't. Even if I did, there's the state of your apron."

Erin looked down and realized she wasn't wearing it anymore. Of course not. Terry had taken it away. Because it had been smeared with red. "Right. I forgot."

"I know that you saw something, that you were down there and got blood on your apron. But I'm telling you, there's no one down there now. So, something about your story doesn't square. There wasn't long enough for someone to get a body out of the basement. Bodies are not easy to move. And it means that someone was in the bookstore when you were there. Probably more than one person, to be able to get it out so quickly."

Erin shook her head. "There wasn't anyone else there."

"How do you know that?"

"I didn't see anyone," Erin insisted. "I looked through the store before I went down to the basement. If there had been anyone there, I would have seen them."

"They could have ducked behind a shelf so that you couldn't see them. Or hidden in the bathroom. Did you check? And there is a back room on the main floor, just a small one, with a coffee service counter. And the loading dock. Did you go in there?"

Erin nodded. "I looked out the back door because I thought Naomi might be taking her trash to the bins. So I had to walk through the back room."

"And there was no one there? No one could have been hiding anywhere?"

Erin shook her head. She didn't want to think that there could have been anyone in the store with her. Watching her. Maybe wondering if he were going to have to stab her to death too. She shuddered. "I didn't see anyone. I walked through the whole store. If someone else had been there, I would have known it."

Terry made a couple more notes in his notepad. But Erin was afraid that he wasn't writing down what she said, that there couldn't have been anyone else in the store. Instead, he was writing down how she was wrong. How there must have been someone else in The Book Nook just waiting for her to leave again so he could remove the body from the scene.

"Vic, maybe you could get Erin a cup of coffee?" Terry said, raising his voice slightly. "Hot and sweet. For shock."

"I don't need anything. I'm fine."

"I can see you shaking. You should have something to calm your nerves and keep you focused."

She wasn't shaking because of fear, but shuddering at the thought of someone else being in the bookstore. Over what she had seen in the basement. Over the idea that the killer had probably stood just a few feet away from her, watching and waiting to see what she would do.

"Have something to warm you up," Terry insisted. "I really think you need it."

"In this heat? I need something to cool me down, not warm me up. I was soaking wet when I got back here." Erin plucked at the sleeve of her limp blouse. "I don't even remember my feet touching the stairs."

"Well, they must have," Terry gave her a smile. No dimple this time. He was too serious, too concerned about her. "I'm pretty sure you didn't learn to fly overnight."

"I wish I could. That would be really convenient." Erin's mind wandered, thinking of all of the things she could get done more efficiently if she could fly from one place to another instead of having to drive or walk. Zip here, zip there. Quick as a wink.

Vic brought two cups of coffee over to the table, setting them down gently in front of Terry and Erin. Erin picked hers up and took a tiny sip. It was too hot. She didn't want to scald her throat.

"There's really no one in the basement?" she asked Terry, not sure she believed it.

"Well, Stayner is over there now. Whoever else has arrived since I left. But a body… no, I'm afraid not."

CHAPTER 5

*E*rin had answered all of the questions she could, posed first by Terry and then by Sheriff Wilmot as they tried to sort out what had happened to the body between the time Erin had abandoned it and the time that Terry and Stayner went down the stairs to look for it. And what had happened before that—how the man had gotten into the basement in the first place and been stabbed, and by whom. None of it made any sense. So after having answered everything she possibly could, Erin went home. Terry asked Vic to keep an eye on her, which wouldn't be hard, since Vic lived in the loft above Erin's garage and spent much of her time in the house. She wouldn't have left Erin alone anyway. She didn't need anyone telling her to make sure Erin was okay.

"This is crazy," Vic said, putting the kettle on to boil. "How could a body just disappear like that? And what was it doing down there in the first place? It isn't like Naomi killed someone! There's no way."

"No," Erin agreed. It was true that anyone could be a killer if pushed far enough, if the stakes were high enough, but if someone had been pushing Naomi like that, they would have known about it. They would have seen the stress in her life, how she was becoming increasingly desperate. But Naomi was always pleasant, relaxed, and laid back. When things when wrong for a library event,

24

she always made lemons into lemonade and came out on top, smiling away and not even breaking a sweat. Erin admired her for her poise.

They would have known if something was wrong.

"Do you know who it was?" Vic asked.

Erin looked at her, not following the question. "That killed him?"

"No, who the victim was. You didn't say. Just that there was a man, a body, it wasn't anyone you knew?"

"No one from Bald Eagle Falls," Erin confirmed, shaking her head.

"Yeah. That's really weird. What would some out-of-towner be doing in the basement of The Book Nook to begin with? He just walked into the bookstore and went downstairs? No one noticed him come in or sneak off?"

"I don't know… Naomi wasn't there. No one was there. Why would the door be left unlocked with no one there to mind the store?"

Vic picked up the whistling teapot and poured water into a couple of mugs. She was frowning. "You don't think something happened to her, do you? To Naomi? Is she missing? Was she abducted by whoever killed the man?" She placed one mug on the table in front of Erin.

"No." Erin picked a teabag and dangled it into her cup. "Terry called her and she was okay. She just had an appointment this afternoon. She wasn't planning to be there. She said that Dave was supposed to lock up."

"And was Terry able to get ahold of him?"

"He was trying. He didn't answer, but people don't always answer right away. He might have turned it off for dinner or a movie, or be out of the calling area."

"Terry doesn't think that anything happened to him?"

"There wasn't any other sign of violence. No sign that there'd been a fight or burglary or abduction."

"Just a dead guy in the basement," Vic summarized, shaking her head.

"Yeah. Perfectly normal, right?"

Vic rolled her eyes. "For Bald Eagle Falls? I'm beginning to think so."

They sipped their tea in silence for a few minutes.

Orange Blossom finished eating his dinner and, seeing as Erin was still in the kitchen, he rubbed against her legs and yowled, waiting for her to realize that she hadn't given him enough food. Erin shushed him and scratched his ears. "You've had plenty. It's time to curl up and have a nap."

But he kept getting progressively louder. Erin winced. She hated it when he got so loud and she had to start worrying about neighbor complaints. Besides the fact that she couldn't hold a conversation in the same room with him or hear herself think.

"Blossom. Blossom!"

The cat quieted slightly to see what she had to say.

"Be quiet! You're finished eating. No more."

He gave a long, low, drawn-out meow that was almost a growl. Erin shook her finger at him. "That's enough! Go find Marshmallow. Have a nap."

Marshmallow, the rabbit, never begged for more. He was always placidly happy with whatever she gave him and would lollop back into the living room when he was done, to lie down on his side in front of the couch. Or behind it, if there were too many people around or he didn't want any attention.

Orange Blossom started to yowl again, and Erin pushed him away with the side of her foot. "No more. Be quiet now."

Each time he started to make noise, she pushed him away, until he finally withdrew into the living room in a huff, leaving Vic and Erin to their tea.

"Do you think Dave forgot to lock up?" Vic asked. "Could he have just walked away without locking the front door?"

"I guess anything is possible. Some people are forgetful or easily distracted."

Erin had never known Dave to be absent-minded, but anyone could be distracted by bad news, or excitement over his evening plans, or could be on a medication that made him forget things he would otherwise have remembered.

"Someone could have picked the lock," Erin said. "It wasn't very secure."

"Who would know how to do that? And wouldn't the police be able to tell if the lock was picked?"

"More people than you think. On TV, the police can always tell, but if a person is careful, he can pick a lock without scratching it. Or if it is old, it already has a bunch of scratches and nicks. They can tell if it was forced with a crowbar—but it wasn't. But if an expert picked it, they wouldn't know the difference."

"Could you have picked the lock?"

Erin shrugged. "It wasn't very secure," she repeated.

Vic gave a knowing smile and chuckled. She sipped her tea. "So it was unlocked when you got there, right? You didn't decide to pick the lock instead of waiting until tomorrow to get the trays back?"

"Why would I do that? They weren't that important. And why would I go poking through the rest of the store? I would just grab the platters and lock the door again. Naomi had already washed them and put them to the side for me."

Vic sighed dramatically. "Well then, why do you think someone broke in?"

"Maybe they didn't break in. Maybe the victim let them in. Maybe he had hidden out in the basement just so he could let his accomplice in. And then…" Erin tried to think of the next step. "Then they met…"

"And the victim's accomplice stabbed him? For no reason?"

"I'm sure he had a reason. I just… don't know what. They were fighting over something of value. Maybe… a rare book. A first edition or a misprint, or something that just came out and he had to get his hands on it." Erin knew that none of her ideas made any sense. Naomi didn't sell used books or antiques. She sold new books. Popular stuff that would sell well. If she had to special order something obscure, she demanded upfront payment, so that the person couldn't change their mind when it got there. Naomi might complain about the skyrocketing prices of books with the pulp shortage, but she didn't have a bunch of really valuable books lying around or a lot of cash in the till any more than Erin did.

CHAPTER 6

"So…" Erin stared through the kitchen window behind Vic, which looked from the kitchen into the backyard, eyes lingering on the gravel parking pad on the other side of the fence where Willie's truck would have been parked if he were home. She wanted to talk about something other than the man who had been stabbed in the basement of the bookstore. Really, anything other than that. "Where's Willie tonight?"

Vic looked over her shoulder as if she, too had to check to see if Willie's truck might be there. "I don't know. He didn't say what he was doing tonight."

"You're not expecting him?"

"No. He said he probably wouldn't be around. Working late or going on a trip, I guess. I don't know."

Erin would have found it challenging to live with a man who was as secretive as Willie. Private was probably a better word. It wasn't that he had anything to hide, just that he saw his business matters as his own business. And when someone worked in mining precious minerals, he had to keep things to himself to keep anyone else from jumping his claim. Did people still jump claims like in the westerns? Or was that a thing of the past with modern land title registries?

She liked Willie and had once considered pursuing a deeper relationship with him, but Erin had backed off when it had become clear that Vic was interested in him. Erin had also been interested in Terry, so it seemed like the gracious thing to leave Willie to Vic. On reflection, she was glad that she had. Vic's temperament was better suited to someone as independent as Willie. She wasn't concerned that he wasn't home every night and didn't tell her everything he was doing. Erin was afraid she would have given up on the relationship long ago.

"What?" Vic asked, looking at Erin. "I don't need to know where he is every minute of the day."

"I didn't say that you did."

"No, but you get that look."

"What look?" Erin shrugged and tried to blank her face, to keep any "look" from settling there.

"That look that says I'm being naive or should be worried about it. I'm not worried. He can do what he likes."

But Vic sounded like she did care. She sounded like she was trying to cover up what she was really feeling. Normally it was okay if Willie wasn't going to be back overnight, but maybe something was going on this time that made Vic anxious.

"So... it's okay?" Erin asked. "Everything is okay?"

"Of course."

"You didn't have a fight?"

Vic opened her mouth to deny it, then stopped, saying nothing, her mouth still open. Maybe Erin had hit on it. They had fought and Vic was concerned that Willie was still mad, which was why he wasn't there tonight.

"We had a *discussion*," Vic said finally.

"The kind where you don't both agree with each other?"

"The kind where... you are each calmly laying out your differences of opinion."

"Calmly?"

Vic sipped her tea, hiding her face behind the mug. "Initially, yes."

"What about?"

"Nothing." Vic's shoulders rose and fell. "Personal stuff."

"Okay." Erin accepted this and tried to redirect the conversation as if she weren't worried about whether her friend was happy or not. "What's he been working on lately, anyway? He always has so many projects on the go. But always at least one really good one."

"Mining. Some odd jobs around the house. A few things to finish up home renovation jobs where Mr. Monroe had left people in the lurch. Some computer stuff." Vic's voice trailed off.

Some of the *computer stuff* Willie had been working on a year before had been for Nelson Dyson, one of the members of the Dyson clan, though Nelson said that he had split off his own organization. Erin didn't know whether that was good or bad. Was his new organization still organized crime? Was Willie involved in anything illegal or unethical in his dealings with Nelson? Was there any personal danger? Not just of being arrested, but being caught in the middle of some kind of violence?

"He's good at search and rescue. Maybe we could get him involved in the search for the dead man," Erin suggested with a short laugh.

"I don't think it counts as search and rescue if they're already dead. I think then it becomes recovery."

"Or zombie hunting." Erin giggled.

"What kind of tea did you have?" Vic asked, pretending to be serious as she looked at the tag on Erin's tea. "What did they put in there? Jimson weed?"

"No weed," Erin assured her. "Just nice, calming lavender."

Vic shook her head. "Even if someone did pick the lock or break into The Book Nook," she returned to the previous topic as if there had been no intervening conversation, "how would they get a body out of there so fast? You would need at least two people to get a body up the stairs, wouldn't you? Unless he was a giant, and then I don't think he'd fit on the staircase. That stairway is pretty narrow."

Erin had been thinking about that herself and, at first, she had not been able to come up with the answer, but then she had remembered how Naomi normally got cases of books—which could also be very heavy—down to and up from the basement.

"The elevator."

"The elevator?" Vic repeated. "The Book Nook doesn't have an elevator."

Erin nodded. "It does. From just inside the loading dock down to the stock room. Can you imagine if Naomi had to take every case of books up and down the stairs one at a time? Or a partial box at a time if it was too heavy for her?"

"She has an elevator?" Vic repeated.

"Yes. It's not big. But big enough for a couple of stacks of delivery boxes. If she gets a delivery of six cases of books, she can just put them all straight on the elevator, send the elevator downstairs, and unload them in the stock room."

"That's very smart. I wish we had an elevator at Auntie Clem's. I hate having to take those big bags of flour down the stairs. Or back up again. It would be so much easier if you could throw the bags on an elevator and then unload them at the bottom."

Erin had envied Naomi her elevator more than once, and agreed with Vic. She really hated carrying heavy things on the stairs, going up or down. She was always afraid she would overbalance and topple down to the bottom, ending up in a heap at the bottom.

In her mind's eye, she again saw the splayed limbs of the man's body. She rubbed her eyes.

"I guess I should be going to bed soon."

"Probably," Vic admitted, covering a yawn. "Have you had anything to eat? You really should have some supper before you knock off for the night."

"I don't like going to bed on a full stomach." Erin looked toward the fridge. "I'll find a light snack." She stood and gathered up their teacups and the other tea things. The meaning of the gesture could not be mistaken. It was time for Vic to go home. They both needed to be up early in the morning.

CHAPTER 7

*E*rin slept restlessly, but the visions of the man crumpled in The Book Nook's stock room with a knife in his chest kept repeating in Erin's head, over and over again. She knew that Terry hadn't returned home, and she really wanted him to be there. He would probably work through the night if there were things he could do. Maybe not interviewing witnesses, but organizing a search for the body, looking into the backgrounds of each of the employees of The Book Nook, and trying to identify the man who had been killed.

At some point, Orange Blossom came into the bedroom and jumped up on the bed to snuggle against Erin. She couldn't keep tossing and turning with him against her, so it forced her to be still for long enough for her body to start settling into sleep, even though her brain was still whirling with thoughts and problems.

She tried to redirect them, thinking instead of the waffle contest. The different blends of flours that might work best for waffles. She wanted a flour that was light and would crisp up properly in the waffle iron. She might use superfine rice flour as the base, which would provide the crispness. Rice flour was hard, though, and would need to soak overnight for the best finished product. It would require a starch like tapioca to keep it light and provide flexibility. And a gum to hold it all together and retain moisture. Xanthan gum and guar gum were falling out of favor, with less processed ingredients like flax or chia seed taking their place. Psyllium powder, maybe?

Pumpkin pulp would provide a lot of moisture and the hearty flavor she wanted. If she did it right, she could avoid eggs, which many gluten-free products relied upon for a protein lattice structure. But eggs were a top-ten allergen and were also shunned by those following a vegan diet. She wanted the waffles to be a good choice for the widest variety of people as possible. Her business plan hinged on not only serving the gluten-free community, but other special diets and conventional diets as well. Products that were good for the whole family, no matter what their varied restrictions.

She remembered Bertie Braceling fondly. He had been such a challenge to bake for, and she often evaluated a new recipe by how many ingredients it contained that Bertie would not have been able to eat. A Bertie allergen rating scale. He would not have been able to have the rice flour or tapioca starch she intended to try for the waffle recipe. Choosing psyllium over the processed gums was a good choice. He would have been able to have that. But she couldn't remember if she had ever discussed pumpkin with him. Had he been able to eat pumpkin or was he allergic? He was okay with most vegetables, so they were a good idea to use as the base in a recipe. Pumpkin, sweet potato, white potatoes, zucchini—they could all be used successfully in baking.

Before she even knew that she had fallen asleep, Erin was roused by the ringing of her alarm. She turned on her lamp and looked around blearily. She felt like the bed should be scattered with papers, with the notes of the various ingredients and recipes she had thought about the night before, trying to escape the visions of the man in The Book Nook and to trick her brain into slowing down and going to sleep.

But the bed was clear, occupied by just her and Orange Blossom, who stretched all of his toes out, then got to his feet and arched his back, sending shivers all the way from his neck to his tail. He gave a couple of trills of greeting and sat back to have a bath, starting by licking his back toes. Leaving him to his ablutions, Erin got started on her own.

She didn't like how empty the house felt without Terry and K9 there overnight. But Terry often took the night shift, so it wasn't like she was used to his being there every night. Sometimes their schedules did not mesh together well for a few days or weeks.

But that didn't mean she couldn't miss him.

She showered and did her hair, then pulled on some clothes and went to the kitchen to turn on the kettle and throw a slice of bread in the toaster. As soon as she was in the kitchen, Orange Blossom began singing for his breakfast, rubbing against her legs and wondering why she was taking so long. He never could seem to understand that she needed to eat as well, and her food did not come ready to eat from a can. As far as he was concerned, his needs came before hers.

She carefully measured out his food for the day. He was now eating "weight control" formula, having grown too heavy for Doc's liking. And when Erin picked him up, she had to admit he was getting to be quite an armful.

Marshmallow hopped into the kitchen and waited patiently for his pellets and fresh vegetables.

"You see how nice he is?" Erin asked Orange Blossom, "Marshmallow doesn't need to make a racket and trip me up all over the kitchen before he gets his food. He just waits until he gets it, and he still gets it just as fast as he would if he was harassing me."

Orange Blossom looked up from his dish and glowered at her. He obviously didn't believe a word of it. He knew that if he didn't yowl like the world was ending, she would never remember to give him his food. Or she would wait until it was convenient for her, and who knew when that would be?

She knew that things would be crazy at Auntie Clem's Bakery that morning. It always was when there was shocking news or gossip, and Erin finding a body definitely qualified. She and Vic had joked many times about how a murder always improved the bottom line at Auntie Clem's. It was sad but true.

As expected, when she opened the door first thing in the morning, there was a larger-than-usual morning crowd waiting with their coffee cups outside. They filed in, already chattering with each other about the latest news.

"I don't know how you do it," Betty Thompson declared. "If there is a dead body in Bald Eagle Falls, we know exactly who will find it!"

"It's all so mysterious." Melissa's dark curls bounced as she moved her head around to make sure that everyone was paying attention to her. She worked part-time at the police department, so she often had important tidbits to share at Auntie Clem's. Information that she was not exactly authorized to release. "How could a body appear in The Book Nook and then disappear before the police could get there to investigate? I mean, it was like magic. There one minute, gone the next."

Erin shook her head and kept a smile pinned to her face, trying not to show any irritation to Melissa. Melissa seemed to consider Erin her best friend, and Erin didn't want to make her feel bad by showing her irritation at the comment. "There's nothing magical about it. Someone—or more than one someone—just managed to move the body in the time it took me to get back here, make a call, talk to the dispatcher, and for the police to get here and enter the building. That's not exactly instant."

"When you're talking about moving a dead body, it is. They're heavy! And awkward. It isn't like picking up a box with handles. It's a two-person job, unless you're really big or they are very small."

"But it isn't impossible," Erin repeated. "There's nothing mysterious or paranormal about it."

She could just imagine what story her foster sister Reg would have come up with to explain the body's disappearance. She always told the best ghost stories but, when they had been growing up together, her paranoia about conspiracies and wildly imaginative explanations for the most mundane things had been aggravating.

"Maybe there wasn't a body," Lottie suggested, looking sideways at Erin to watch for her reaction. Lottie wasn't usually at Auntie Clem's two mornings in a row. Erin suspected she was there just for the gossip. Auntie Clem's was the place to go to discuss the latest tragedy.

Erin wasn't sure where they had gone before she had opened the bakery. Had they gone to Angela Plaint's bakery to discuss such things before Erin had come to town? Or had they just gotten into the habit of coming to Auntie Clem's because she was so often involved in the investigation on one end or the other? Or maybe it was just because she was with Terry, and they figured she could get information about the police investigation from him and pass it on to them.

"What do you mean, 'maybe there wasn't a body'?" Vic demanded. "You think that Erin just made it up? Looking for attention?"

Lottie shrugged. "I'm just considering all of the possibilities. What proof is there, after all, that there was a body there in the first place?"

"Well, there was the blood," Melissa pointed out.

"Blood isn't the same as a body. Someone could have cut themself. Erin could have seen the blood and made up the rest."

"It wasn't just a little bit of blood," Melissa told her, shaking her head. "There was too much for it to have just been a little accident—someone stabbing themself with a box cutter or getting a paper cut from one of the cardboard boxes. Someone was badly hurt down there; that was obvious."

Lottie was smiling like the cat who caught the canary. Maybe she hadn't really doubted that Erin had found a body and was trying to get more information about the crime scene. If so, she was sneakier than Erin had ever thought. She always believed that Lottie said everything she thought without a filter. But maybe she did hold some things back. Maybe she just liked to aggravate people but had other thoughts that she kept to herself.

There were murmurs among the women about this detail of the crime scene. Even though Erin was trying not to keep picturing what had happened, she tried to visualize what the crime scene had looked like after the body had been removed. She hadn't seen a lot of blood, but it had probably pooled under the body. A stab to the chest could be expected to bleed a lot, unless it was directly to the heart and stopped it from pumping.

She was glad she hadn't seen how much blood there was.

"Who do you think it was?" Melissa asked. "You must know pretty much everyone in town now. It wasn't anyone you had ever seen before?"

Erin shook her head. "It wasn't anyone I've ever seen around Bald Eagle Falls. I don't know everyone, but I think he must have been an out-of-towner. If it was someone associated with the bookstore, I think I would have seen him going into or coming out of there sometime."

"If he was from out of town, how are the police ever going to figure out who he was?" Betty asked Melissa. "It isn't like Erin saw his identification. They can't check his fingerprints."

"They took fingerprints at the scene," Melissa said. "He may have left prints while he was there if he wasn't wearing gloves. And he wasn't, was he, Erin?"

"No. I don't think... no," Erin agreed. Her stomach was tight. If they managed to find the man's fingerprints in The Book Nook's stockroom, it wouldn't take long to identify him. Even without a body, they would know who he was. The investigation would move forward.

"Or there could be a missing person report," Vic offered.

"He could have come from anywhere," Betty pointed out. "Can they check for missing person reports all over the country? Or even Canada? It isn't impossible that he came here from Canada, you know."

"I'm sure if there's a fingerprint record or missing person report from Canada, we'll find it," Melissa said firmly, but the frown on her face indicated otherwise. An international investigation would take on all kinds of new complexities.

CHAPTER 8

"What can I get for you today?" Erin asked Lottie.

Normally, she would have served Betty first, since she was the oldest and used a walker. Erin didn't like to keep her waiting on her feet for too long. But if Lottie was going to come to Auntie Clem's just to gossip or make more trouble for Erin, she wouldn't get away with sneaking out of the store when no one was looking and not buying anything.

Lottie met Erin's eyes and seemed to understand what she was doing. She shrugged and chuckled. "Well, something decadent," she suggested. "Something like 'Death by Chocolate'?"

Erin reviewed the selections to see what might qualify. "I have double fudge brownies. You could warm them slightly in the microwave and top them with ice cream or whipped cream and chocolate sauce. Or I have a nice Black Forest cake," she pointed to the chocolate cake under glass, with plenty of creamy icing, cherries, and curls of bittersweet chocolate.

Lottie pondered the two possibilities, finger to her chin. She took a deep breath and sighed. "I guess it had better be the double fudge brownies. I don't think I can eat a whole cake before it begins to go off. Two double fudge brownies."

Erin nodded and got them out for Lottie, making sure they were generous portions. As far as she knew, Lottie lived alone, which might explain why she came to Auntie Clem's to gossip so often.

~

It was a while before the flow of traffic into the bakery slowed and Erin and Vic could take a breather. They took a few trays of cooled cookies from the kitchen and restocked the display case, enjoying the momentary quiet.

The bell on the door jingled. Erin looked up and saw that it was Dave Wolfe, one of Naomi's part-time employees. He was around her age, maybe a little younger. In his late twenties or early thirties. He was a nice-looking young man with a preppy style that fit with the bookstore, and he had always been pleasant with Erin when she stopped by The Book Nook and he was there. She had conversed with him once or twice when she'd had to wait for Naomi but, usually, a wave and nod of greeting was about as far as their interactions went.

"Oh, Dave. How are you?" Erin searched his face for any sign of distress. He would have had to talk to Terry or someone else in the police department after Erin discovered the body the day before, and Erin already knew from Naomi that he was the one who had neglected to lock up after closing. Or he had remembered to lock up and someone had come along and picked the lock.

But the lights had been on, and Erin assumed he would have turned the lights off when he closed up, and a burglar would not want to turn them on and draw attention to the store.

Dave's expression was serious, but he didn't look too upset about whatever had transpired during his interview with the police. And he was in the bakery, after all. He had not left town or crawled under his covers to hide for the next week. His clothes were neatly pressed as usual. A good sign that he was taking care of himself and had not, at least, slept in his clothes or been up all night.

"Um… I'm okay, I guess." Dave swallowed and shook his head. "I can't believe that all of this really happened. It seems like it should be the plot of some TV movie, not my real life."

"Or maybe you're dreaming or someone is pulling a prank on you?" Erin suggested.

He laughed and nodded. "Yeah, exactly; how did you know?"

"Been there," Erin assured him. Had she ever. Been there, done that, got the t-shirt *and* the mug. Even with all of the unusual deaths she had dealt with in the past couple of years, it was still a shock. She was better at dealing with it than she had been. Things had been bad there for a while, but she was learning to adjust and be more resilient.

For poor Dave, this was probably the first time he'd had to deal with an unexpected death. At least he hadn't had to see the body. Everything might feel slightly unreal for him because he hadn't actually seen it, but it was better that way. Better than having to deal with nightmares about what he *had* seen.

"I guess you have," Dave admitted. He had moved to town shortly before Erin, so he would have heard about everything she had been involved with while she'd lived in Bald Eagle Falls. He should have known not to take a job so close to her bakery. Things happened around Erin.

"I guess you've talked to Terry by now. Or one of the others."

"Yeah." Dave's voice was low. He glanced at Vic, unsure about talking in front of her.

Vic raised her brows. She turned toward the kitchen. "There's the timer; I'd better take care of the next batch of cookies." She stepped through the doorway into the kitchen and out of sight. Dave took another step toward Erin, looking intently into the display case as if he were one of the children in the Kid's Club trying to pick out the best cookie. Erin leaned forward on the edge of the display case on the other side so that they were close together and Dave could talk to her quietly without worrying that anyone else might overhear him.

"I can't believe this all happened," Dave said. "And I'm so sorry… Naomi said I must have left the door open, but I'm sure I didn't. I would never have put you through something like this on purpose. I'm so sorry."

"I know you didn't set it up," Erin assured him, laughing at the ridiculousness of the thought. "If you had known what was going to happen, you would have done anything you could to prevent it."

He nodded, giving a heavy exhale in his relief. "Yeah. That's right. I would never have allowed something like this to happen." His shoulders were hunched and he tried to relax into a less tense posture. "I'm just afraid that you won't be able to come to The Book Nook anymore. Because of what happened there."

"Well… I've still been able to come to my own bakery, and things have happened here too. I'll be fine, Dave. I might not ever go down to the stock room again, but I don't exactly need to. Naomi can get me whatever I need. And if she ever needs someone to go down there to help her rearrange boxes or something… well, she can find someone else."

They both laughed awkwardly. Erin was doing her best to put Dave at ease, but wasn't sure it was helping.

The door opened, the bell jingling loudly, and Dave and Erin both jumped. Dave whirled around to see who it was and looked stricken when he saw his boss standing there.

"Dave," Naomi said, impatience in her tone.

"I was just returning Miss Price's platters," Dave protested. Then he looked down at his empty hands. He looked at Erin as if he might have already given her the platters. But he hadn't had anything in his hands when he entered the bakery. "That is, I…"

Naomi held up the trays. "These platters?"

"Uh…" A red flush was creeping up Dave's tanned neck. Erin felt bad for him, wishing there was something she could do about his embarrassment. But the more she focused on it, the worse it would be. "I guess… I forgot them. I don't know where my head is today."

Naomi nodded. She swept her long hair away from her face with her forearm, then strode forward to place the platters on the top of the display case. "Thank you, as always, for putting together such a nice treat for the book club."

Erin nodded. "Always glad to help. Is there a theme for the next meeting?"

"I think maybe we're going to do a back-to-school theme. Talk about young adult books, explore the genre a bit, make some suggestions for books they might want to read to better understand what kids these days have to deal with at school and at home."

"Hmm." Erin thought about what she could bake with a back-to-school theme. She didn't want to do cliched items that were found in school lunches. Jell-O cups. Twinkies. That was too depressing. "How about 'an apple for the teacher'? I can put together some apple tarts and bars."

"That would be wonderful! You always have such great ideas."

Erin smiled. She enjoyed the creativity of finding a food that would fit with the book that the book club was reading or the theme they were discussing. Sometimes she would pick a food that a character in the book had eaten, something traditional from their culture, or something historically accurate. It was fun. "I enjoy doing it."

"Well, you should. You do such a good job of it."

They both looked at each other for a minute, unsure what to say. There was a big pink elephant in the room.

"So... are you okay?" Erin asked. "With everything that happened over there? You've probably had police all over the place all night and interviews and everything..."

Naomi nodded. "It's been pretty crazy. I've never been at the center of a murder investigation before. It's... kind of surreal. Like it's happening to someone else. I've only ever seen this kind of thing on TV before."

"I was just talking to Dave about that. How it seems so unreal. Your brain tries to rationalize it."

"Yeah. Because if it's real..." Naomi shuddered. "It's just too much. How do you go on if it was all real?"

"You find a way."

"I hope so. But..." Naomi squared her shoulders. "Luckily, I wasn't there when it happened. That could have been me. I could have been killed. Or been the one to find the body. It was only dumb luck that I wasn't there. My own mistake."

Erin raised her brows, not understanding. "What do you mean?"

"I had to go into the city to see my lawyer. Just for some business stuff, nothing to be concerned about," Naomi waved away any questions about legal trouble she might be in. "But I got the date and time of the appointment wrong. The meeting isn't until next week, but I wrote it down wrong, and I ended up being away when all of this happened. I was in shock when I got the call from Terry Piper, I'll tell you!"

"I'll bet," Erin agreed. "That was lucky. I'm glad you weren't there. That you didn't get hurt."

"Yes, me too. Though I'll bet you wish that it was someone else who found him."

Erin wasn't sure what to say about that. It was true that she didn't want to stumble across any more dead bodies. She hated the anxiety and nightmares as well as the reputation she got from always being the one who seemed to be magically drawn toward the bodies of the dead. But she wouldn't wish that on Naomi either. Erin had been through enough that she could hold it at a bit of a distance. Though it was a shock to her system, she was sure that it would have been much harder on Naomi if she had been the one to find the dead body. She might have gone into hysterics. It might have changed her forever. She might have been sick and depressed and traumatized for weeks, months, or even longer.

But she hadn't had to go through that because Erin had been there and found the body instead. As much as she didn't enjoy that part of life in Bald Eagle Falls, she didn't wish it on someone else.

"It's hard," she admitted. "But it does get easier. You get more... not *used* to it, exactly but find ways to handle it better. Usually. I've had my problems."

"Well, thank you for finding this one for me." She started to turn toward the door. "Except, maybe neither of us was supposed to find it. If you hadn't been there exactly when you were, you would have missed it. It would have been gone."

"Oh... I guess so." Erin hadn't thought about it from that perspective. She'd had a half-formed belief that the body had disappeared *because* she had found it and called the police, and that if she hadn't been there, it would have just lain there until it was discovered during the ordinary course of events. But that wasn't necessarily true. The body hadn't disappeared because she had seen it. And if she hadn't seen it, no one would have been the wiser. No one would know that someone had died in the basement of The Book Nook.

CHAPTER 9

Erin had only been booked for the opening shift at Auntie Clem's Bakery and had given herself the afternoon off to work on other things. She could have stayed at the bakery to do the books, which she was getting a little behind on, but she didn't really want to stay there. She wanted to be home where she could relax and maybe catch a nap to make up for the poor sleep she'd had the night before. She might even be able to catch Terry napping, if he had finally decided to take a break from the case and catch some shut eye. Either way, she knew she needed to rest for a while and get recharged.

Terry was not home, but had left a sticky note on the fridge indicating that he had been home while she'd been on her morning shift, had caught a few hours of sleep and had a bite to eat, and had headed out again. Heading off all of the questions she would ask him to make sure he was taking care of himself. Erin read the note through again, folded it in half, and threw it in the garbage.

She made herself a sandwich. She needed to follow Terry's example and take care of herself too. Though she was already doing that by coming home to rest instead of staying at the bakery to do her accounting or pitch in on the next shift because she couldn't keep her fingers out of the pie. Her employees were fully capable of looking after the regular shifts without her there to supervise them all the time.

She sat on the couch to read—which she knew she shouldn't do because she would get crumbs on it, and then complain later about certain people eating in front of the TV and getting crumbs on the furniture. But she would be sure to clean up after herself so that wouldn't happen. She wanted to be somewhere comfortable to eat and read through her email on her tablet.

Erin yawned, rubbed her eyes, and put down the half sandwich that remained, scrolling through the emails to look for anything important. But she knew that what she was looking for wasn't in her inbox anymore. It was in the trash. And she wasn't looking for it; she was trying to avoid it, pretending to herself that she wasn't looking for it, but just scrolling for anything new.

Orange Blossom got up from his spot on the easy chair, yawned widely and stretched, then jumped up on the couch beside Erin and curled up against her leg. He didn't even show any interest in the half sandwich, though he might have been trying to lull Erin into believing that he wasn't going to go after the people food the first opportunity he got.

"Hi, sweetie," Erin greeted him, and scratched his ears and neck. "You're very cuddly today."

He purred. Erin closed her eyes, enjoying his warmth against her leg and the rumbling purr that made her feel at home.

She looked at her email again. She couldn't help herself. She clicked on the email trash and scrolled down. She should empty the trash. That was what it was there for, after all. A place to put things that you never wanted to see again. To destroy them forever.

But there she was, scrolling down and skimming for the familiar string of characters.

She missed it the first time. She could feel that she had gone down too far and scrolled back up more slowly, eyes fixed on the screen. And there it was.

Meet me at Canyon Park Wednesday afternoon at 2:00

She knew better than to do it. She had said that she never wanted to see him again, and that hadn't changed. She really didn't want to see him again. Or talk to him, or respond to his emails. She had assumed that if she never responded, he would eventually give up.

That was what the foster moms and dads had always said about bullies, wasn't it? Just ignore them and they will eventually go away.

But it never worked that way. At least, it hadn't for Erin. Maybe she was just a target, like Reg had told her. She looked too vulnerable, acted too tentative, and people thought that meant they could take advantage of her. If she were tougher, if she showed people that she wasn't the type of girl who could be pushed around, they would respect her.

But that had never worked either.

She wasn't going to the park. There wasn't any point because she knew he wouldn't be there. It was a pointless gesture and would just prove that she had never managed to get him completely out of her life, no matter how far away she had moved.

Instead, Erin would lie down and have a nap, get caught back up on the sleep she had been short on the night before. She would take care of herself and get the rest and relaxation that she needed so that she would be able to bounce back from her gruesome find quickly and move on with her life. She didn't need to dwell on it. Life went on despite damaging and traumatic experiences. If she'd learned anything in life, it was that.

But she knew she wouldn't be able to sleep when she lay down in her bed. As much as she wanted to, it just wasn't going to happen. Her mind was going like a hamster wheel. Between replaying the discovery of the murdered man in the basement of The Book Nook and the email requesting her presence, there was no quieting it. The hamster was determined to keep running, even if he wasn't actually getting anywhere. What made them keep running, anyway?

Erin tried for twenty minutes, and probably tossed and turned at least twenty times in the process. She couldn't stop twitching, let alone lie in the same position for more than thirty seconds at a time. She looked like some jumped-up meth freak.

She decided to go for a walk. That would help to calm her down. A walk in the woods was always calming and refreshing. It was the hottest part of the day, in the hottest part of the Tennessee summer, but the woods were shady and it was time she got acclimatized to the weather conditions in Tennessee. She was never going back to Maine.

Vic wasn't home yet, or Erin would have invited Vic and her fluffy white dog, Nilla, to go along with her. The dog's need to sniff every leaf and tree trunk along the way would keep them moving slowly, even if she felt like she always needed to be productive and keep things moving as quickly as possible. With her tai chi practice, she was learning just to breathe and let the rest of the world flow around her. A person needed more than productivity. She needed rest and meditation as well.

Erin began to walk. The woods behind the house were quiet, as they always were. A buffer between Erin and the rest of the world. Her own little piece of paradise. Bugs buzzed and whirred, but the rest of the animals were quiet, resting during the heat of the day just as she had planned to.

In a few minutes, she was passing Adele's cabin. Adele, a practicing witch, was Erin's gamekeeper, keeping trespassers out of the woods where they could harm others or themselves. And then sue her because she had allowed it to happen. She liked to sit and visit with Adele, who sometimes seemed wise beyond her years. But Erin wasn't going to knock on her door in the afternoon. Adele was usually up late at night to perform her gamekeeper duties or religious rituals, so she would probably be asleep in the afternoon. Maybe on the way back to the house, it would be late enough to see if she were up and around.

Erin had looked up the address of Canyon Park. Just in case she ever wanted to go there someday. Through online satellite and street-level photography, Erin could see that it was a small park, out of the way, without any playground equipment for the children. A little place to enjoy nature, maybe have a picnic, maybe take dogs for a walk, but there wasn't really anything to do there.

Which was probably why there was no one there now. And likely why her email correspondent had picked such an isolated spot in the first place. With nobody around to eavesdrop, he could talk to her about whatever he wanted to talk about, and no one would overhear, and he could persuade Erin to his way of thinking. The secluded location provided a perfect opportunity for the two of them to talk without interruption.

But she knew he wasn't going to be there. That would be impossible.

CHAPTER 10

$\mathcal{E}$rin suppressed a shudder. Goosebumps popped up all over her arms, and she rubbed them as if she were cold, despite the oppressive heat. Her shirt was nearly drenched with sweat, and she wished she hadn't walked so far from home and was back there so she could shower and change without having to walk all the way back.

It was familiar from the satellite pictures but a little larger than Erin had thought. Some walking paths where people could go to enjoy nature, much like the paths through Erin's own woods.

She looked around. There was no one waiting there for her. She had known there would not be. But she'd needed to reassure herself. Nothing but trees, with the songs of birds that seemed far away and cheerful, as if it were a perfectly normal day. She walked around the small clearing. There was a large sandstone rock with the words Canyon Park chiseled into it. There was a single bench for someone who wanted to take a break to sit down.

She sat. She looked around at the trees and the blue sky and the brilliant green grass. It was all so beautiful. So peaceful. So quiet. Like nothing bad could ever happen there.

She heard a rustling in the trees. She turned her head watched a deer walk into the clearing.

It looked at her with liquid brown eyes for a long moment, then it turned and disappeared in a flash, back into the shadows of the trees. Erin let out her breath.

She knew she couldn't stay there forever. It was only a matter of time before someone would be looking for her. Terry would call her, or someone from the bakery, or someone who hadn't been able to make it to the bakery and still wanted to ask her about the body in the basement of the bookstore.

Erin stood with a sigh.

Approaching the rock from the other side, she could see a shoe lying beside it. Who would leave a shoe in the park? It wasn't a hiking or walking shoe. Maybe someone had changed before they went for a walk.

And had just left it lying there?

Then she realized it looked familiar. She'd seen that shoe before. A shiny black shoe like she had seen in the basement of The Book Nook.

Her stomach knotted tightly, Erin got closer and pushed back the bushes that obscured the rest of the shape behind the big rock.

A startled noise escaped her mouth. Not quite a scream, but a little yelp that she couldn't stifle.

The face was obscured by the bushes, but she knew who it was.

She reached for her phone with nerveless fingers and pulled it out, searching for the buttons she knew so well. The phone felt hard and cold in her hands instead of responsive, every tap taking several tries before she managed to get it to do what she wanted. She was afraid that it would be just like before—that she wouldn't be able to get a signal, wouldn't be able to reach out for help and would have to go somewhere else to place the call.

And then what would happen? Would it still be there when the police arrived? She knew it was irrational, but she couldn't take her eyes off of the form lying in the shadows of the brush and the rock. If she looked away, it could disappear. Just like before.

She finally managed to tap Terry's name enough times that the call started to go through. Then was canceled because she'd also managed to hit the hang-up icon. Erin swore under her breath, tried to hold the phone steady, and tried again.

"Erin?" Terry's voice finally sounded in her ear. "Everything okay?"

Erin stifled a sob. She took a deep breath, let it out, and tried to sound as calm and collected as possible. "Well… *I'm* okay."

"What's going on?"

"I'm at Canyon Park. Do you know where that is?"

"What are you doing at Canyon Park?"

"I… went for a walk."

He didn't answer, probably considering the fact that he'd never known her to go walking to random parks before. She usually stayed in the woods behind her property when she went for a walk. Or walked between Auntie Clem's and the house.

"Terry, I found him."

"You found who?"

"The… man who was in the basement. At The Book Nook."

"You found him. Does that mean he is alive?" Terry's voice was cautious, not accusatory, but he must have thought she was crazy. Either she thought that a live man had been dead, or that a dead man was wandering around the neighborhood.

"No… he was dead. I mean, he was dead when I found him in the bookstore, and he's dead now, but he's here. In Canyon Park."

"How did you—" he started to interrogate her, then broke off. "No, never mind. I'm going to hang up and call the dispatcher. You'll stay there?"

"Yes."

"I'll be five minutes. Don't…"

"Don't take my eyes off of the body?"

"Well…" In her mind's eye she could see his helpless shrug. "Yeah. One of us will be there in a few minutes. I don't know who is closest."

"Okay." Erin hung up so he wouldn't feel guilty about disconnecting her when she might be distressed.

She stood there, staring down at the body, not taking her eyes off of it despite her instinct to look away. She didn't want this moment impressed on her memory. But like Terry, she also couldn't dismiss the fear that it would be gone by the time he arrived.

A siren sounded in the distance. She hoped that Terry would be the first to arrive, but, of course, it didn't matter. All of the Bald Eagle Falls police department would be on their way, whether they were on shift or not. They would all be there within a few minutes.

As the siren drew closer, she could also hear a truck engine. The truck that sped into sight was Terry's. She sighed in relief and looked back down at the body, realizing in an instant that she had looked away from it. But it was still there.

Terry jumped out of the car and hurried over to her, K9 running at his side. He got in close where he could see the body and seemed to relax. He put a warm hand on Erin's back, which felt incredibly comforting.

"Are you sure it is the same body?" he asked, studying it closely from top to toe. The hilt of the knife still stuck out of the chest and looked like Erin had described it. The shoes she had recognized from The Book Nook were on his feet. Or at least, one of them was. She didn't see the other nearby, but she wasn't about to start poking around the bushes or under the body to find it. Some things she didn't mind leaving with the police.

"Yes. It's the same one."

"Good. Always nice to find what you have misplaced."

Erin knew he was trying to be lighthearted and distract her from the gravity of the situation, but it didn't seem funny to her.

"You don't have to keep looking at him," Terry said. "If you want to sit down for a while until one of us can interview you…"

Erin sighed and walked back over to the park bench and sat down. Her sweat-damp clothes stuck to her. She didn't want to sit and wait to be interrogated again. She wanted to go home and pretend that nothing had happened.

Why had she insisted on coming to the park? She had known that she shouldn't, and she had anyway.

CHAPTER 11

$\mathcal{E}$rin felt Terry's gaze on her, and she glanced at him. However, he didn't say anything to her. He, the sheriff, and Stayner cordoned off the area and started the initial processing of the scene. When someone came to sit on the bench and talk to her, it wasn't Terry, but Sheriff Wilmot.

"Miss Price. How are you doing?"

"I'm hot and sticky and want to go home."

He took the opportunity to remove his hat, wipe his sweaty brow, and put the hat back on again. "It is a warm one," he admitted.

"When can I go? You can come to the house to talk to me."

"Soon. We'll cover the preliminaries here before we let you go anywhere so that everything is still fresh in your mind and you haven't had a chance to be influenced by anything else."

"There isn't really anything to tell. I just came here, out for a walk, and I saw the shoe…" She pointed to the shoe of the corpse, which extended just beyond the big rock. "I went over for a closer look and saw him there."

"Did you touch the body?"

"Why would I?" Erin shuddered. "No."

"Maybe to turn it to get a better look at his face. Or to make sure that he was dead."

"I already saw his face when he was in the basement of the bookstore, and I already checked to make sure he was dead then. I didn't need to check again today."

"You were sure it was the same man."

"Yes. I was sure. I could see him. Same clothes, same knife. Same body."

"You didn't need to see his face."

"No."

"Are you sure you don't want to take a look so that you can confirm one hundred percent that this is the same man as you found in The Book Nook? There isn't anyone else who can confirm it is the same body. You were the only one who saw him."

"And whoever took him away."

"Well, I suppose so, but whoever that is, they aren't going to tell us anything. They didn't want anything to do with the police in the first place, so why would they now? If they were inclined to go to the police, they would have done it in the first place, like you did, not take the body away." He shook his head. "I don't know what they intended to hide, moving him from there to here. Exactly what does moving him accomplish?"

Erin shook her head. Nothing that she could see. Other than to make everyone think she was going crazy. If they were going to leave him somewhere that he would be discovered anyway, why do such a thing? If it had been Erin, she would have dumped him down a mine shaft or left him somewhere deep in the woods where no one would ever find him. It was ridiculous to remove him from the bookstore just to dump him in a public, easily accessible park where anyone could see him and he would be found within hours or days, depending on how much foot traffic went through the park.

Wilmot grunted. "I don't know either. But not all killers are very bright. It isn't like on TV, where they are all criminal masterminds. Actual criminals tend to be pretty stupid. They have poor impulse control and never think they will get caught. But of course they do."

"You'll figure out who killed… whoever this is."

Wilmot looked at Erin sidelong. "Do you know who he is?"

"Not anyone I've ever seen in Bald Eagle Falls before."

He grunted again. "Me either. Out-of-towner. Someone looking for trouble."

"Didn't he... have a wallet? Identification?"

"No. No wallet, no phone, nothing to identify him. We'll have to check missing person reports to see if we can figure out who he is. Maybe he'll have a criminal record and his fingerprints will pop something."

Erin stared off into the trees. "Maybe."

And when they did manage to identify him... what then? "Do you think that who he is has something to do with why he was killed?"

"What do you mean?" Deep wrinkles formed between Wilmot's eyes.

"I mean... do you think it was just random, like any victim would do? Or do you think that he was targeted because of what he did or who he was?"

"Oh... well, that's a good question. I'm not sure I can answer it." Wilmot considered the question for a minute. "He has no wallet, so it could have just been theft, a mugging. Except for the fact that he was found in the basement of the bookstore. Not out on the street or in an alley, where it might conceivably be a mugging. He was in the basement, and no one knows why; what he was doing down there, who let him in, or why his body was removed. That says something about it being personal. Someone knew he was going to be there and intentionally followed or met him. It couldn't just be some random person who happened to wander by."

Erin nodded slowly. Who could have known the out-of-towner? Had he come to case out The Book Nook, thinking they had something valuable on-site? Who had known that he was coming or why he had shown up?

It was disturbing. There were too many questions.

"Then whoever killed him had some kind of connection with him."

"Yes, that's what I'm thinking. And as soon as we can identify him, hopefully we will be able to identify who the connection was. Through phone or text records, an email trail, something from his past. When we find out the connection, we'll know the *why* and the *who*. It will just be a matter of getting enough evidence to prove it."

Erin rubbed her forehead. She swallowed, but her mouth and throat were so dry. "Do you have any water? I sweated so much on the way over. I think I'm getting dehydrated."

"I surely do." Wilmot smiled at her. "Be back in a tick."

Erin watched him walk over to his car. She took a quick look at Terry, but he was occupied with whatever evidence he was cataloging. He didn't give her another of *those* looks.

Wilmot opened his trunk and pulled out a bottle of water. He brought it back to Erin, cracking the top open on his way.

"It ain't cold," he warned, "but it's wet."

The water was lukewarm and tasted flat and stale from sitting in the warm trunk of Wilmot's car, but Erin didn't complain. It felt good going down. She swished a mouthful around and swallowed again. She poured a small amount into the hollow of her hand and then wiped it over her face and neck to cool down a bit. She should have known to bring a water bottle when going for a walk in the Tennessee summer heat.

"What possessed you to venture out for a walk in the middle of the afternoon in this heat?" Wilmot asked, his mind obviously following the same track.

Erin took a deep breath. "I just… needed to get out and clear my head. I was thinking a lot about finding the body in the bookstore, you know… I needed some exercise and fresh air."

He looked around, thinking. "Do you come here often? It's sort of off the beaten path."

"No. Someone mentioned it the other day and I thought I would check it out. Give myself something to do."

"Uh-huh. Who was it that mentioned it?"

"Umm… I don't know. Someone at the bakery, I guess. I don't remember what we were talking about. But I hadn't been here before, so today, when I was looking for something to do to keep my mind occupied, I thought why not check it out?"

He nodded slowly. Erin shifted. "Is that everything? Can I head back home now?"

"I suppose so. You should probably get a ride, if you're already dehydrated. No point in trying for heatstroke."

"I guess." She looked at Terry's truck. Was Wilmot suggesting that Terry could take her home, or was he expecting her to call someone to be picked up?

"Maybe Miss Victoria could pick you up?" Wilmot suggested.

"Well... I could try Willie." Erin knew Vic did not have a driver's license, although she sometimes borrowed a vehicle to get where she needed to go. It was probably best not to let Terry see her driving. Just because he had overlooked it once before, that didn't mean he'd give her a break again. And even though the sheriff had been the one to suggest it, he might remember later on that Vic didn't have a driver's license and decide to give her a ticket.

Wilmot nodded. "See if you can get someone. I know it isn't far, but I'd feel better knowing you weren't trying to make the hike back when you're already feeling poorly."

"Okay."

Wilmot stood up and went back to the other law enforcement officers to help with the investigation. Erin toyed with her phone for a moment and then tried Vic's number. It rang a number of times, which told Erin that she was probably serving a customer. She had tried to train her employees not to answer phone calls when they were on shift, but particularly not when actually in the middle of serving a customer.

"Hello, boss," Vic answered eventually, sounding slightly breathless. "What do you need?"

"I just wondered what Willie is doing today. I need a short ride, and if he's in town...?"

"You need a ride?" Vic sounded confused. "Did your car break down?"

"No. I went out for a walk, but I went too far and I'm tired and overheated. I was hoping I could get a ride back home from somebody."

"Well… you'd better take Willie off your list. I think he's out of town today. Sorry."

"It's okay. He's the first one I tried. I'm sure someone else will be able to help out."

"Do you want me to leave Charley to mind the store and I'll come and get you?"

"No, you'd better stay there," Erin said immediately. Charley, her long-lost biological sister, was older than Vic, but Vic was more dependable. Erin wasn't comfortable leaving Charley without some kind of supervision. Vic might only be nineteen, but she was more responsible than many thirty-year-olds. "I'll call around to see if anyone else is available. Or I'll walk. It's not really that bad; I've had a rest and a drink."

"Don't do anything stupid. You didn't grow up around here, and heatstroke is a real thing. You don't want to end up dead in the middle of the woods."

"I'm not going to do that."

"Call me back if you can't find anyone else. Where are you?"

"Canyon Park."

"Where is that?"

"Just a little park a couple of miles from home." Erin was going to describe it as peaceful or undisturbed or something else to indicate that it was isolated and not a busy place but, looking around at the busy cops, she decided that peaceful was not the word.

"Okay. I'll look it up. Just promise me you won't walk home alone."

"I won't."

"Good. Text me when you get back home, because I'm going to be worrying about you now."

That had not been Erin's intention. She looked through the other names on her favorites list. Most people worked or had other commitments during the day. She didn't like disturbing anyone.

Beaver? Adele? Adele might be asleep. Rohilda Beaven worked, but she wasn't on a nine-to-five schedule like an office worker. She was an agent for a federal agency, and Erin thought she had a lot of control over the hours she worked. Depending on what she was investigating at the time, of course.

Beaver might be a good choice. She was a down-to-earth, savvy woman who wouldn't mince words and could give Erin advice on what she should do, stuck in the middle of this investigation.

CHAPTER 12

$\mathcal{B}$eaver answered after just one ring.

"Erin?"

Erin could hear her chewing her gum. Beaver was constantly chewing a wad of gum. Erin sometimes wondered what it did to her jaw. Would it make it stronger because she was always chewing, or break the joint down because it never got a rest? Erin suspected that the reason Beaver chewed was not that she'd had an addiction to chewing tobacco in the past, but because she needed something to keep her busy, or because she ground her teeth when she had to be still. Beaver moved languidly, as if she were calm and relaxed and nothing could affect her but, underneath that, Erin knew she was coiled like a viper just waiting to strike. Chewing gum made her appear casual and unconcerned, but she knew that Beaver was anything but.

"Hi, am I interrupting you from anything important?"

Beaver might have answered right away because she was awaiting a call. It might mean it was a bad time for her to talk.

"No, everything is quiet. What can I do for you? I hear you've been out tripping over bodies again."

"Again?" Erin repeated. Had word of the body in the park spread that far already? She supposed Beaver might be listening to a police scanner and know what was going on the instant she had called Terry for help.

"I heard something about a body in the basement of the bookstore? Or have you found too many lately to remember such an insignificant thing?"

"Yes, that's right. I did find one there. And then again…"

"Again?" It was Beaver who repeated the word this time.

"Yes. You heard that the body I found in the bookstore disappeared before the police could get there?"

Beaver chuckled. "I did hear something about that. Sounds like something from an old *Three Stooges* flick. Or *Keystone Cops.*"

Erin was gratified that Beaver was blaming the police department rather than her. "Well, as it turns out, I found him… again."

"In the bookstore?"

Erin laughed. "No. In the park this time. Canyon Park."

"Don't know it. Is it close?"

"It's in Bald Eagle Falls." Erin suddenly wondered whether Beaver was even in town. She was often in the city or elsewhere in the state for an investigation. Though she spent a lot of time in Bald Eagle Falls with her boyfriend Jeremy—Vic's brother—she didn't actually have a residence in town. "Are you… around?"

"I haven't been called in by the boys in blue to consult. Do they need my expertise for something?"

"No. I just need a ride home from the park and was wondering whether you were even in town."

"Ah. I could do that. Though I would need to harass the locals first," Beaver warned, laughing. "They need someone keeping them on their toes."

"I think you could say I have been doing that already."

"So you have. Two bodies in two days. Or one body in two different locations in two days. Now, why did you find him and not them? They should have been all over it today."

"I'm just lucky, I guess."

"Will Canyon Park show up on my GPS, or is it too small of a place to matter to the GPS gods?"

"It should show up, I think. I looked it up on the internet, and it was on their map with all the access roads and satellite imagery. Even street-level pictures."

"It should be on the GPS then," Beaver agreed. "I'll see you in a few minutes."

When Beaver showed up in her clunker a few minutes later, Erin heard Terry swear and ask, "What is *she* doing here?"

He had worked together with Beaver plenty of times in the past. But Erin supposed he still didn't like to find that she was on a case he had thought his, or that a seemingly innocuous death was something bigger that the feds were already interested in.

Erin stood up to walk to the car and get in, but Beaver had already warned that she intended to harass the local police department about the case, and she hadn't just been joking. After getting out of the car, she loped over to the cordon taped off with a slow, lazy gait.

"What's up, Beaver?" Sheriff Wilmot asked. "Haven't been told you have any involvement in this case."

"When have the higher-ups ever told you I was involved in a case before I showed up at the scene?"

"Well… not very often," Wilmot admitted.

"Probably never. What've we got?"

"DB. No identification yet, so I don't see how you could be involved. Unless you already knew who it was when Erin found him in the bookstore."

"It's not anything to do with any of my cases." Beaver shrugged and chewed her gum, mouth partially open. "I'm just rubbernecking."

"Well, don't be asking questions about the case if you're not involved. You can get it from the newspaper like everyone else."

"Will this even make the news?"

Wilmot laughed sharply, like a cough. Had Erin been finding so many bodies in Bald Eagle Falls that it wasn't even noteworthy anymore?

"I'm sure there will at least be a footnote," he said. "Maybe a letter to the editor."

"About how you need to be keeping the parks clean?" Beaver

suggested. "Free of trash like this." She gestured toward the dead body.

"Trash?" Wilmot repeated, looking at the shiny shoe that was visible from where they were standing. "Doesn't seem to me like you are in a position to be making that kind of judgment."

"Just a joke, Sheriff."

"Hmm. What are you here for, if you don't have any involvement in the case?"

Beaver nodded toward Erin.

"Ah. Good." Wilmot nodded. "Glad she's got someone to take her home. Now don't you go putting any ideas in her head. We don't want her contaminated or biased by anything you might have to say."

"Would I do that? I told you it isn't my case."

But Wilmot's suspicious look suggested that he was not convinced of the fact. Just because Beaver said she didn't have any interest, or didn't *yet* when the body had not yet been identified, that didn't mean that she didn't know something that he didn't, or that it wouldn't become a case that she was officially interested in in the future.

Beaver gave a nod of acknowledgment or farewell. "See you later, Sheriff."

He nodded and turned back to the body. Beaver strode over to the bench and Erin stood up. Despite the fact that it was hot and she had warmed up her body with the walk, her knees and back protested at having to get up from the bench after sitting there for a while. Erin straightened and stretched.

"Thanks for coming to pick me up."

"No bother at all, Miss Erin."

"I appreciate it."

"Always good to see what's going on in the neighborhood."

"I didn't interrupt you from anything important?"

Beaver didn't answer as she led the way to the car and climbed in. She looked over at Erin as she slid into the passenger seat.

"If I couldn't get away from what I was doing, I wouldn't say yes. I would tell you no, and you could go to the next person on your list."

Erin nodded, feeling a little better. She didn't like to impose on anyone and didn't want Beaver to help her out just because she felt obligated by her relationship with Jeremy or because of something Erin had done to help her out in the past. But Beaver was one of those people who was upfront about how she felt and didn't make her guess.

"Okay."

Beaver pulled out. "What's your relationship with this guy?"

"What? With Terry?"

Beaver snorted. She chewed her gum and her eyes roved back and forth when she drove, as if she were waiting for something to happen. A sniper, maybe, or a drive-by.

"Your relationship with the guy with the knife in his chest."

"I didn't put it there. I've never even seen the guy around Bald Eagle Falls before."

"That's not what I asked."

Erin shrugged and stared out the window. It was quiet. Despite Beaver's vigilance, there wasn't anything going on outside to distract Erin's attention or explain why she wasn't answering Beaver.

"You just happened to find this guy in the park," Beaver said, in a tone that told Erin she knew it wasn't true.

"I wasn't expecting to find him there. There's no way I could have known that someone would dump his body there."

"Yes. Makes you wonder, doesn't it?"

"I didn't put him there. I'm the one who called the police, remember? If I had something to do with it, do you think I would have called the police? I especially wouldn't have called the police to an empty basement, telling them that there *used* to be a body there. And then dump it somewhere else and call the police again to tell them that I'd found it *again!* You think I want to end up in this kind of situation?"

"Nope. Which is why I'd be interested in finding out exactly what is going on."

"Nothing is going on. This doesn't have anything to do with me. I appreciate the ride home, but I really don't want to talk about it all. I already talked to the sheriff about it, and I know he's going to want to talk to me again, and I know Terry is going to want to talk to me about it when he gets home. Whenever that is. I don't want to have to discuss it with you, too."

"You're not going to be able to mislead everyone."

"I'm not trying to."

"No? Huh. Could have fooled me."

Erin looked at her sharply and almost repeated that she didn't want to talk about it with Beaver. But then she didn't. That would be denying it too much. Beaver would want to know why she was so resistant if she hadn't had anything to do with the death. If Erin just kept it casual, and shrugged off any of Beaver's theories, she would be in a much better position.

It only took a few minutes for Beaver to drive her home. Erin climbed out of the car. "Thanks again. I really appreciate it. Now I'm going for a cool shower and fresh clothes. And maybe a nap."

Beaver chewed. "Sounds like a plan." She shifted the car into drive. "You know how to reach me if you want to talk."

CHAPTER 13

Of course, Erin was right about Terry wanting to talk to her about the case when he got home. She wouldn't have expected him to be home early, but he finished in plenty of time to make it home to dinner, leaving the others in the police department with whatever other processing and paperwork needed to be done. Terry had, Erin supposed, been elected as the person most likely to be able to get the full story out of Erin.

She had been thinking of what to say to him but still hadn't come to any decision. She couldn't lie to Terry, and she couldn't tell him the full story, and that left her in a difficult position. It had been the same since she moved to Bald Eagle Falls. Terry knew that Erin didn't want to talk to him about her past, that she had things she didn't want to be part of their relationship, and he'd had to accept that. But he never really had. He'd kept quiet about it, played along with her, and pretended he was happy with her, but she knew all along that he had doubts. He wanted to know the whole story, no matter how unhappy he might be to hear it.

And when he found out, how was he going to react? Would he dump her? Tell her that things weren't working out? Say that he just couldn't live with her, but it was his own fault and not hers? She would be alone again. Just she and the animals. And she would miss K9.

But maybe it was better to be alone than in a relationship that wasn't open and equal. She'd been deluding herself into thinking they could be happy together.

Terry walked in the door and saw her in the kitchen, putting the finishing touches on dinner.

"I'm going to have a shower," he told her, pinching his uniform shirt between his fingers and making a face. "Change into something more comfortable. I'll only be a few minutes. You can keep it warm?"

"It will keep," Erin agreed.

He was true to his promise and didn't take long to shower off the day's sweat and dust and change into a light t-shirt and shorts to keep cool. Erin fed K9 and the other animals while he washed up, so she was ready to eat once he sat down at the table.

Terry ate without any comment. He probably couldn't even have told her what he was eating. He shoveled the food in steadily and didn't seem to enjoy it or even notice that he was eating.

"Is everything okay?" Erin asked.

She meant the food, but he didn't take it that way.

"Is everything okay? No, I don't think everything is okay. I keep trying to figure out how it happened and how everything fits together, but I can't. Of course you didn't have anything to do with this man's death, but… what's going on? How did you find him? Not just once, but twice? What were you doing in the basement? What were you doing in the park? You shouldn't have been in either place. Are you trying to cover for someone? Are you trying to mislead us? It just doesn't make any sense."

Erin took a few more bites of her dinner, chewing carefully and pretending to give the food all of her attention.

"I told you what happened," she said finally. "If you don't believe me…"

"How can I believe you? You just happened to go over to The Book Nook when it was supposed to be closed but someone had left the door open, happened to go down the stairs where you shouldn't have been, and happened to find a body. And then lost it. You walk to a park that you've never been to before just out of curiosity or an impulse, and you come across the same body again. You don't have a good explanation for why you were in either place."

"I went to The Book Nook to get my platters," Erin said evenly.

"But you didn't get them. They were on the kitchen counter waiting for you, if that was what you really wanted. There was no reason to go downstairs. If you didn't want to wait around for Naomi or another employee, you could have just gone back to Auntie Clem's."

"I thought I heard a noise."

"But you didn't. By your own account, the man was dead and no one else was down there. So you didn't hear anything. You didn't have a reason to go down there."

"I *thought* I heard a noise. You can *think* you hear a noise when there isn't anyone else there to make it. The house makes all kinds of noises when there is no one else there. Creaking and tapping and all kinds of other noises. Sometimes I think I hear someone on the stairs going up to the attic. But there isn't anyone else at home and no one has pulled down the stairs. It's just the house making noises. Or ghosts, if you want to believe in a supernatural explanation. It's the same thing with The Book Nook. I thought I heard a noise. Maybe it was just the pipes or the ventilation."

He stopped eating for a moment and stared at her. Then his eyes dropped to his plate again. It was obvious that he was trying to avoid seeming confrontational. He was trying to act casual about the whole thing. Like it was just a conversation between couples, not a custodial interview.

"Maybe that's true. But then explain to me what you were doing in the park today. Exactly what you were doing there, in a park you had never been to, where someone just happened to have dumped the same body again."

"Bald Eagle Falls is a small place."

"Not that small. I patrol this town regularly, and I can't think of the last time I walked around that park looking for any trouble. I've never found a body over there."

"Well, I hadn't either. Until today."

"You'd never been there before. You just happen to hit the jackpot the first time?"

"It wasn't exactly the jackpot. That would imply that it was something I wanted to find. Trust me—it was not. That was the last thing I wanted to find in the park today."

Almost the last thing. The second-to-last thing.

"Why were you there? What possessed you to go there today on this little walk? A walk that took you out of the way in the heat of the day, so far from the house that you couldn't make it back safely."

"I could have made it back. I just… didn't think it was a good idea to push myself too hard."

"Why, Erin?"

"I just wanted to check it out. I wanted to see what kind of a park it was. If it was nice. Someone mentioned it when we were talking about places to go and things to do around town. I thought I would go have a look."

"Places to go and things to do in Bald Eagle Falls? I have never heard anyone put Canyon Park on that list. There is nothing to do there. Literally nothing. It is some grass and a pathway through some trees. You have more wildlife in your backyard."

"There was a deer," Erin argued.

"What?" Terry was momentarily derailed.

"In the park. I saw a deer. It didn't stay long, but… there is wildlife there. I don't usually see deer in the woods here." She pointed toward the woods beyond the back fence.

She was too noisy when she walked through the woods. She was clumsy and always seemed to put her feet in the wrong places, rustling the leaves, breaking dry sticks, rustling through the bushes. The deer didn't stay long enough to see who was there. Only when Erin stopped and was quiet and still like she had been sitting in Canyon Park.

"I'm not talking about the wildlife." Terry shook his head irritably. "I'm talking about you going there for no reason and finding a body. Like you knew it was there. Like you went there looking for it. How are you involved in this? How did you know that's where the body had been dumped? Who told you?"

"Reg would tell you that I just happen to stumble across these things," Erin said. "I attract trouble. Like… karma or something. I don't know. My psychic energy."

"Reg? Reg Rawlins? You think I want to hear what some scam psychic has to say about it? That would settle things for me?"

Erin shrugged. She nibbled at her meal. "No. But sometimes there are coincidences. You can't explain why something happens; it just does. You believe in miracles, don't you? I know you're not very religious, but you believe that those stories in the Bible really happened. And you believe in people in modern times being healed, or guided to do something, or protected."

He'd never said much to her about it. She was an atheist, so why would he share those things? But Erin had heard him talk to others. She had gone to church with him once for a Christmas Eve service and had seen the look on his face when they talked about the Christmas story and faith and miracles.

Terry scowled. "This wasn't a miracle. You didn't pray to be guided to his body. Nothing… *spiritual* led you there."

Of course he wouldn't believe that. Even if he were an ardent churchgoer, he wouldn't think that God could guide an unbeliever, would he?

"I can't explain it to you," Erin said finally, shaking her head. "You know me. You're just going to have to trust me when I say I didn't have anything to do with that body being dumped in Canyon Park."

The look he gave her was not reassuring.

$\mathcal{E}$rin was studiously avoiding discussing anything that had happened the afternoon before as she and Vic worked together in the kitchen to prepare the day's morning breads and muffins. Erin really didn't want to spend any more time answering questions about the body that had now reappeared or how she had just happened to be the one to find it.

Instead, she was talking waffles.

"I have a few new recipes to try out. Some different flour combinations to see how they will hold up. I really think that the pumpkin spice idea is a good one. If I totally liquefy the pumpkin in a blender, it can act as most of the liquid for the waffles and shouldn't make them too heavy. Maybe I'll add a bit more baking soda or cream of tartar to make sure it has enough rise."

"You always need a bit extra for gluten-free recipes anyway," Vic agreed.

Erin smiled and nodded. Vic was picking up on some of the nuances of gluten-free baking. She wasn't making any of her own recipes yet but, like all of the Auntie Clem's employees, she made plenty of suggestions as to things they could make in the future, variations on favorites, and holiday or promotional treats that would keep people coming back again and again, interested in the variety rather than being bored with brown rice bread and chocolate chip cookies. Erin often discussed the possibilities with Vic, talking about what things she might have to tweak in a new variation to make it work. And Vic was clearly picking up on and remembering the details.

"You're getting the hang of it," she commented. "How you need to adjust for different flours and ingredients, I mean."

"Well, not like you, but I'm getting more of the basics."

"One day you'll be coming up with new recipes all on your own."

"As long as I document them." Vic nodded to the recipe binder on the counter.

They couldn't be casual about the recipes. They needed to replicate it exactly every time, and customers needed to know exactly what ingredients were in each baked good. Some people were only following a gluten-free diet and could have anything in the bakery, since no gluten-containing ingredients were allowed in the kitchen. And the majority of the bakery customers weren't actually following a gluten-free diet. Because Erin's was the only bakery in town, they chose to go there rather than to drive all the way into the city to get to a regular bakery or settle for the mass-produced loaves of bread and boxes of cookies at the grocery store.

But more often than not, those who had a problem with gluten also had other allergies or intolerances and needed to be very careful about what they ate. A single purchase could involve a careful review of half a dozen different recipes to find a product that was suitable.

"I don't think I'll ever be as good as you," Vic said. "You really have a knack for it. And there aren't a lot of people around who know how to bake for gluten-free diets like you can."

Erin shrugged modestly, feeling a flush creep up her throat. "Not in a small town like this. I know Mrs. Foster did some gluten-free baking before I opened up Auntie Clem's, for little Peter, but she must be so busy with all those kids. I don't think she makes much anymore, and it was just the bare basics when she did."

"Aunt Angela never got the hang of it," Vic referred to Angela Plaint, who had died shortly after Erin had moved into town. "Even though she was a baker and ended up with a wheat allergy. She mostly just bought that awful stuff off the shelf."

"Most of the commercial stuff isn't that awful anymore," Erin said generously. "You can hardly even tell that some of it is gluten-free."

"Hmm. Not to hear Aunt Angela tell it. She was miserable when she started reacting to wheat."

It had affected Angela's living—being the owner of The Bake Shoppe at the time Erin moved into town—as well as her health and ability to enjoy the foods she loved, so Erin could understand it. She knew other people who had reacted that way. Who were so miserable eating a special diet that every meal was a chore and a cause for distress. It was no wonder Angela Plaint had been such a grouch, so miserable to everyone else around her.

Though from what Erin understood, Angela had always been a hard woman. Tough on her kids, maybe even abusive. She had been accepted into the church ladies' group that met at Auntie Clem's every Sunday after the Baptist services but, as Erin had discovered after Angela's death, no one had really liked her. It was hard to embrace someone who was so prickly.

"There is Lacey," Vic said, "Lacey Moore."

Erin looked toward the door but didn't see anyone waiting outside yet. "Lacey Moore?" Erin repeated.

"Not actually *here*. I just meant that she had a knack for special recipes, like you."

"And who is Lacey Moore?" Erin knew she'd heard the name before but didn't know where. One of the older ladies, she thought. Not a regular customer. Of course, if she were a good baker herself, there wouldn't be any reason for her to patronize the bakery.

Vic raised her brows in surprise. "Bertie's sister."

"Bertie Braceling?"

Vic nodded as she started one of the big mixers running. "You know how challenging *he* was to cook for."

"I didn't even realize he had a sister." Erin had been at Bertie's funeral, but she couldn't remember much about it. She had probably still been in shock at the time, after Davis Plaint had tried to run them down. But Bertie had pushed Erin away and he was the only one who had ended up being hit. Bertie had been coming to Auntie Clem's in the weeks preceding his death. Erin wouldn't have guessed that he had someone cooking for him at home. "Why did he come to the bakery if she cooked for him?"

"I don't remember. Something was going on at the time. She had to go look after their ailing mother or something like that. She was away for a few months. Came back after Bertie and her mother died."

"Oh, the poor woman. That's too bad."

"Yeah. I don't imagine she has anyone to cook for now. No one who needs her special touch, anyway. She's getting on in years, though, and probably isn't sorry not to have to do that anymore."

"It can be a big job, especially with someone like Bertie who had *so* many allergies. He wouldn't be able to have anything packaged or off the shelf. Everything had to be made from scratch."

"She must be in her eighties now. She's probably happy for a break. Though… of course, she wouldn't see it that way." Vic gave a little grimace.

"I know." Erin kept her eyes on the cupcake batter she was pouring rather than on the images that sprang into her head.

CHAPTER 15

The door burst open, sending the bells swinging and jingling madly. Melissa swept in like a tornado. Dark spirals of hair bounced around her face.

Erin pressed her hand to her heart. "You want to give us a heart attack? What's going on out there? Are you being chased by a bear?"

Melissa laughed. "No… nothing like that. I was just… really eager to get here."

The only time that Melissa was that eager to get in the door at Auntie Clem's was when she had some bombshell news she wanted to share. She loved the drama and basked in everyone's reactions to good, bad, or shocking news.

Since she worked part-time with the police department, the information she had to share was often not the kind of things she was supposed to be telling anyone, but some little tidbit she had learned of an investigation while she was filing reports, reading or perhaps overhearing something that was going on in the office.

"Well…" Erin pretended not to know that Melissa was only there because she wanted to burst whatever bombshell she had and watch the destruction. "What are you looking for today?" She looked down studiously at the contents of the display case, bringing up Melissa's personal baked good preferences from her brain's filing cabinet.

"These double chocolate brownies have been very popular this week. Or maybe some salted caramel fudge?"

"Oooh." Melissa was distracted at least momentarily from her news as she considered the possibilities. "Have you ever considered selling the two together in some kind of package? Or maybe adding a layer of salted caramel on top of the brownies?"

"Two very good ideas!" Erin approved. She would have to remember them the next time she was working on a new variation. "Would you like one of each, then?"

Melissa nodded, her lips slightly parted. At least she wasn't actually drooling. Not down her chin, anyway.

"Anything else?" Erin raised her brows and looked over the rest. "Some crusty bread to have with soup for a simple lunch or dinner? Rosemary herb breadsticks?"

"Maybe half a dozen of the breadsticks," Melissa decided. "Do you have garlic oil to go with them?"

"Of course." Erin packaged up the breadsticks and added a small condiment container of garlic oil for dipping. "Just put them on parchment and heat them gently for a few minutes."

Melissa knew that, of course. It wasn't the first time she had purchased Erin's breadsticks in one of their many variations. Maybe sun-dried tomato next time...

As Vic tapped the register's keys, Melissa's eyes slid back over to Erin.

"Did you hear," she asked in a low, confidential tone, "that they have identified your dead body?"

Erin swallowed. This was not welcome news. She kept her face blank. "It's not *my* dead body," she pointed out.

"You've found him twice." Melissa laughed, her generous mouth a wide grin showing off plenty of teeth, "I think that makes him yours."

"I don't have anything to do with him. That was just... a weird coincidence."

"Mind your manners, Miss Melissa," Vic warned. "You wouldn't want to bite the hand that feeds you." She passed Melissa her bag of baking, raising her brows significantly at the word "feeds."

Melissa laughed again, but more repressed this time.

"Well, whether you want to call him yours or not, we have a name for him now."

Erin nodded and didn't ask the obvious question.

"Well?" Vic took up the opportunity instead. "What is it? He was an out-of-towner, right?"

"His name is Brandon Quayle. And he is from Maine." Melissa looked at Erin expectantly.

Vic's eyes turned to Erin as well, surprised by this news.

"Huh." Erin shrugged. "Do they know anything else about him?"

"He's from Maine," Melissa repeated.

"Yes… do you know everyone who lives in Tennessee?"

"No," Melissa laughed. "Of course not. But Maine is much smaller."

"Well then… do you know everyone who lives in Bald Eagle Falls? Would you know everyone's names? Anything about them?"

Melissa frowned. "No. But I thought… since he came to Bald Eagle Falls from Maine, and you came to Bald Eagle Falls from Maine, that you probably knew each other. We don't get a lot of people here from New England. Maybe you were brought here by the same thing."

"He was brought here by his aunt leaving him a bakery or storefront?" Erin asked dryly. "I'm sure there are other people in town who come from Maine or New England. It's just a coincidence."

"That you kept finding him *and* he was from Maine?" Melissa looked doubtful. She had obviously been expecting Erin to immediately volunteer that she knew the man and was disappointed by the lack of response.

Erin looked from Melissa to Vic and back at Melissa again, waiting for her to recognize that it was time to leave. She had purchased her baked goods, dropped her bomb, and there was nothing else for her to do.

The silence drew out awkwardly. Erin could have made things easier on Melissa by asking her how she was doing now that she was married. If she had been happy with the way the wedding and reception went, if Davis was happy, if she felt any different being married instead of single—which Erin thought was unlikely since none of their living arrangements had changed. Davis remained in the penitentiary; it wasn't like he was going to move in with Melissa any time soon. Or within the next decade or two.

But she didn't want to make things easier on Melissa or help her to make a graceful exit. She just wanted Melissa to leave.

"Well… thank you for these," Melissa said, holding up her shopping bag. "I'm really looking forward to dinner tonight."

"Enjoy." Erin gave her a genuine smile. She was happy to see a customer enjoying her wares.

Vic gave a little wave, and Melissa left the bakery, the bells jangling more sedately as she left than they had upon her arrival.

Vic glanced toward Erin after Melissa was gone. "You don't think there's anything significant about him being from Maine? You don't think it's anyone you know… or who knows you?"

"That man and his death have nothing to do with me," Erin said firmly. "It doesn't matter how many points of similarity you find between us or how many lines you draw connecting us, his death didn't have anything to do with me. I wish everyone would just drop it." She tried not to think about the man in the bookstore basement or let the memory of his face and the knife seep back into her thoughts.

Vic pressed her lips together and nodded.

"Sorry. I wasn't thinking about how annoying it probably is for everyone to be asking you about him like you should know him. I know you didn't have anything to do with his death. I saw you when you came back here to report it. You were as white as a ghost."

Erin gave a small smile. "Thanks. I really just want to put this behind me. But…" She looked toward the door, "I know that's not going to happen now. If they know that he was from Maine, then it's just a matter of time before they come to ask me more questions."

CHAPTER 16

As Erin had expected, it was not long before the police department wanted to speak to her about her possible connection with Brandon Quayle. Sheriff Wilmot wanted her to come in but, when she arrived, it was not Wilmot who was waiting to interview her, but Rod Stayner.

Erin had never been particularly comfortable around Stayner. Her first few experiences with him had not been positive, and she knew that had colored her opinions of him. She was sure he was a fine law enforcement officer and was well-trained and had what it would take to be great at what he did one day. But from the beginning, she had seen only his flaws.

He covered up his shortcomings with a bold, brash attitude that said he couldn't do anything wrong, and anyone who suggested it didn't know what they were talking about. If he missed taking fingerprints, touched something before it had been processed for evidence, or made a wrong assumption, that wasn't his fault and he wasn't responsible for the consequences. He made sexist or racist comments without any indication that he understood it was wrong and could hurt someone.

On the other hand, she knew that he did show some compassion toward crime victims, and still treated Erin with respect although she had been a suspect in the past.

But now she was facing him again. He had grown and matured since his first arrival in Bald Eagle Falls to cover Terry's position while he was recovering from an assault. He was no longer brand new. His overconfidence had been replaced with real knowledge and experience, and he would probably be more insufferable than ever—a bully with experience and training in how to intimidate and interrogate.

"Uh, I thought I was supposed to talk to Sheriff Wilmot," Erin told him. "I think I'll just wait for him."

"No, you're here to talk to me," Stayner told her firmly. "Just come in here and have a seat, and we'll have a little chat."

Erin shook her head again. "Maybe Terry, then, if the sheriff isn't free."

"Miss Price. You're here to talk to me, and I'm the one you are going to talk to. Please come in and don't waste my time."

His square jaw clenched. He apparently did not appreciate her attempts to get out of the interview or to see someone else in his place. Now she had insulted him or hurt his feelings, but hadn't gotten out of talking with him, so he would hold that against her.

Erin reluctantly followed Stayner into the interview room, her stomach tied in knots. She knew that she could refuse and go home. She wasn't under arrest and if she didn't want to talk to him, she didn't have to. But she didn't want to look guilty and didn't want them to think they had to investigate her further because she was trying to hide something. She wanted them to be satisfied that there was nothing in the coincidence that both she and Brandon Quayle came from Maine. It was not that big of a deal. There could be hundreds of people in Bald Eagle Falls who had come from Maine. Or dozens, anyway.

"Thank you for coming in," Stayner said formally as he sat down across from Erin. He turned on a digital recorder on the table and dictated the date, time, and persons present. Erin looked at the security camera in the corner of the ceiling and wondered whether Terry was watching on his computer or in another room with a monitor in it.

"I don't think there's really anything to say to you," Erin told him. "I told you guys before that I didn't have anything to do with this guy's death. It's just one of those random things. Just a weird coincidence. Things like that happen, you know. Like when two twins do the same thing at the same time even when they're a whole world apart and haven't coordinated it. Sometimes you run into the same person twice in two different places, two days in a row. You might think they're stalking you, but it's just a coincidence."

"How did you know Brandon Quayle?"

Erin closed her eyes and shook her head. "I don't think we've established that I did," she pointed out. "Just because we both came from Maine, that doesn't prove anything."

"You said that you had never seen him before you found his body in the basement of The Book Nook."

Erin was pretty sure she hadn't said that. She waited for him to actually ask her a question. He was fishing, that was all. Trying to get information from her by twisting what she had said. She had been pretty careful of what she had told them previously.

"Did you know Mr. Quayle in Maine?"

"We might have met. I lived there for a lot of years."

"You didn't know him well?"

Erin shook her head. She looked over his head, trying to keep her expression blank. Stayner studied her, his eyes narrowed.

"Were the two of you in a relationship?"

Erin opened her mouth to answer him, but Stayner cut her off. "*Any kind* of relationship."

She closed her mouth again. She took a deep breath and let it out again. "I never told you I didn't know him at all."

He blinked at her.

"I've read through Sheriff Wilmot's and Officer Piper's notes… and I'm pretty sure you did."

"They may have misunderstood me."

"If they misunderstood, it was because you deliberately misled them."

Erin couldn't exactly argue that, so she just kept her mouth shut.

"What was your relationship with Mr. Quayle?"

"We were… it was never really formalized. I was with him for a while, but we were… it was more casual. It wasn't like there was a *defined* relationship."

"You were 'with' him."

Erin tried to find a way to clarify what she had meant or take it back, but couldn't think of a way.

"Uh, we knew each other."

"Casually."

She shrugged.

"What does that mean? That you had friends in common?"

"Some, yes."

"Did you ever date?"

"We never…"

"Never *defined* that," Stayner guessed. "If you didn't call it dating, then what was it?"

"Just… going out with friends. Or later, we went together because…" Erin foundered, trying to find an explanation that wouldn't make it sound like she and Brandon had been what they were.

"Because you knew each other casually."

She nodded.

"But then after a while, if you were seeing each other alone, you got to the point where you weren't just going out with each other as casual friends."

"Uh…"

"You were intimate partners?"

"Sometimes."

"Did you live together?"

"Not… exactly…"

"You had separate residences? But you slept over?"

"No… I crashed with him… because I lost my place. But it wasn't like… *that*."

"You just slept on the couch," Stayner said sarcastically.

"Sometimes, yeah."

"And sometimes with him."

Erin swallowed hard. "When I had to."

Stayner cocked his head slightly, considering that. "What do you mean, when you *had* to?"

"If I had to… in order to stay there. Or if he was… drunk or violent."

There was a long silence.

"Why would you stay with someone who treated you like that?"

He was so young. He had seen so little of how the world worked, sheltered in rural Tennessee. She was sure it happened there too, but he hadn't been exposed to it as a boy. If he had, he wouldn't have sounded so surprised.

"Survival." Erin shrugged. She couldn't explain it all to him in detail. The way that the world worked for people who didn't have families, money, or homes. People who did their best to make it in the world without relying on homeless shelters, stripping, or selling drugs. American society was not set up for people who had to make it on their own without anything.

"Survival," Stayner repeated.

"If you want a roof over your head, a warm place to sleep, maybe even food or companionship, you do what you have to. Guys like Brandon… depend on that. That you won't leave because you don't have anywhere else to go."

"So. Despite what you told me, you did know him well."

"No. I…"

"Lived with him."

"Not like… a couple."

"How was it not like a couple?"

"We didn't… we weren't friends. We didn't share interests or spend time talking with each other. I never considered him a boyfriend."

"But you went out together, shared friends, and slept together."

"Some of the time."

"Some of the time," Stayner repeated.

Erin nodded and shrugged, looking down at the table. Stayner considered this in silence. After a few minutes, he stood up and walked out of the interview room. He shut the door behind him, and the latch clicked loudly in the emptiness of the space. Erin blew out her breath. She had done everything she could to avoid having to tell them about Brandon, but she had known from the time she first saw him in the basement of The Book Nook that she was in trouble. They would find out and would immediately jump to the conclusion that she had been the one who killed him.

CHAPTER 17

It seemed like a long time before Stayner returned to the room. It probably wasn't as long as it seemed—just a short conversation with Sheriff Wilmot or someone else to figure out what he should do next. Erin half expected him to return with a pair of handcuffs and inform her that someone would be coming to take her to the penitentiary and lock her up.

The same place as Davis Plaint and other men she had been instrumental in having arrested were incarcerated. But they wouldn't be allowed in the women's wing. Still, she might have to face women like Kim Brandon, who she did know.

When Stayner finally returned, he held a card in his hand, which he read to her. The Miranda warning. She'd heard versions of it so many times in cheesy TV mysteries and dramas, she was tempted to look around for a movie camera and the audience. It seemed unreal to hear it here, in safe, sleepy Bald Eagle Falls.

Terry had walked in the door behind Stayner, and he listened to Stayner's recitation of the warnings on the card. He nodded when Stayner was done, approving it.

He sat down at the side of the table, around the corner to her right rather than directly across from her like Stayner was. K9 sniffed at Erin and lay down between them. Terry reached for Erin's hand, but she pulled it back with a jerk.

"Erin, do you understand what is happening?" he asked.

"Am I under arrest? You don't have any evidence that I had anything to do with Brandon's death."

"No, we don't. You're not under arrest. But this is what we would call a custodial interview. Rod is interviewing you about a crime you might have played some part in, and you need to understand your rights."

Erin nodded.

"I'm not here as a law enforcement officer," Terry assured her. "I'm here for you. I'm here to make sure that Rod does everything by the book and that your rights are not compromised. I'm here to support you."

Try as he might to divide the two roles, he couldn't turn off what he heard in the interrogation room and not use it at home, or turn off his cop's brain and not see the things she did at home that might implicate or clear her in the case. He was still a cop. Like he'd been ever since they had met that first day and had confronted her in Auntie Clem's Bakery, demanding to know what she was doing there.

"Do you understand that?" Terry repeated.

Erin shrugged. "I heard you."

Terry looked at her for a minute, then decided it was okay for Stayner to go on. He nodded at his fellow officer.

"Did you know that Quayle was in Bald Eagle Falls?" Stayner asked.

"No."

The two cops looked at each other. Erin pretended she hadn't seen them exchange looks. Terry was there for her? Communicating nonverbally with Stayner? Analyzing whether Erin was telling the truth or not, whether she could be trusted?

"He had not been in contact with you?"

Erin didn't answer.

"Had Quayle been in contact with you?"

"No."

Another look passed between the men.

"When you went into The Book Nook, was it to meet with Quayle?"

Erin was taken aback by the question. She shook her head. "I didn't know he was going to be there. Why would I expect him to be in The Book Nook basement?"

"You don't know why he was there?"

"How would I?"

"I'd like a straight answer. You don't know why he was in the bookstore?"

"No. I was shocked to find him there. As shocked to see it was him as I was to find a dead body there. I had no idea that he would be there."

"He was right down the street from you. And you didn't know he was there?"

"No."

"He didn't tell you he was going to be there?"

"I don't know. Not as far as I know."

"What do you mean you don't know?"

"I don't know what he might have *tried* to tell me. Some message he might have tried to get to me. I didn't know he was going to be there. I don't know if he tried to tell me that or not."

"What does that mean?"

Erin turned her face away from Stayner to look at Terry. "How hard is that to understand?"

"What Rod is asking is, how would Quayle have tried to contact you? How would he have gotten you that message?"

"I don't know. Calling, texting, emailing, getting someone to give a message to me. Sending it by carrier pigeon. I don't know, since I didn't get it."

"He had your phone number?" Terry asked. Funny how quickly he had gone from observing and being there by her side to protect her from Stayner to being the one asking her questions.

"I don't know."

"Did he ever phone you?"

"I don't know. He could have. I don't answer… anything with a 207 area code."

"In case it could be him."

"In case it is anyone from my past. I don't have anyone there I want to keep in touch with."

And if she did, if someone from her past reached out to her that she wanted to be in contact with, they could leave her a voicemail. There was no need for Erin to answer an unrecognized number.

"You never talked to Quayle about meeting him at The Book Nook?"

Erin shook her head. "No."

"Or why he might be going there?"

"No."

She gave Terry a long look, and then looked at Stayner. She shifted in her seat. "I want to go home."

The two cops exchanged glances. But Terry had said that she wasn't under arrest, and she didn't have to stay there and talk to them and give them more details that might incriminate her. She had already done enough damage to herself and her reputation in Bald Eagle Falls.

It had taken the church ladies a long time to get over the fact that she was an atheist, without even the slightest inclination to join one of their churches. And that she had ensnared one of the town's most eligible bachelors, who was at least Christian in name. And had taken a transgender runaway into her home and employed her in the bakery. A gluten-free bakery, at that, where a family couldn't even get a normal loaf of bread. It had taken time for them to come around and accept her as she was, with all of her quirks and shortcomings.

How were they going to feel about her when they found out that she had been involved with someone like Brandon Quayle up north and was a suspect in his death? It wasn't just a shocking story of discovering a body in The Book Nook basement anymore, or the fact that it had disappeared and reappeared. Now they would hear the rest of the story, as far as the police knew it. Her business at Auntie Clem's Bakery might not survive the blow. If they boycotted her and went into the city or to the grocery store for their baked goods, Auntie Clem's would fold.

Neither of the cops told her that she couldn't leave. Erin pushed herself to her feet. "I'm going to go home. Have some supper. I need to get to bed."

She didn't know what time it was. But she was completely wrung out and didn't want to deal with the world. If she could sleep, at least she could turn it all off for a few hours and maybe recover her equilibrium.

"I'll take you home," Terry said, also standing up.

Erin looked at him for a moment. Did he really think that he could swap roles like that? Go from being one of the cops interrogating her to being her boyfriend?

But maybe he didn't mean he was going to drive her home as her friend and partner. Maybe he was just offering to drive her home like he would any other suspect who was at their offices without a car. A courtesy.

"Fine," she said eventually, "you can drive me home."

They went out to Terry's truck in silence. Maybe Terry just didn't want anyone else in the office—Clara or Melissa—to hear the discussion between them. Or perhaps he wanted to say something to her that he couldn't say in front of Stayner. Whatever his reason was, it was fine with Erin. She didn't want to talk to him either. Both because she didn't want to spread her business all over the town grapevine and because she was upset with him.

She tried to decide as they walked out to the truck and got in whether she was justified in being upset with him. Did she just feel like that because she was tired? Having an emotional reaction that was not rational? She didn't think so. Terry had excused himself from investigations that involved her in the past. That was what he was supposed to do, even if her connection to a case was only tenuous. If he didn't pull himself off, the sheriff would do it for him.

But this time, he had pretended to be on her side and not involved in the case and then had participated in the interrogation, trying to pry extra details out of her. He hadn't been doing that as a supportive partner trying to help her.

They didn't speak on the drive home. When Terry pulled up in front of the house, Erin had her door open before he was even fully stopped. She got out without a word and headed up to the front door without pausing to look at him or speak to him. He could pull back out and go straight back to the police department offices to continue investigating her background and anything that tied her and Brandon together. He could verify what she had said, start making phone calls to track down Brandon's friends to ask them about his relationship with Erin. He could dig deep and turn over as many of her secrets as he could, exposing them to the light of day.

She was nearly to the front door when she heard Terry's truck door open. He didn't call out to her, but followed her up the sidewalk into the house. Erin went into the house, shutting the door behind her, not waiting for him and holding it open as she normally would.

There wasn't anywhere she could go to escape him. She couldn't lock him out of the house when he lived there with her. It wouldn't be morally right or legal. If she tried, he could just call the sheriff, who would force her to let him in to at least remove his possessions from the house. And Erin didn't want to involve anyone else in their drama.

The door opened and closed quietly. Erin could hear K9 panting and, in a moment, he galloped across the house to catch up with her in the kitchen, which meant that Terry had released him from duty and was planning to stay rather than going back to the police department to continue the investigation. He needed his sleep too.

Erin talked to Orange Blossom and K9 as she got out their treats. Nothing that was going on was their fault. She tried not to treat them any differently from when she'd had a good day.

She opened the fridge and looked for something appetizing. Terry stood in the doorway of the kitchen, watching her.

"Erin."

She bent down to open a couple of containers of leftovers to see if there was anything she felt like eating, keeping the fridge door as a barrier between them.

"What?"

"We need to talk."

Erin shook her head. "I don't think so."

"I don't want things to be tense between us. We need to talk it out."

"I don't think that's the best solution."

He continued to stand there, waiting until Erin straightened up and closed the fridge door. "What do you think we should do, then?"

"Pretend that nothing happened. You can go back to work if you want. I'm going to bed."

She attempted to go into the walk-in pantry. He caught her by the arm, stopping her. His grip was not tight, but Erin stopped, her heart rate speeding up, just waiting for it to escalate.

"I don't want to go to work. I want to stay here and support you. But you need to let me do that."

"You can do what you want." Erin shrugged and tugged away from him, pulling out of his grip. "I didn't say you had to go back to work. It's up to you."

She looked at the various cans lining the shelves of the pantry. Eventually, she settled on a can of peaches. They would be sweet, go down easily, and be gentle on her stomach. She wouldn't eat much. She didn't want a full stomach keeping her awake. But she didn't want to lie awake hungry or wake up after a couple of hours needing something either.

Of course, all of that assumed that she would be able to sleep at all. She might not.

Terry watched her open the can and spoon some peach slices into a bowl. He helped himself to a few after she sat down at the table. He opened the freezer and added a small scoop of vanilla ice cream to the peaches. "You want some?"

It looked good, but Erin shook her head. "No."

He looked at her for a minute as if she were just being difficult and would change her mind if he waited her out. But Erin started to eat her peaches, and he put the ice cream back away. He put the remaining peaches into a plastic bowl with a lid and put them in the fridge before sitting down to eat his snack.

Hopefully, he would eat more later. He would order a pizza after Erin went to sleep or settle in front of the TV with a couple of beers and a bag of chips. But she wasn't going to offer to cook him anything or insist that he had to eat more, because that would just bounce back to her, with him suggesting that she had to eat more too.

Erin didn't have the energy to argue that her stomach simply wasn't prepared for anything heavier.

"You never told me about Quayle," Terry said after the room had been filled with nothing but their clinking spoons for a few minutes.

Erin didn't look at his face. "We haven't discussed our previous relationships."

She didn't know all the details of who he had dated in Bald Eagle Falls, either. She'd heard some rumors and knew some of the women he had dated in high school or since then. But they'd never discussed details with each other. Maybe he figured it would be too awkward for her to deal with those women as customers at the bakery and community events.

"I would think that you would have told me about something like that. About… the difficulties that you'd had before. It might have come up."

"Why?"

She glanced up at Terry's face for a moment. His brow crinkled and the corners of his mouth turned down. He was clearly upset; she had never seen him like this before. Usually, when he was upset, he kept a blank, stoic expression, giving nothing away. The revelation of her past relationship with Brandon had obviously bothered him significantly.

"Because… it sounds like a pretty traumatic experience. You might have wanted to talk about it. Or to work through it with a counselor. Or… to let me know if anything in our relationship… bothered you. Triggered a traumatic memory."

Erin ran her spoon through the leftover syrup in the bottom of her bowl, swirling it in circles and figure eights.

"I don't see why I would do that."

"When you're in a relationship… you share things."

"About past relationships? Why?"

He couldn't seem to come up with a reasonable explanation, demonstrating to Erin that it wasn't something that a normal couple would have discussed. He was just trying to get more information out of her as a suspect.

"I didn't know that things had gotten quite that bad for you,"

Terry said, approaching it from another angle. "I know you said that things were tight when you aged out of foster care. You had to start working immediately and couldn't always get something stable."

Erin nodded her agreement.

"But you didn't say… that you had moved in with someone like that in order to survive."

"I wouldn't share that."

She could feel his eyes on her. "No. You don't share much from your past."

Erin rubbed her forehead uncomfortably. "You've known that from the start. You knew… that I'd had trouble. You ran background on me when you were investigating Angela Plaint's death."

He had to admit this was true. "I knew that you'd faced charges a couple of times. That you had gone by other names. I guess once we got to know each other I thought that if it was anything big, you would talk to me about it. You said you'd had trouble with families thinking that you had stolen things from home care patients you had worked with, or the patients themselves thinking that. And kids in foster care often go by several different names. I just… didn't anticipate anything like this."

"Like what?" Erin challenged. K9, lying on the floor next to Terry raised his head at her sharp tone. "I didn't do anything wrong. This isn't… you make it sound like I broke the law by being with him. I didn't. I just needed somewhere to live."

"No… I didn't mean that you did something wrong. Just that you went through something a lot worse than I thought. You only talked about trying to keep a steady job, having to move when a client died, because your job had included board. You never said that you had lived with anyone else. I thought… maybe a shelter for a few days to get back on your feet, or sleeping in your car until you could find an apartment."

"And that would have been okay?" she demanded.

At least living in a shelter or car would not have resulted in her being suspected of murder. Did Terry and the others really think that she'd had something to do with Brandon's death? That she had coldheartedly set up a meeting with him and then stabbed him in the chest? Did he really think she was that kind of a person?

"You're taking this the wrong way. I'm not accusing you of doing anything wrong. I'm just... a little hurt that you would not share something so important with me."

"That's a part of my life that I would rather forget."

Though she wasn't looking at him directly, she could see him nod his head. "I can understand that. I'm sorry if you think that I'm being intrusive or asking about something that's none of my business. But couples who live together usually share. They have more... emotional intimacy."

"They don't tell each other everything. Do you think that Willie tells Vic everything? She doesn't even know where he is half the time. Or that she tells him everything about her past? Or Beaver tells Jeremy about her previous relationships or stings?"

"Sorry," Terry muttered. He was silent as he ate his last few slices of peaches.

When he was finished, he ran his hand over his face, a fatigued gesture. He'd been short on sleep while he'd been investigating Brandon's murder. Or the disappearance of his body. He needed to get to sleep and not to be up another night.

"What do you want me to do?" Terry asked tiredly.

"About what?"

"Do you want me to sleep in the guest bedroom? Or leave?"

He looked at her, waiting for her response.

CHAPTER 19

"No, you don't need to leave," Erin said quickly, as if she would never think such a thing. As if she hadn't already been thinking about whether she could keep him out of her house, now that she was a suspect and Terry was being a cop instead of her boyfriend.

"The spare room, then?"

Erin didn't know what to say. It was good of him to suggest that he sleep somewhere else. There was a rift between them, and she didn't know if it could be repaired. He chose to be a cop over being there for her in a supportive role like he had first suggested. She had turned out not to be the person he thought she was. Someone who had sunk lower than he had ever imagined. Who might have killed a man to hide her past.

She wanted him to be there in her bed and to hold her tight and to say that it didn't matter and that he forgave her and didn't think she had killed Brandon Quayle. She wanted his warmth beside her, anchoring her. But that was a dream. It wasn't going to happen. They couldn't just erase what had been said over the last hour or two.

"Yeah, I guess," she conceded. "There are fresh sheets—"

"I know where everything is. I'll get out of your way."

He stood up and took his bowl to the dishwasher. Then headed out of the kitchen and down the hall to the spare room. He shut the door with a soft click, and Erin heard K9 whine in confusion. Terry opened the door again, and K9 exited, running back out to Erin and then heading toward her bedroom, where his kennel was.

But then he looked around and ran back to Terry in the spare room.

"Sorry," Terry apologized from within the room. "He's confused. I can move the kennel in here so he knows where to sleep."

Erin's heart gave a tug. Not only was she keeping Terry from her bed, but she was also upsetting K9. It wasn't his fault that his master had chosen the investigation over his relationship. Erin wanted to tell Terry that K9 could sleep in her bedroom, but she suspected that still wouldn't be a good solution. K9 would want to be in his kennel and near Terry. He wasn't used to sleeping in a different room.

"Yeah, I guess."

Terry came back out of the guest room and went down the hall to retrieve K9's kennel from Erin's room. He looked at her face for a moment when he returned. Was he wondering, as she was, whether this would be a permanent separation? He was probably running through his options, figuring out how quickly he could get his own place again if he needed to. Or maybe things would settle down and go back to normal and he would only be sleeping in the guest room for a day or two. K9 still ran back and forth between Terry and Erin, whining. Terry called him into the room, ordered him into the kennel, and shut the bedroom door.

K9 was a well-trained dog, and he would stay there, but Erin was afraid he would be unhappy all night, wondering why things had changed and he couldn't sleep with both Terry and Erin like usual.

K9 wasn't Erin's dog. She had known him for a much shorter time than Terry had. His loyalties were clearly to Terry rather than to Erin. She had never considered him her dog, but couldn't help the feeling that he was being torn away from her. She was attached to all of the animals in the household and would miss K9 if she and Terry did not work things out. And the other animals would miss him too. Orange Blossom took hissing and growling at K9 to a high art, but Erin suspected that he enjoyed the rivalry with K9 as much as his friendship with Marshmallow and would not be a happy kitty if his enemy no longer came around.

~

"I take it you didn't sleep too well last night?" Vic asked as she watched Erin pour coffee into her tall travel mug. Erin didn't normally consume that much caffeine.

"No. Not very well. I was tossing and turning all night, don't feel like I got a wink of sleep, though I know I must have gotten some."

"You should just stay home," Vic urged. "I can start the morning routine and call Charley to see if she's still up. Then one of the others to help out with the afternoon shift. No point in you being miserable all morning instead of just staying home and having a rest."

"I need to work. I need to throw myself into something and keep my mind off of… things."

"I heard that you knew Brandon Quayle," Vic said, her voice quiet, eyes down and away from Erin. She didn't ask for details, though it was pretty evident from her manner she was curious.

"Yeah. I'm sure that will all come out now. We can talk about it later. We'd better hit the road."

Erin grabbed her purse, heavy with her stuffed planner and tall travel mug, and headed out the door. Vic followed her out the door without complaint. They probably should have walked, but Erin chose to take the yellow VW bug instead. When they were on the way, Vic looked sideways at Erin.

"So, Brandon Quayle?" she prompted.

Erin looked back at her. "What about him?"

"I just wondered. You said before that you didn't know everyone in Maine, so you didn't know him. But… there are rumors that you did know him. The police department was questioning you about it yesterday."

"Someone needs to learn to keep her mouth shut."

Vic nodded philosophically. "Yeah. She does. So… they were asking you about him? And things went south?"

"I didn't kill him."

"Well, of course not!" Vic exclaimed. "I was there! Well, not right there in the basement, but I was there when you left Auntie Clem's and when you came back. I know you didn't have anything to do with it."

A huge weight lifted from Erin's shoulders. The police could suspect her all she liked, even Terry, but *Vic* knew that Erin hadn't had anything to do with Brandon's murder. She would stand up for Erin no matter what. And maybe others would too. Surely the residents of Bald Eagle Falls that she had rubbed shoulders with the past two years knew something about her by now. They knew that she wouldn't have done something like that.

If she had, she would have done a much better job at covering it up, and would not have moved the body, called the police, and then done it all a second time just for her own entertainment. Who did something like that? She had a hard time understanding why Brandon's body had been moved in the first place. And she was baffled at why it had been left in Canyon Park.

"I know you didn't kill the guy, Erin," Vic assured her. "There's no way. You didn't have enough time and, even if you did, why would you kill him? What motive did you have?"

"I don't know. I left him…" Erin shook her head, "before I ever came to Bald Eagle Falls. I haven't had anything to do with him since I left. So why would I do something now? All of that stuff, anything that happened between us, is way in the past."

"It doesn't make any sense," Vic agreed. "You didn't even know he was in town."

"No." Erin studied Vic. "I didn't."

"I knew it. If he was an ex, there is no way you would have gone over to The Book Nook to meet with him."

"Of course not."

Were there other exes that she would have met up with? Erin went through them in her mind and shook her head. She couldn't think of one of them that she would have agreed to meet with. Or one who would have wanted to meet with her. Who would come to Bald Eagle Falls to see her? It wasn't like she was a lottery winner and everyone wanted a piece of her. She was comfortable for the first time in her life but didn't have money to burn. Or to give away to anyone.

They reached the back door of Auntie Clem's Bakery, and Vic stepped aside to wait as Erin unlocked it and opened the door.

"Melissa said that Quayle was writing a memoir."

CHAPTER 20

$\mathcal{E}$rin turned to look at Vic as they walked into the kitchen and turned on the lights.

"What?"

"Brandon Quayle was writing a memoir."

"A memoir?" Erin let out a laugh. "Why would he do that? Who would read it?"

"He didn't lead a very interesting life?" Vic asked. "I gather he wasn't anyone famous."

"An interesting life?" Erin echoed.

She didn't say anything while she pulled the bowls of batter out of the fridge and lined them up on the counter. Vic started turning on the ovens.

An interesting life? She supposed Brandon's life had been interesting. Certainly more interesting than she had liked. He certainly wasn't someone to hold up as an inspiration to others. He had been an addict, a liar, someone who was frequently in trouble with the police, and abusive.

He was a charmer. He had a way of making people think he was something he wasn't. But that only lasted for so long, as eventually people came to realize the truth about what he was—someone who manipulated others for his own gain. He got jobs and money from unsuspecting folks, used women for his own pleasure, and convinced people that his clothes were designer names and that his car was actually his. Yet in reality, he was not only behind on rent—but had been taken to court three times by his landlord to have him removed.

"Why would he write a memoir?" she asked aloud. "What exactly was it supposed to be about? A life he made up?"

"I don't know anything. Just that Melissa said that's what he was doing. Maybe that's why he was at The Book Nook."

Erin couldn't figure that one out. "Why?"

"To… read other memoirs or a book about writing memoirs. Or meet an agent or publisher."

Erin couldn't remember Brandon ever reading a book while she had known him. Not even a comic book. And he thought he could write one?

There was a knock at the door, which made both of them jump.

CHAPTER 21

It was so rare for anyone to knock on the back door while they were open. And even more rare so early in the morning, before they had opened. One day, Beaver had dropped by early in the morning looking for something to eat after an unexpectedly long stakeout. She had not planned to be overnight and had not been prepared with the food she needed.

That had ended up being a pretty stressful day for anyone at Auntie Clem's or any of the businesses along Main Street, so Erin's heart was in her stomach as she walked over to the door to answer it.

"Who's there?"

"My name is Adrienne. I don't know if you remember me."

Erin opened the door slowly, trying to sort through her memories to find someone named Adrienne. She remembered as she opened the door and saw the woman standing there—one of the rural homeless around Bald Eagle Falls. There were families who squatted in the woods, trying to make enough to provide for their needs. People who couldn't afford the rental cost of an apartment or basement suite. Who maybe couldn't manage more than a tent over their heads, or living out of a car, as Terry had suggested the day before.

Erin knew what it was like not to have a proper place of her own. Maybe that was why she had felt so strongly the need to help and support the poor in and around Bald Eagle Falls when other successful business owners in the town did not.

"Adrienne. Come in." Erin let her step inside the door. "What can I do for you?"

Adrienne looked nervously in Vic's direction, but Vic didn't stare at her or ask questions. She just went back to her work.

"It's okay," Erin assured her. "Do you want a coffee? Warm you up inside?"

Even though it wasn't cold outside, people who were malnourished often didn't have the fat to keep their body temperatures up and were constantly cold. Adrienne was thin. Her children were as skinny as sticks, but still seemed to have the energy to play all day, so they must be getting enough to eat. Adrienne probably skipped meals herself to put food on the table for them.

Adrienne shook her head, still looking around as if someone might attack her or might have seen her and followed her there.

"I just wondered… I know about your day-old bread program."

"Of course," Erin agreed. "I have so much in the freezer right now; I'd really be grateful if you could take some of it off my hands. We try not to make too much more than we need in a day but, of course, you have to keep food in the display case right up until closing time, so there has to be extra each day."

Adrienne nodded as Erin explained this and followed Erin over to the large chest freezer along one wall. Erin opened it up, and Adrienne's eyes popped at the variety of goods stored there. She had probably thought that Erin was kidding about needing someone to give the excess food to.

"Some bread and muffins, first of all," Erin said briskly, taking out several bags of frozen goods. "And what else do the children like? Some cookies? Chocolate, oatmeal, gumdrop, gingersnaps…"

Adrienne's eyes went over the possibilities. "Chocolate chip." She pointed at one of the bags. Erin pulled them out.

"And maybe some pizza shells? Bagels? The pizza pretzels are popular, so we always keep them well-stocked throughout the day and have a few left over after closing."

"That sounds nice."

"Let me get a shopping bag for you." Erin took a couple of bags of pizza pretzels out of the freezer and took a few shopping bags off of a shelf. She started loading the baked goods into bags. "Now, what else?"

Adrienne's eyes were big. She shook her head. "It's too much. I can't take all of this."

"Do you see anyone else taking it?" Erin motioned to the kitchen, occupied only by the three of them. "I take more home than I can eat with Terry—Officer Piper. Only a little bit of our day-old gets claimed, and I have to take the rest into the city for the shelters there or throw it in the garbage. And I hate throwing anything in the garbage."

Adrienne nodded, her eyes still big and skin pale. Erin would have expected her to be tanned or sunburned, with the amount of time she must spend outside but, if she wasn't getting enough to eat, starvation might have caused her pallor. "Of course. You can't throw good food away."

"Exactly. Are you sure I can't get you anything else?"

"No, this is plenty. We can afford to go to the grocery store." She said it defensively as if Erin had accused her of being unable to feed her family.

"Okay. Well, when you've used this up, just stop by. Or if you know someone else who could use it. It's so much easier for me if someone will take it off my hands."

Adrienne took the bags from her slowly. Her fingers were long and thin. For a moment, their eyes met.

"You are a nice woman," Adrienne said softly. "Most people don't understand."

"I think there are others who would… but they don't have as much to give as I do."

"*They* don't know what it's like to have nothing." Adrienne tossed another glance in Vic's direction, unsure of speaking in front of her.

"Vic understands," Erin countered. "When I first came to Bald Eagle Falls, she was living in the basement of the bakery. Hiding. She didn't have anywhere to go."

"Oh?" Adrienne looked at Vic for longer this time, and her shoulders lowered as she relaxed. "I didn't know."

"How would you? It was a couple of years ago, probably before you moved here."

The woman nodded, her lips pursed. She put her hand briefly on Erin's arm. "*We* know what it's like. Vic and I." She glanced over at Vic to elicit a nod. "Living how you can. Surviving. It isn't like people think it is. I wouldn't take my kids to one of those places. Catching fleas, getting molested, never being able to get a good night's sleep. You want a *home*. A place of your own." Her hand fluttered to indicate the direction of her camp. "Even if you have to start out living in a tent. Or with someone who..." Her eyes went to her feet, away from Erin. "Someone willing to help you out."

For Vic, that had been Erin. She had taken the younger woman in and invited her into her home. Vic was now more independent with her loft room over the garage, paying Erin a small amount in rent out of her earnings at Auntie Clem's. Erin didn't expect anything from her. But it had been different when Erin had been left with no job, no income, and no roof over her head. There were no savings to fall back on. No Clementine back then, before Alton Summers had come looking for her to tell her of her inheritance.

She'd had to survive somehow. It had been Brandon who had given her a hand, letting her crash with him while she tried to get back on her feet. Living in his apartment, eating his food, and trying to find another job when her last employer couldn't give her a reference and his family had refused to. Managing to find casual labor for a day or two, or saving nickels and dimes from panhandling. It took a long time working that way to put away enough money for a down payment on an apartment. And then she would need a job that paid enough to maintain it.

That's why it was better to find a job caring for someone who needed a companion, a position where she could board. Until that job ended, and the bottom fell out, and she was left again with no place to go.

"You did what you could at the time," Adrienne said, reminding Erin she was there, drawing her back from the memories.

Erin realized with a start that Adrienne wasn't just there for herself. She wasn't just there because of Erin's day-old baking program, though she appreciated the donation. She was there for Erin, to tell her that there were people who understood. It was hard for people like Terry and Stayner, who had always had a home, always had a roof over their heads, men with good jobs to support themselves. They'd had the stability, family support, and education needed to move into their chosen professions. They couldn't understand why she had stayed with Brandon and appreciated him despite his emotional instability and abuse.

"Thank you," Erin said softly, and put her hand over Adrienne's. She didn't know how word had gotten to Adrienne so quickly and still resented Melissa gossiping about the personal, private details of Erin's past. But she was thankful for Adrienne's empathy, even when everyone else only saw her as the prime suspect in a murder.

CHAPTER 22

$\mathcal{E}$rin had known that it would be a busy day at the bakery, as it always was after a murder or other tragedy. Initially, they had been curious about the disappearing body—the shock of first discovering it and then its disappearance. Then there had been the rediscovery of the body in the park. Now, they were even more titillated by the fact that the victim was an ex-boyfriend—what else were they going to call him?—of Erin's. They wanted to see Erin and her red-rimmed, baggy eyes to speculate on how she felt about Brandon and his death and whether she might be his killer.

They hoped she would give them some salacious details to feed the Bald Eagle Falls grapevine and keep it chattering away. And if she didn't give them any, they would make it up.

There was a moment of startled silence when Dave Wolfe walked in the door, and then the whispers and giggles started. Erin found herself looking questioningly in Dave's direction to find out why he was there, even though there were several ladies ahead of him in line.

"I just thought I'd get a muffin," Dave offered. "And… Naomi had some questions about the next book club theme…?"

"Oh." Erin shook her head. "Things are pretty busy here today."

"Go ahead," Vic told her. "You look like you need a break. I can handle things here for twenty minutes."

"Are you sure? It's been so…"

"Go," Vic repeated firmly.

Things would probably quiet down once Erin left and they didn't have anyone to direct their curiosity at. Maybe they would follow her to The Book Nook and give Naomi some business. Had she been getting more customers since Erin had discovered Brandon's body in the basement? People had probably started their back-to-school shopping early. Any excuse to scout out a murder scene, even if they couldn't go down to the basement.

The Book Nook had just barely opened. Booksellers did not need to be up as early as bakers. There were no cars parked out in front of the store yet, even though Auntie Clem's had been buzzing with activity for several hours.

The door was unlocked and the Open sign up, so Erin walked in. The tinkling bell drew Naomi's attention, and she smiled at Erin, raising her brows as if surprised to see her.

"Oh, hi, Erin. What can I find for you today? Some more breakfast recipe books?"

Erin laughed. "I think I've already got a copy of everything you have. And a couple you don't. Dave said you wanted to talk to me about the next book club theme? We were going to do 'an apple for teacher,' right?"

Naomi walked across the floor to her. "I think it was probably more that he's just been concerned about you and wanted me to make sure you were okay. We've *both* been concerned about you since… you know. I just wanted to make sure that… things weren't going to be awkward between us. And you coming here… sometimes people can get kind of a phobia about going back somewhere that something bad or scary happened. And I thought… finding a body in the basement is *kind of* traumatic and you might feel… anxious about coming back here."

Erin had been distracted by wondering what Naomi's concern over the book club theme was and hadn't even thought about the bookstore being the location where she had found Brandon's body the first time. Now she looked around, actually thinking about it, testing out how she felt about being there.

She had been at The Book Nook many times before and had always had good experiences there and positive feelings associated with it. The fact that she had found Brandon in the basement, a place she had never been before and would probably never be again, made it a little bit easier. She could imagine it was some other world, some-place far away rather than right under her feet. A sort of a nightmare world that she had been dropped into once, but would never dream of again.

"No, I think I'm okay with it, actually. As long as I don't have to go down to the basement."

Naomi smiled, her face lighting up like the sun had just broken over the horizon. "Oh, I'm so glad, Erin. I wouldn't want to lose your friendship or your help with the book club just because... something unfortunate happened."

"It's not your fault." Erin gave a shrug. "I don't think you invited him over here or killed him in the basement. Why would you? You didn't even know the guy. Now if you had known him..." Erin tried to keep a teasing tone and not let her voice get serious or malicious. What *would* Erin have done if she had seen Brandon again? She had never been violent toward him. She couldn't see herself ever trying to hurt him.

And she would never have the opportunity to find out. Brandon Quayle was gone.

And good riddance.

Erin visited with Naomi for a few minutes, made sure they were both onside with the plans for the next book club meeting, and then Erin headed back to the bakery. She could see when she reached the door that the crowd had thinned out and only a couple of customers were at the counter waiting to be served. Vic had things well under control. There were a number of coffee cups, wrappers, and dispos-able plates on the little tables at the front of the store, where the women had gathered to gossip or catch up with one another's lives.

She figured her time would best be spent tidying up so that it didn't look like a pigsty for the next group of customers. She picked up the various detritus and threw it into the nearby garbage. It shouldn't be that hard for customers to take two steps over to the garbage to throw their own trash away instead of leaving it on the tables. That was just common courtesy.

Erin picked up a folded piece of lined paper that looked like it might be a school assignment and unfolded it to see what it was. If one of the students who stopped in for a quick treat had left it behind, they might be looking for it by the end of the day. Finding out that Erin had thrown it away—and having to dig through the garbage to find it and see if it were salvageable—would not be a good experience.

It was not a school assignment, but a recipe. Interested, Erin skimmed through it to see if she could figure out who had left it behind. She read through it a second time, more slowly, her heart racing.

"Vicky... do you know who left this here?"

"What is it?" Vic studied the paper in Erin's hand and shook her head. "No, I didn't see. Where was it?"

"On one of the tables. I was just clearing up."

"No. There were a lot of people over there in the past hour. It could belong to anyone."

Erin walked slowly over to the section of the counter that folded back on a hinge and let herself back into the "employees only" section.

"What is it?" Vic asked.

"It's a recipe."

"One of yours?"

"No. Not one of mine. I don't know whose it is."

"Well, if it's important, I guess they'll come back for it. Probably not anything you can use, huh? It would be nice if it was. A nice little gift from the gluten-free fairies..." She giggled. "Or brownies!"

"It actually is."

"What?"

"Gluten-free. It uses buckwheat. You don't know of anyone else in Bald Eagle Falls who was entering the waffle contest, do you?"

"No, not that I've heard."

Erin had been talking about the waffle contest to customers for a week. She thought that if anyone else had been interested in entering the contest, they would have mentioned it. Or asked her how to submit an entry to the contest. But no one else had expressed any interest in it, other than to ask her what she would be submitting.

"It's a waffle recipe?" Vic asked. She counted Mary Lou's change out loud and handed it over. "A gluten-free waffle recipe?"

"Yes." Erin looked toward the table again as if the person who had left it there might have materialized.

"Maybe it is the gluten-free fairy," Vic laughed. "She heard you wishing for a gluten-free waffle that would win the contest, and *behold!* There it is."

"That's weird." Erin shook her head. "Weird that someone would just leave something like that here."

"You're not going to use it, are you?"

"No. Not without knowing where it came from. I don't want to jeopardize someone else's chances of winning the prize."

"Though why anyone else would want to make twenty waffles at once, I don't know," Vic shook her head. "Who but a restaurant or bakery owner would want to win one?"

"Well… someone who wants to save time and put a bunch in the freezer for the kids to use for breakfasts and lunches. Someone with a big family. You know, if you've got six kids, twenty waffles don't really go far. Especially if a couple of them are teenagers. Sometimes it would be convenient to make a whole bunch of waffles all at once."

"Okay, you got me there. Maybe it was someone who is entering the contest. But why would they leave the recipe here? It seems to me that if I wanted to enter a contest, I wouldn't leave my recipe in my rival's house or place of business."

"No. It's probably not that. Just… a coincidence."

"Or the waffle fairy," Vic joked. She sobered up. "Or… someone who wanted to give you a chance at winning the contest. Maybe it isn't for someone else's entry, maybe it's for you."

"Then… why not give it to me? Or leave a note saying that it's for me to use? Just leaving it here like this…"

"I hope you solve your mystery," Mary Lou said with a smile, turning to leave the shop.

"Oh, I didn't even say hello to you," Erin realized. "I just barreled in here and completely ignored you. How are you, Mary Lou?"

"We are getting along fine, thank you," Mary Lou said with a small nod, pausing in the doorway. "I think you can be forgiven for ignoring a customer when you discover that the gluten-free fairy has left you a gift." She gave a small chuckle at their conversation.

Vic turned pink, grinning. "It isn't every day that the gluten-free fairy comes by." She wiped tears from the corner of her eyes as she tried to keep from laughing. "Although if there is any place in town that she should bless with her offerings, it would have to be Auntie Clem's."

"Of course," Mary Lou agreed. "It's only fitting." She shook her head and pushed the bar on the door to leave. "Have a nice day, ladies."

CHAPTER 23

*E*rin was left to puzzle over the serendipitous appearance of the waffle recipe for the rest of the day. At home, she and Terry came and went without much comment to each other, did not eat dinner together and, as evening drew on, Terry retreated to the guest bedroom again. It was earlier than he usually went to bed, so Erin could only assume it was a declaration of his intentions. He would continue to sleep separately until she talked to him about it and indicated she wanted the situation to return to normal. He wouldn't push her, wouldn't get in her way; he would wait until she told him she didn't like the status quo. Either to invite him to return to her room and her bed, or to tell him that she didn't want him in the house anymore.

She hated to think of him leaving and didn't intend to kick him out. Not yet, anyway. She felt the situation could be salvaged. She hoped that it could be. The two of them were not incompatible. They had just run into a speed bump in one area. When it was resolved, they could move on together again.

At least, that was what Erin hoped.

She heard K9 whining, and then the dog gave two sharp barks. She hovered outside of the guest room door uncertainly.

"Do you want me to take him out?"

There was a pause before Terry answered from the other side of the door. "I can take him outside, Erin. You don't need to do that."

"He's probably confused about why I'm not doing anything with him. I don't mind taking him outside for a few minutes. Let him know that I'm not mad at him or something."

"Well… if you want to, of course."

After a moment, Terry opened the door. He clicked his tongue at K9 to call him to the door.

"Come on, K9," Erin invited. "Let's go outside."

K9 bounded over to her and rubbed against her leg, his head repeatedly pressing into Erin's hand so that she would give him pets and scratches.

"Okay, okay," Erin laughed. "I'm right here. I'm not going anywhere. Let's go outside for a run."

He ran to the back door. Erin nodded at Terry. "We'll just be a few minutes."

"Sure. I'll leave the door open until you're back."

That way, she didn't have to knock to get him to open the door again to let K9 in. He was trying to make things convenient for her and not cause extra awkwardness, which made Erin feel more awkward about the whole thing.

Erin let K9 into the backyard. To begin with, he went straight to the dog run on the other side of the house. He and Nilla were trained to use the area so that they didn't have to worry about cleaning up after them in the rest of the yard. Erin kicked off her sandals and started practicing her tai chi forms. After a few minutes, K9 ran over to her with a ball in his mouth and deposited it at her feet. Erin picked it up and threw it for him. K9 chased after the ball and brought it back again. Erin continued to alternate tai chi forms with throwing the ball while K9 bounded around excitedly.

She was glad she had offered to take him outside for a while.

"Miss Price. I wonder if we could talk."

Erin turned her head, startled, and saw Sheriff Wilmot standing at the gate between the front and back yards. She often visited in the yard with Vic, Willie, or Adele, but she hadn't been expecting Wilmot.

"Uh… I don't know. It isn't really a good time."

"I think it's important. You probably want to get this case solved as quickly as possible."

Erin hesitated. Even though she recognized he was trying to manipulate her, she *did* want it all to be over. The sooner they could figure out who it was that had killed Brandon Quayle, the sooner she could go on with her life and she and Terry could get back on track if that was possible. K9 brought Erin the ball back again. He glanced over at Sheriff Wilmot, but didn't tense or act worried about his being in the yard. He saw Wilmot at work every day, so he knew he was not a threat.

Erin threw the ball again. K9 jumped up to catch it, but it was just a little beyond his reach. He snapped at it again once his feet hit the ground and managed to catch it on a bounce. He brought it back to Erin, his pointed ears and wagging tail showing that he was proud of himself.

"What do you want to know?"

"Could you come down to the police department?" At Erin's look, he changed his mind. "Or maybe we could sit down inside? I don't think *this* is conducive to a conversation." He indicated K9 and the yard and Erin starting another tai chi pose.

"Could it wait until tomorrow?"

"Are you able to come by in the morning?"

"Well…" Erin stretched her arms out, eyes on a distant spot on the fence. "No, I work in the morning."

"You work long hours. And I don't want to disrupt your schedule. That's why I thought that maybe now… you could take a few minutes with me."

Erin sighed. "Okay. Fine. I guess we can talk inside." Erin motioned to K9 to return to the house and started in that direction herself. K9's tail drooped, and he reluctantly followed her into the house. Erin gestured for Sheriff Wilmot to sit down at the kitchen table. She got K9 a cookie. "Good boy. Go see Terry."

K9 obeyed, taking the cookie in his lips and bounding off to the guest room. Erin turned her attention to Wilmot, but she didn't want to have to sit there with him at the table with no choice but to either look him in the face so that she seemed engaged, or not look at him and make him think that she was hiding something. Instead, she went to the counter and put on the kettle to boil.

"Have you heard that Quayle was writing a memoir?" Wilmot asked, watching her work and apparently deciding he might as well start on his questions rather than waiting until she was done.

"Heard that today."

"Yes, a lot seems to have gotten out today," he admitted.

"You really should do something about that leak."

He shrugged with one shoulder. Erin knew that Melissa had worked with the police department since she was sixteen, long before Sheriff Wilmot had started there, and before that her dad had been a cop. So she got a certain amount of leeway just because of her long history with the department. But Wilmot didn't seem too worried about the leaked information. Erin had her suspicions that he sometimes wanted information to be leaked. Maybe it was his way of shaking the tree to see what would fall out of it.

He didn't say anything, and Erin went back to his comment. Brandon was writing a memoir. She had been shocked when Vic had revealed that information. It certainly wasn't something that the old Brandon would have done. She couldn't imagine him taking on anything as serious as writing a memoir. Jumping off a bridge while drunk to get his name in the paper, maybe, but a memoir? A whole book? She couldn't imagine what he had been planning to put in it. What accomplishments did he have to tell about? It wasn't like he was a famous musician or actor. He hadn't discovered a scientific principle or new planet. Brandon had been much like Erin. Undereducated. Working class. He could make ends meet and pay the rent most months, but he wasn't the type who was getting ahead. He'd never achieved anything really big, so far as Erin knew. And she thought she would have heard if he had. Brandon had never been very motivated to do anything more than get out of bed in the morning, sometimes not even that.

"What was he writing a memoir about?" she asked Wilmot finally. "What did he ever do that he would write about?"

"It was a tell-all," Wilmot explained slowly. "All about his life before he sobered up and turned things around."

Who would care about his life before he sobered up? Erin shook her head.

Wilmot studied her. "Can you think of anything you wouldn't want him to write about you?"

CHAPTER 24

*E*rin felt the blood drain from her face.

Stuff about her? What could Brandon write about her?

It wasn't like she had been involved in any criminal behavior that she was afraid he would reveal. They hadn't been knocking off liquor stores or doing drug deals together. Brandon had done a lot of crazy things, but Erin hadn't been a part of that. If he said that she had, he would be lying. But when had the truth ever been the barrier to a good story?

Despite her thought that he didn't have enough material in him for a memoir, Brandon had been a good storyteller. He had an endless supply of stories, mostly things that had happened to other people with some extra embellishments. It wasn't unusual for him to have the whole room on the edges of their seats or in stitches. He reveled in the spotlight.

"I have no idea what he might have written," Erin told Wilmot, shaking her head. "What makes you think it would be the truth?"

If the police already had Brandon's manuscript and were reading through it, she didn't want there to be any doubt that every word in there was probably a lie.

"Brandon liked to get people's attention. He liked to tell stories.

I'm sure that's all he's done if he's really written something that he called a memoir. He's made up a bunch of stories and put them together like it really happened."

"And does that worry you?"

Erin swallowed and kept her face blank and unconcerned. "No. Why should it? Anyone who knows Brandon will know that it isn't true. And it's not like he's some famous person or bestselling author. Why would anyone care about the stuff he did when he was drunk? That's not literature."

Sheriff Wilmot nodded slowly. He wrote a few notes in his pad. "You wouldn't be concerned if he got a big book deal?"

"A *big* book deal?" Erin repeated. "I doubt he'd get any book deal. A *big* book deal? How would he get that? No one knows him. You can't get into those big publishers just because you send them your manuscript. You have to have an agent and... something really good. Not some no-name telling all of his favorite drunk stories."

"We haven't heard the details of the deal yet. We are following up on that. It's slow going because we don't have the name of his agent or who the deal is with. Just that he had been telling people he got a big deal."

Erin poured boiling water into cups and took them to the table with the rest of the tea things. "I'd take that with a grain of salt. The guy isn't known for his honesty."

"Wasn't."

"What?" Erin sat down and picked out a teabag for herself. Something herbal that wouldn't keep her awake.

"He *wasn't* known for his honesty. You said isn't."

"Oh." Erin shook her head, thinking about it. "I guess maybe I haven't accepted that he's dead. I mean, I know he is, but... talking about the way things used to be... I guess it hasn't really sunk in."

Erin heard the guest room door open and knew Terry was listening, trying to catch their conversation. She didn't know what she should do. Invite him to join them? Pretend she didn't know he was there? Wilmot didn't give any sign that he knew anyone was listening in on the conversation.

"So it didn't concern you. That Quayle might publish a tell-all book that included information about you. Or stories about you that weren't true."

"No. Nobody who reads it is going to know me, and anyone who really knows me will know what's true and what's not. Besides, when they publish stuff like that, don't they change the names and say it's been fictionalized? I mean, I heard that they merge several different people together to make one character or change things about people to make them more interesting or to fit with the story better."

"I've heard that."

"Then why would I care? He can say whatever he likes. And if it was a big publishing company, their lawyers wouldn't let them publish anything libelous. Nothing that they could be sued for."

Wilmot sipped his tea, a ginger orange blend with some notes of nutmeg. He seemed to have stalled in his questions. Maybe he was just regrouping or figuring out what to ask her next. Had he really thought she would be concerned about what Brandon might be threatening to publish about her?

"Did Brandon tell you that he was publishing a book?"

Erin shrugged. "No. I didn't know anything about it. I didn't talk to him."

"When was the last time you talked to him?"

"I don't know. More than two years. Not since I moved to Tennessee. And before that, I was doing the best I could to avoid him. I didn't move in those circles anymore."

"Why not?"

"I just… didn't. I wasn't interested in being part of that group. They did a lot of stupid stuff. Once I could get a job that would let me leave… I did."

"We would like to access your computer. Do you think I could have a look at that now?"

Erin stared at him. Did he think he could just walk in and get a look at whatever he wanted? She shook her head. "I don't have a computer at home. Just the one at the bakery that I do my book-keeping on."

"That's your only computer?"

"Yes."

"You must have another way to pick up your email and communicate with people. Your phone?"

"Yes, sure. Of course."

"Could I see that?" Wilmot put his hand out as if he expected Erin to hand it over.

She didn't move. "No."

"You said that you haven't had anything to do with Quayle, so you don't have anything to hide," he reasoned.

"No. You don't need to see my email or my phone. There's nothing on there to do with the case. I have my right to privacy."

"If we are going to figure out who killed Quayle, we are going to need access to these things."

"No," she told him again. "That's private."

"I will come back with a warrant."

"We'll see."

He would need to go into the city for that, or at least to call a judge in the city. They didn't have one in Bald Eagle Falls. And he would need to prove that he needed access to it. That she was a good suspect in Brandon's murder. She didn't think that the facts supported him. Yes, she had known Brandon, and she had been the one to find his body, but it wasn't like she'd been caught hanging over him with the murder weapon in her hand or that her fingerprints were on the knife that had killed him. She had called the police about finding the body—twice—and that was what good citizens did, not murderers. Wilmot didn't have any evidence that she had been in contact with Brandon since moving to Bald Eagle Falls. That was what he was looking for. It was a fishing expedition.

"I think you're done here."

Erin and Wilmot both startled slightly and turned to look at Terry, standing in the kitchen doorway. Erin was torn between being grateful for his intervention and irritated that he had stepped in to take control of the conversation. She was handling it just fine, and she was going to get rid of Sheriff Wilmot herself. She didn't need him interfering.

Wilmot looked at Terry, scowling. "Why don't you see if you can talk her into letting us have a look at her emails? If she has nothing to hide…"

"She's not going to give you access to her email."

Sheriff Wilmot took another long sip of his tea and put the cup down. "I'll be back, Miss Price. You can count on that. This won't end until we figure out who killed Mr. Quayle."

"That's fine with me," Erin said flatly. "But that doesn't mean you're getting access to my personal property."

He nodded to her and Terry and slipped out the back door. Erin stood up and began gathering the tea things and putting dishes into the dishwasher.

"You shouldn't have invited him in," Terry said from the doorway.

"I didn't exactly. He said that he needed to talk. Kind of invited himself."

"You shouldn't have let him in. Don't talk to him voluntarily anymore. He doesn't have enough evidence to arrest you. And if he does, you still don't talk to him. You only talk to your lawyer."

"You think I did it?" Erin asked. "You think I killed Brandon?"

"No. I don't think you did," he scoffed. "No matter what he did to you years ago, why would you kill him now? You didn't invite him to meet with you in the basement of The Book Nook. You just told Wilmot that you don't care what he put in his memoir. That's not a motive. But you need to protect yourself. Don't talk to him. Don't give him anything to use against you. If he gets that warrant, you have to comply, but you don't have to talk to him. Get a lawyer and keep your mouth shut."

"You think he would railroad me?"

"I think it's been done many times. Not by Wilmot," he hastened to add. "He's a straight shooter. But that doesn't mean he couldn't be misled or make a wrong judgment. I don't want anything to happen to you. You need to protect yourself."

Erin nodded. "I will."

He stood there for a moment longer, then went back to the guest bedroom.

Erin waited a few minutes, puttering around the kitchen but not really getting anything done. She armed the burglar alarm and shut off the lights. Orange Blossom rubbed against her legs and chatted with her in low meows. After getting ready for bed, Erin pulled out her tablet and opened her email.

CHAPTER 25

*A*untie Clem's was closed on Sunday, as were the rest of the shops in town. But it opened for a couple of hours for the ladies' tea after services. Women came over to chat and gossip and relax with coffee, tea, and cookies. It was a low-key affair. There was nothing to do on Sunday but open, serve food and drink, and clean up after the ladies were gone. And while Erin frequently did this herself so she could keep up with the local news and visit with the women in a relaxed environment, it was a duty that any one of her employees could easily handle, and today Bella was taking the shift.

Erin slept in as much as she was able. It was later than she normally would have been able to sleep, which told her that she had not been getting enough sleep lately. She needed to make sure that she got to bed in plenty of time and was nice and relaxed, so she could get enough hours of good quality sleep to keep going. She made herself a slice of toast and cup of tea and sat at the kitchen table, reviewing her planner and working on her schedule and tasks for the next week.

Vic tapped at the back door and entered. Erin had already unlocked it for her and disarmed the burglar alarm.

"Morning, sunshine!" Vic greeted.

She was still in a pair of pajamas, with her fine blond hair pulled back into a ponytail, brushed but not styled.

"Hi. Grab yourself a cup of tea," Erin invited. She motioned to the teapot. "It's still hot."

Vic made herself at home and sat down across from Erin. "How is next week looking?"

"Not too bad. I hope to have the time to try a few waffle recipes."

Vic licked her lips. "I love waffles."

"Well, you should get your chance to test several varieties!"

"Did you find out anything about that waffle recipe you found on the table at Auntie Clem's?"

"No." Erin frowned, thinking back to her investigations so far. She had asked a few people she knew had been at the bakery that afternoon, but no one claimed the recipe or knew who had left it there. No one had come back looking for it. "It's all really weird. I don't know... why anyone would have left it there. I mean, it's one thing when the kids come for a snack and leave their homework on the table. That's understandable. But who brings a waffle recipe to a bakery? And then just leaves it there? Why did they bring it? Why did they forget it there? Why are they even making gluten-free waffles?"

Vic laughed. "It's a mystery, all right."

"It is," Erin agreed. And a much better one than trying to figure out who had killed Brandon Quayle. Of course she wanted to clear her name, but she didn't want anything to do with the investigation or Brandon. He was a part of her life long past, and she had not expected to ever see him again. Now she had, twice, but she would never see him again. She would much rather solve the mystery of the unknown waffle recipe owner than anything else. Except maybe making waffles.

"You should try out the recipe. See whether it is any good."

"Well... I thought of that. Just because I'm curious to see how it turns out. But I don't want anyone accusing me of stealing their mee-maw's old recipe without permission. Or competing against someone who enters the same recipe into the contest. What would they do if they got two identical recipes?"

"It probably happens all the time. Some guy thinks his mom's pie crust recipe was her own invention, without knowing that she just got it from the back of the shortening package. Or the Toll House cookie recipe was on the chocolate chip bag. Or in the Better Homes and Gardens recipe book for like, a hundred years."

"I suppose," Erin agreed. "Well, if I ended up using it, I'd have to rewrite it. Make sure the instructions are my own and maybe even adjust the number of servings so that the ingredient amounts change."

"Double it," Vic agreed with a nod. "Triple it. Or ten-times it so you can use it on that fantastic new waffle maker."

Erin sighed, picturing the waffle maker and how quickly she could turn out dozens of fragrant waffles. "I might just have to buy one if I don't win it."

"You're a sucker for new kitchen equipment."

"I know. But wouldn't it make it so easy… making ten waffles at a time…"

"Much easier than waiting five minutes for each one," Vic admitted.

Erin had folded the recipe and put it in the back of her planner with several other pieces of paper that she wasn't sure why she was still carrying around with her. She thumbed through the pages to find it, unfolded it, and smoothed it out on the table in front of her.

"Is that it?" Vic asked.

She nodded. "This is it."

"Can I see?"

Erin handed it over. Vic started to read the ingredients aloud. Erin closed her eyes, visualizing how the ingredients would work together.

"Wait… that's not gluten-free."

Vic's eyes dropped back to the page. "What?"

"Malt vinegar. That's barley. It isn't gluten-free."

"Oh." Vic considered. "Maybe whoever wrote the recipe didn't know that. You could use another kind of vinegar. I think it is just to react with the baking soda to make the batter lighter."

"And a little bit of deeper flavor." Erin pondered on this. "Maybe some caramel flavor… though it can be difficult to find caramel that isn't derived from corn or dairy."

"You could make your own caramel with sugar and non-dairy milk. Coconut, maybe?"

"Coconut can trigger people with tree nut allergies. I'll have to think about it. It's probably fine without the malt flavor. I can bump up the amount of vanilla."

"Okay. So then you can try this one next week. Or are you going to do it today?"

Vic was pretty good at reading Erin. Erin couldn't help the flush of embarrassment that spread from her neck to her face. "Well… I was wondering if I could swing it today."

"If you don't have a bunch of errands that you have to go into the city for, you should have time. Unless you've got a bunch of stuff to do that you didn't tell me about."

Erin's life was pretty much an open book for Vic. They were around each other for so much of their time, Vic probably knew Erin's schedule better than she did herself.

Erin took the recipe back from Vic and looked it over. Being a baker had its advantages. She could be reasonably sure she would have all the ingredients she needed on hand, either at home or at Auntie Clem's.

The recipe called for a commercial pumpkin pie spice mix that she wasn't familiar with. Erin pulled out her phone and tapped the description in along with the keyword "ingredients" to find a listing of the ingredients and guess at the proportions of the various spices. She would make it from scratch rather than relying on someone else's mix.

"That's weird."

Vic sipped her tea. "What's weird?"

"This pumpkin spice mix." Erin moved the paper over so Vic could look at it with her.

"Grandma Jo's Pumpkin Spice."

"Yeah. I just looked it up, and it's not gluten-free either."

Vic shook her head. "People just forget that they have to look at all of the ingredients in everything. If you're adding something from a box or a bottle, you have to see what's in it too."

"Yeah. Plenty of spice mixes have flour in them to bulk them up, thicken the dish, or make the spices flow better. Lots of people think they have to look for the word 'wheat' on the ingredients for it to have gluten in it, but that's not nearly enough. I can even remember people trying to tell my foster sister Carolyn that she could have white bread, just not whole wheat bread. As if the white bread you get at the store wasn't made of wheat too."

"You don't know about all of the other things to look for until you start cooking for someone who is strictly gluten-free. You want to avoid poisoning them."

Erin nodded her agreement. Anyone who thought following a special diet was easy was in for a big shock when they tried it.

The back door opened, and Willie walked in. Erin was startled. She looked at his black-stained face and smiled. "Morning Willie! I didn't know you were even around."

He smiled and bent down to give Vic a kiss. "You were already gone when I woke up."

"Baker's hours," Vic said with a shrug. "My body doesn't think it's possible to sleep past six."

"You could have woken me." He winked.

It was Vic's turn to blush. She looked away from Willie, shaking her head. "We're just in here talking baking. Grab a cup of tea or make some coffee."

Willie proceeded to do exactly that.

Even though it was Erin's kitchen, they were all so used to being there to visit or share a meal together that she didn't feel the need to make Willie's coffee or even invite him to do so herself. They were all comfortable looking after themselves.

Erin frowned as she studied the recipe again. Vic raised her brows. "Another bad ingredient?"

"No. There's just something about this recipe."

"Something about it?"

"Something… not wrong, exactly, but…" Erin tried to tap into the feeling at the back of her brain. "Something… familiar…"

Willie leaned against the kitchen counter, waiting for the machine to brew. "You think you've seen the recipe somewhere before?"

"I don't think so. I think I would remember if I had seen this one before. Especially with the malt vinegar and spice mix in it. But even if someone who didn't know about those containing gluten added them later, I don't remember ever seeing waffles with this combination of..."

Then it all came together.

CHAPTER 26

"Oh." Erin looked at the recipe with fresh eyes, suddenly seeing clearly what she had missed before. "That's it."

"What's it?" Vic and Willie asked in unison.

They all looked at each other and laughed. Erin let the recipe lay on the table, tapping it with her forefinger.

"Bertie."

"What?" Vic and Willie exchanged glances and then looked back at Erin, none the wiser.

"Bertie Braceling. This combination of flours is what we used for Bertie's tortilla and pancake mixes. Because he was allergic to or intolerant of so many different ingredients. Buckwheat, arrowroot, and psyllium."

"Really?" Vic looked down at the recipe and glanced through the ingredients. "How would you remember that?"

Erin laughed. "I know my customers. Bertie was really hard to bake for, but I enjoy a challenge. I was always trying to find combinations of ingredients that would work for him. And I remember that being the flour blend we used for most of the stuff I made for him. No grains of any kind, so no rice, cornstarch, sorghum, or oats. Tapioca starch caused him neurological issues. He couldn't tolerate xanthan gum or guar gum."

"So, buckwheat, arrowroot, and psyllium."

"Just like this recipe," Erin tapped it again. "I haven't seen that particular blend in anyone else's recipes."

None of them said anything for a few minutes.

"But Bertie is dead," Vic pointed out finally. "So whose recipe is it? And if it was for Bertie, it wouldn't have had malt vinegar or a spice blend that included flour in it."

"Maybe it's a recipe that started out as Bertie's," Willie suggested slowly, "but then someone else adapted it to their tastes and they didn't have the same restrictions as he did."

"Yes, that could be it. Cooks are always adapting other recipes, putting their own spin on them. What about his sister?" Erin looked at Vic. "Tracey…"

"Lacey Moore." Vic shook her head. "She's out of town. Mrs. Peach mentioned she's been feeding Mrs. Moore's cat."

"Does it matter where the recipe came from?" Willie asked.

"No, I guess not. I'd like to know, but it doesn't really make any difference. Unless I want to submit it to the contest. Then I should know where it came from and get permission before I submit it. And make sure that whoever left it at Auntie Clem's isn't submitting it themselves."

Vic nodded. "Right. It's really weird that it just showed up at Auntie Clem's."

"It is, isn't it? But it could have just been a coincidence. Or maybe someone wanted to show it to me because they knew I was developing a recipe to submit to the contest. And then… I wasn't there, so they left it behind. Or they had to go somewhere and forgot that they had put it down… maybe they haven't realized yet that they lost it, or maybe they're planning to come back and ask for it later."

"Or they don't even need it because they already have a copy," Vic suggested.

"Yeah. Would they have left it in Auntie Clem's if it was their only copy? You're right; it probably isn't. They wanted to share it, and I wasn't around, so they just left it there."

"They should have said something. I was there. They could have handed it to me. Told me to give it to you."

"It was probably still busy and they had to go. Didn't want to interrupt you. Maybe they'll be back next week and ask if I got it."

"Yeah. Maybe."

"Do you want me to see if I can find out who it came from?" Willie asked. He had poured himself a cup of coffee and took a tentative sip.

"Well… sure. But how are you going to do that? I've already been asking around, and no one has said anything. You don't even know who was in the bakery that day."

"But if it was originally a recipe for Bertie, I knew him. And some of his friends and family. I can ask around about his waffle recipe."

"Oh! Yeah, that's a good idea. Thanks."

Willie nodded. He glanced toward the living room and then back at Erin. "So… Piper around? What's going on with you guys?" he asked bluntly.

Vic reddened and made a motion for him to shut up. She had undoubtedly been aware of the tension between Erin and Terry and had mentioned it to Willie. But she hadn't meant for Willie to bring it up to Erin.

Erin sighed. She ran her finger over the crease in the paper the recipe was written on, smoothing it out. "Well, you know what it's like. When he suspects you of something, it doesn't really matter who you are. That's his first priority."

"Is that why you're fighting? Because you're a suspect? He doesn't believe your story?"

"He says he believes me. He says that he won't be involved in the case or question me about it. But he does. And he's upset that I never told him about Brandon."

Willie approached the table and sat down. "What about Brandon? That's the dead guy?"

Vic leaned forward, her eyes bright with interest.

Erin didn't know what to say. "I never talked about Brandon to Terry, and I guess he thinks that I should have. That I should share everything about anybody that I've been with in the past. But… he doesn't go out of his way to tell me about every person in Bald Eagle Falls that he ever dated. He'll say something every now and then, but

I don't really know anything about any serious relationships that he's had. He hasn't told me all of that stuff either. I didn't think… that it was required."

"But now he's acting like it is."

"Terry knew about my life before I came here. He knew that I was in foster care and that I'd been in a lot of different places doing a lot of different jobs since then. He knows that… I'm a private person. So why would I tell him everything about Brandon? You wouldn't tell Vic everything about everyone you were ever with, would you?" Erin raised her brows. Willie too was a private person and it had caused a definite hiccup in their relationship when Vic had found out from someone else that Willie had been a member of the Dyson clan. Even though he knew that Vic was from a rival clan, Willie had not bothered to fill her in on that little detail and the five years that he had spent as a soldier for the family.

Willie looked at Vic and then back at Erin. "Are you trying to get me in trouble? Is that my punishment for opening my mouth?"

"You haven't sat her down and told her about everyone you've ever dated, have you?"

"No… I don't think that's the way it's usually done. You tell a little bit here and a little bit there. Casually. Building on it as you get to know each other better."

"You know everyone I've been with," Vic declared.

Willie shrugged. "Considering you weren't even legally an adult when you came to Bald Eagle Falls, it's not a very long list. I've been a bachelor for as long as you've been alive."

"Old man," Vic teased.

"That's right. And I honestly don't think it would be good form to make a list of everyone I've ever had an interest in and go through the circumstances of each one at a time."

"No. I suppose not." Vic looked sober, maybe considering for the first time the long history that Willie had had before the two of them had gotten together. It was one thing to acknowledge that he was older than she was. It was another to think about what that actually meant in terms of life experiences.

"So…" Erin brought the conversation back around. "He thinks

I'm obstructing the investigation *and* keeping important secrets from him. And since I don't trust him…"

"You're not sharing a room anymore?" Willie filled in.

Erin looked reproachfully at Vic. She wasn't even sure how Vic had figured it out so quickly. It wasn't like Vic went snooping in the bedrooms when she was over. Her visits were usually confined to the kitchen and living room, and Erin didn't see how she could have figured out that Erin and Terry were no longer sleeping in the same bed together so quickly.

Vic held up her hands. "I'm sorry. I didn't mean to pry. I just used the facilities the other day, and I noticed when I went down the hall that K9's kennel and Terry's things were in the second bedroom, not in yours where they usually are. I haven't said anything to anyone else, I promise."

"I don't know. I can't really explain all of what happened. We were both tired and frustrated. It wasn't a fight. I wasn't happy with him, but it wasn't a fight. But if he doesn't trust me, if he puts the investigation before our relationship… maybe we're not supposed to be together. He offered to move to the guest room and I said yes. I didn't kick him out. He asked."

"He's just being a gentleman. If you ask him to come back to your room, he will,"

"I know."

They were all quiet.

"But you're not ready to do that," Vic said finally.

"No."

"Where is he now?" Willie asked. "On shift? At work?"

"No." Erin swallowed. "He went to church."

"What?" Vic's voice climbed up several notes. She made an effort to keep it calm and lower it again. "I know Terry's Christian, but he goes to church what, twice a year? Easter and Christmas?"

"And apparently… when he's having problems with me."

"You think he's being passive-aggressive? This is… getting back at you somehow? You're an atheist, and the two of you are on the outs, so he starts going to church again?"

"It's only once. Maybe he needed to say a prayer that... I'll come around and start behaving more like a Christian wife."

"Or praying for understanding," Willie said, his tone serious. "To be able to understand what you went through with this guy, and why you didn't share it, and what he needs to do next if he wants to keep you."

Erin sipped her tea, pondering this. Was that why Terry had gone to the church he barely ever frequented? Not to punish her somehow, or alienate her, but to find a way to get closer to her?

"I don't know. I never heard anything like that at any of the churches that I went to as a kid."

"Would you have? If you were in a children's Sunday School, they would not have been talking about intimate relationships. And if you were with a general congregation, would you really have listened to it and understood what they were talking about?"

"I probably wasn't the best listener at church."

Willie chuckled. "Few kids are. You go to hear the exciting stories like Noah and the Ark or Daniel in the Lion's Den, but most of the stuff that you really go to learn... you don't get until you're much older."

CHAPTER 27

$\mathcal{E}$rin enjoyed her day off from Auntie Clem's Bakery but, after a day, she was ready to go back to work. She really did love her work, and it was paying the bills. What more could she ask? Maybe there were things going on in other parts of her life that were difficult, but she still loved baking at Auntie Clem's and talking to her customers.

Willie dropped them off in the parking lot behind the bakery and Erin strode up to the door, her key out, to let them in. It wasn't until she was right up to the door that she could see that the door was hanging open an inch in the dim lighting from the streetlights. It had been forced, Erin could immediately see by the marks on the door-frame and the edge of the door. A pry bar and a good yank, and out it had popped.

Vic ran into Erin from behind because she had stopped so abruptly.

"What's going on—" Vic saw the door and turned back toward Willie's truck. He was pulling away, but she managed to bang on the side of the truck and stop him before he got out of the parking lot. Erin could hear Vic talking to Willie in urgent tones, but they seemed like they were far away or underwater. She used one finger to push the door open wider. No movement on the other side. Not a sound.

Erin's heart was pounding and her legs were so weak she had to hold on to the doorframe for support. Who would have done such a thing? She thought that she was well-liked and respected in Bald Eagle Falls. That no one would ever do anything like this.

But that hadn't always been the case. And she was afraid that there might be more than one person still harboring a grudge against her for her hand in exposing the students in the burglary ring at the school, or for someone else who had been put behind bars at the penitentiary. She had been in too many cases to really believe that no one resented her for what she had done.

And then there was Vic. It could be a hate crime. There might be all kinds of slurs against trans people painted on the walls of the kitchen or even the public space out front. She didn't smell any paint but, if there was something like that, she needed to see it first and keep Vic from seeing it.

She had to know. The bakery was dark and she needed to find the light switch, which didn't seem to fall right under her hand like it usually did as she walked in the door. She inched her way along, one hand on the wall, her eyes wide open and searching, her heart pounding in her chest as if it would jump right out of her body.

"Erin!" Willie's sharp whisper behind her made her jump. "You shouldn't go in there. Someone could still be inside. You stay out here until the cops get here."

"I have to see," Erin insisted. "There isn't anyone here."

She finally touched the light switch and flicked it on.

Erin squinted in the sudden brightness, blinded for a moment. She forced her eyes open, though tears started to run down her cheeks from the light. There wasn't a mark on the walls. No vandalism was apparent. No damage. No one was there. The appliances gleamed. The long counters were clear and clean, waiting for them to begin their morning work. She would have thought she was being paranoid and that the shop had been left unlocked, rather than being broken into. But she couldn't ignore the pry marks on the door.

"Erin." Willie was tugging her from behind. "Come on. Wait outside until the police get here."

Erin let herself be pulled back out of the kitchen into the parking lot. Vic was there, pale and anxious.

"It was broken into? Who would break into the bakery? It isn't like we leave money in the till overnight."

"Maybe they heard there was a lot of dough there," Willie offered, deadpan.

Vic stared at him for a moment without smiling. Then she shook her head, the corners of her mouth twitching. "Do you really think this is an appropriate time to joke around?"

"Well, you asked. I can't help that. The joke is going to be pretty lame if I use it on a day when the bakery *hasn't* been broken into."

They could hear an approaching siren.

"If someone was looking for a lot of bread…" Willie tried again. Erin turned her head to glare at him. He grinned and shut up.

"Did everything look okay?" Vic wanted to know. "I mean… it isn't all smashed up or anything, is it? We'll still be able to open today?"

Erin nodded. "It looked fine… didn't look like anything had been touched."

Vic let out a breath. "Good. Glad to hear it. We'll just wait for the boys in blue to clear it and confirm that there isn't anyone else still around, and then we can get to work."

Erin remembered having the police check out the first iteration of Auntie Clem's Bakery, which had been across the street from her current location. Looking for the "ghost" that had moved things around in her office and smashed a coffee mug that had been left on the counter. And the burglar who had pried open a cabinet in the basement. Because there had been a murder in her basement, her reports were taken seriously.

The ghost, it turned out, had been Vic. Sleeping in the bakery overnight. Somewhere safe and warm and sheltered. Though she hadn't been the one to pry open the cabinet. Erin smiled at Vic, remembering her discovery of the slim young woman in her shop.

Vic raised her brows questioningly, probably wondering if Erin was in shock. Why would she be smiling like that after a break-in?

She didn't see the parallel like Erin did. She had been on the other side of the equation, the burglar who was trying to avoid detection.

A police car pulled into the parking lot. Not Terry's truck. Stayner stepped out, releasing his sidearm as he strode across the parking lot toward the door. "Have you been inside?"

"Just into the kitchen," Erin said. "No one in there."

"Stay out here. Don't come in behind me unless you want to get shot."

It seemed like a good idea to do what he said. Erin and the others waited after he disappeared into the bakery, waiting for him to clear the building and confirm that it was safe to go in. Erin felt a little silly about the police being called to the scene when there had apparently not been a theft or vandalism. Someone had pried the door. Maybe kids thinking that they could get something out of the till, not realizing that they cleared it out and made a bank deposit every night.

Or maybe on a dare. Kids did stupid stuff.

Erin had always been a goody-two-shoes, according to Reg. She had tried to follow all of the rules in order to stay out of trouble and have the best possible chance of achieving success when she finished school and was out on her own.

Some kids ended up with foster families that agreed to keep them on after they aged out of foster care, helping them to get through college or getting them to pay rent to contribute to the household expenses. But Erin had not ended up with one of those families. When she aged out of foster care, that was the end of anyone taking care of her. She had to take care of herself, and she wasn't always able to do that.

Kids did stupid things. So did young adults like Brandon had been when she knew him. She wondered what he had written in his memoir. Had he really "told all" about the stupid things he had done while they had been together? The drinking and doping and partying? The abuse, dishonesty, stealing, bar fights, and everything else? Had he ever broken into a bakery on a dare? The record store down the block from them? One of the other little businesses run by hard-working folks trying to make ends meet?

Stayner walked back out of the bakery at a relaxed pace, his sidearm properly secured in the holster. He nodded to Erin. "All clear, Miss Price. No one in there. Would you like to take a walk-through and point out anything that might have been damaged or stolen?"

"Yeah. Thanks."

Her knees were still a little shaky, but it felt better to be walking than standing still. Erin led the way back into the bakery, followed by Stayner, with Willie and Vic behind them. Nothing appeared to have been touched in the kitchen. Everything was as clean and pristine as it should have been. Erin was really glad that they hadn't painted slurs all over the walls. Glad that it wasn't a hate crime.

She went out to the front. The register did not appear to have been touched. Erin pressed a few buttons to pop open the drawer, which was empty, as expected. The mechanism still worked, which she assumed meant it had not been pried open with the crowbar. Everything appeared to be functioning. There was no sign that the burglar had even gone out to the front of the store.

Erin was beginning to think she was right and that it had just been some kids on a dare. She walked back through the kitchen to the stairs and went down to the storage room to see if anything appeared to have been touched or stolen. For a moment, she flashed back to descending the stairs at The Book Nook and finding Brandon in the basement, dead. Having found his body twice already, she half-expected to find it lying in the basement of the bakery. But of course Stayner had already been down there and would have noticed if there were a body. And he certainly hadn't dragged one in there to plant it there himself.

The basement was well-lit, not spooky and shadowy. All modern and bright, with finished walls and floor and gleaming shelves to hold all of their bulk goods. Erin glanced over the goods on the shelves but couldn't see anything that was missing initially. She would have to go through the inventory sheet to be sure, but nothing appeared to have been touched. She shrugged at Stayner, who had stopped partway down the stairs to wait for her response.

"Everything looks fine."

She climbed back up the stairs and returned to the kitchen.

"Your office," Vic prompted, nodding to the tiny room off the kitchen where Erin kept her files and the computer. It was barely big enough for a desk with an integrated file cabinet and had probably been a closet in its previous life, but it was large enough for Erin to get done what she needed to.

She glanced around the room and nodded. Again, nothing appeared to have been broken or messed with. The keyboard and monitor were exactly where they always were. Pencil jar. In box. Writing pad.

Except… taking a closer look, she saw that the computer CPU itself, which sat in the kneehole under the desk, was missing.

CHAPTER 28

The sheriff had arrived to help with the investigation of the burglary. Stayner had agreed that Erin and Vic could begin work on the day's baking as long as they stayed out of the office, which was just fine. They weren't normally in there during their morning baking session anyway. Other than to drop off their purses where they were a little more secure.

Stayner took a cursory look around the tiny room, then guarded the door to prevent anyone from entering until Wilmot arrived.

"The computer was the only thing stolen?" Wilmot demanded.

He looked at the office and took a walk through the rest of the bakery and basement, as if Stayner and Erin might have missed something of importance.

"Well, that's convenient, isn't it?" he asked, brows drawn down in a scowl. "You knew I was getting a warrant for your computer, so it conveniently disappeared."

"Are you kidding?" Vic demanded. "You think that Erin set this all up? She wouldn't damage the door so that she could make it look like a burglary. Who do you think has to fix that door? Who has to work here and worry about whether it is secure until it gets fixed? Erin didn't do this to keep you from looking at her computer."

"Miss Victoria," Wilmot said gravely, "I don't think I was addressing you."

"Well, I still heard and I still had something to say about it. I can't believe you would throw around accusations like that. Erin could sue the department for slander."

Erin wasn't going to sue anyone, and Wilmot would know that. Erin wasn't the type of person who would make waves over something like that being said. It would be far more trouble than it was worth.

"No, it isn't convenient," Erin told him. "That computer has all of my bookkeeping on it. All of my promotional graphics and files for the next few months. Recipes that I've been collecting or developing. This is…" She shook her head hopelessly, her eyes filling with tears. "This is terrible. I don't know how I'm going to replace it."

"Computers aren't that expensive anymore," Wilmot assured her. "You have a backup, right?"

Erin kneaded her forehead. When was the last time she had made a backup? It was always one of the last things on her list. Something she knew she had to get to sooner or later. The backup drives were in the desk, but she worried they would not be much help. She walked into the office, ignoring Wilmot's grunt of protest. He was too far across the kitchen to stop her. She opened the top drawer of the desk to look at the dates written on notes stuck to the backup drives. How much work would she have to redo because she hadn't been doing her backups as often as she should?

But there were no backup drives in the drawer. Erin stared at the odds and ends for several long seconds. She even opened the next drawer, a file drawer, and looked through it as if she might have accidentally filed the backup drives in one of her folders. She swallowed hard and looked at Wilmot.

"My backups are gone too."

"Well, that's conven—" He cut himself off before finishing the statement. "Don't you have any offsite backup? A cloud drive? Safety deposit box? Safe at home?"

Erin wiped at the corners of her eyes. "No."

She fell into her desk chair, helpless to stop the tears. She put both of her hands over her face. Vic moved in, pushing past Sheriff

Wilmot in the doorway, to rub Erin's back and murmur comforting words to her.

"Your accountant has last year's financial files. You can start with that. You have all of the paper files. You can hire someone to enter the bookkeeping for the first half of the year. Email is all online."

That helped a little. It was a lot of work, but it was manageable if she could hire someone to do all of the inputting instead of doing it herself.

"The promos," she said, swallowing. "All of my swipe files and graphics and plans for holiday promotions this year."

Vic stroked her hair and rubbed her back soothingly. "The newspaper office and printer will have all the graphics for what you've done over the last couple of years. We can reuse them. And the paper will have all of your copy for what you've advertised in the weekly. And your promos, we talked about stuff and you wrote notes in your planner. We can reconstruct from there."

The tears started to slow. Vic was right. Erin had been worried that the business would collapse without everything she had on her computer. But they could start with what they had done in the last two years. No one would notice if the promotion graphics were reused. And there was time to start rebuilding her plans for upcoming holiday promotions.

"What about... employee paychecks and shifts, and our client list?"

"Uh... you use a human resources company for the paychecks and withholdings. There won't be any break in that. We'll reconstruct what we remember of the shifts and ask everyone what they remember for hours worked last week and shifts in the next couple of weeks. No one is going to abandon you because your computer got stolen. They know you'll treat them fairly."

Erin nodded. She grabbed a tissue from the box on her desk, blotted her eyes, and blew her nose. "And the client list is online."

"That's right, it is," Vic agreed. "In your CRM manager. You haven't lost that."

"I'll have to reset passwords." Erin sniffled. "I never could remember all of them."

"Resetting passwords is easy."

"Yeah. But my recipes?" Erin tried to avert another flood of tears, but was not successful. She swore. "What is a bakery without recipes?"

"All of the ones that we use are in the binder." Vic referred to the reference binder they kept in the kitchen, with all the recipes in plastic page protectors in case they got spattered with batters. "We can scan them so you have them on your new computer. The ones that you haven't used or are still experimenting with..." She shrugged. "You can start over. You got most of them online to start with. So find them again. We'll try to remember what we can for the ones you've been experimenting with. But everything we make regularly, we've got. You're not going to go under because you don't have any recipes."

"Okay." Erin swallowed and nodded. "Okay, we can do this. We can recover."

"Right now, it's time to get to work," Vic said sternly, looking at the clock on the wall. "We open in half an hour."

That was exactly what Erin needed to galvanize herself and throw herself back into the morning's work. There was no time to cry over spilled milk. She could recover from the lost computer. In the meantime, she needed to get back to work.

CHAPTER 29

"Uh, Miss Price…?" Wilmot was standing outside Erin's office door when she exited, intent on getting the morning's baking done and everything ready to open for the day. "We still need to talk."

"I don't have time right now. I have a bakery to get open."

"The sooner we can get onto this, the better the chances are that we'll be able to recover your stolen property. Can you talk while you get ready?"

"Uh… I guess I can try." Erin went back to the muffin batter she had been in the midst of and started pouring it into cups.

"Do you have any idea who would have broken in here to do this?"

"No. I guess someone wanted a computer."

"I think this was targeted. I don't think it was just 'a computer.' I think it was *your* computer."

She glanced over at him. "Does that mean you don't think that I did it myself? I didn't just ditch my computer so you couldn't find whatever incriminating evidence I have saved on it?"

"Well, there's no need to be snippy about it," he grumbled. "Yes, I'm coming around to your way of thinking. But I still need your cooperation if we're going to figure out who it was and recover it. If you aren't going to help me out, then I have to wonder why."

"I didn't say I wouldn't help."

"Is there anything on that computer that someone might want? Or want to destroy? In particular, anything to do with this case?"

"No. I don't have anything to do with this case on my computer. And you just heard what valuable stuff I have on it—my financial records and recipes. Not... I don't know what you're looking for. Pictures of me and Brandon together? I don't even know what you think you're going to find on it."

"Well, I was hoping to find evidence of whether you were in touch with Brandon or not. But if someone stole it, I would think that it has more than that on it. Something that this case hinges on."

"There isn't anything on my computer to do with Brandon."

"Nothing at all?"

"Why would there be? If I was threatening to kill Brandon, or whatever it is you're implying, why would I have it on my work computer?"

"Does anyone else have access to what's on that computer?"

"No!"

"Victoria, maybe?"

Erin looked over at Vic and shook her head. "She doesn't have my password. I'm the only one who touches the financial files and who sets up the advertising and everything. Vic bakes and works the till. She doesn't run the business."

Vic nodded her agreement. "And happy as a hound dog with two tails that I don't have to do all of that stuff," she affirmed.

Wilmot's mouth twitched.

"If it isn't anything to do with Brandon, then can you think of anyone else who would want your computer for any reason? Someone who is upset with you and might have targeted you? Someone who you told you have something on your computer and they want it? Anything?"

"No. It was just a crappy old computer, Sheriff. Nothing fancy on it. It wasn't a system you could have used for gaming or anything like that. Anyone who needed a computer wouldn't go after a dinosaur like that. They'd want the latest and greatest with lots of memory and a fast graphics card and all that. That one could barely keep up with putting together text and graphics for a flyer."

He smiled. "Maybe I should look into insurance fraud, then. Maybe you're angling to get a new one."

"I wouldn't go through all of this rigmarole for that. I'd just go out and buy one. Take this one home to do email or family history stuff."

He nodded at this.

"And you don't have any clue who might have broken in? You didn't see anyone hanging around the last few days? Smell someone's cologne when you came into the store after the break-in? See that something was moved or taken that might have been connected with someone you know?"

"No… I don't think so."

His mention of cologne got her thinking. *Had* there been a trace of a scent as she had entered Auntie Clem's to turn the light on? Any smells were quickly wiped out by other people moving in and out of the kitchen and by the smells of the batters and baking bread that soon permeated the bakery. Had there been a smell when she had entered The Book Nook? It was all so fleeting, she couldn't be sure. Her other senses had quickly been overwhelmed and she had forgotten anything else.

"Do you know anything about Brandon's manuscript?"

Erin looked up from her muffins, frowning at Wilmot's question. "Brandon's manuscript? What about it?"

"Did he show it to you? Email you a copy?"

"No."

"You haven't seen it."

"No. I can't see why I would have wanted to."

"Maybe so that you could see what he had written about you. How he had portrayed you. The only reason I can think about that he would have come to Bald Eagle Falls is to talk to you."

Erin was baffled as to what other reason he would have had to be there. But whatever it was, it had nothing to do with her.

"I don't care what he wrote in his book. I don't even care if it got a big New York literary deal. So what? It's not about me. If I'm in it, he'd have to spice it up to make it anything interesting. Because nobody cares about the girl who crashed on his couch."

"There was more to it than that, from what you said."

"In your mind, maybe. But that's all it ever was to him. Or to me. Somewhere to live while I found something else."

"It is missing."

"What's missing?"

"His manuscript."

"Because he didn't have it on him? He wouldn't carry it around with him, would he? It's not like a phone."

"We've been in contact with the authorities in Maine. They've searched his apartment there and have his computer. If he had a hard copy, he must have brought it with him."

"Why would he?"

"To show the person who was in it."

"Well, he didn't. I never saw him or his manuscript."

"Until he was dead."

"What?" Erin asked in irritation.

"You didn't see him until he was dead. If I am to believe you. You *did* see him. At least twice."

"Okay." Erin rolled her eyes. "Not alive. So he obviously couldn't show it to me when he was dead."

"Unless it was on his body when you found it."

"Again, why would he be carrying it around?"

"Again—to show you."

"I had no idea he was in town until I found him there. I had no way of knowing he was in The Book Nook."

"We'll see if your email history bears that out."

Erin put trays of muffins in the oven and turned to look at him, wiping her hands on a towel. "My email? My computer was just stolen."

"Yes. But your email is still available in the cloud. Like you and Miss Victoria were just saying."

Erin rolled her eyes and shrugged. She didn't think there was any way for him to get access to it. And if there was, she'd already done what she could to eliminate any trail. He could look all he liked and not be able to prove her wrong.

"How do you know there even *was* a manuscript?" Erin asked. "Had anyone seen it? Brandon didn't exactly tell the truth all the time, you know."

Wilmot considered this, his eyes rolling upward. "Well, that is something I can inquire about. I'm sure someone must have seen it. He wouldn't get a book deal without someone reading the manuscript, right?"

"How do you know he had a book deal?"

"That's what he told everyone."

Erin nodded. "But did anyone see this book deal? Talk to his agent? To the publisher? It could all just be made up out of thin air."

CHAPTER 30

$\mathcal{E}$rin didn't feel up to making supper after a long day at Auntie Clem's. She hadn't realized how much energy the burglary and seemingly endless questions by Sheriff Wilmot would take out of her. She also knew that Terry would be getting off work and didn't want to be home with him, tiptoeing awkwardly around each other, trying to decide if she was still obligated to make supper for him, or if she wanted to have him messing around in the kitchen without her. There really wasn't a winning answer.

Sooner or later things would have to either settle down with Terry or come to a head. She hoped that things would work out, but she recognized that she wasn't putting much effort into it, waiting to see what he would do and how he felt. He was the one who had decided she was not trustworthy. She hadn't done anything wrong. She figured he should be the one making the first move.

A meal at the restaurant seemed like the best bet. Erin decided she was in the mood for Chinese and avoided the family restaurant, which was Terry's favorite. If he decided to go out to dinner too, in order to avoid her and having to make his own meal, she didn't want to run into him there.

Erin only had to wait for a few minutes to be seated and was given an empty booth in the back. Too close to the kitchen to be considered a prime spot, but she was happy to be out of the way and have some relative privacy instead of being at one of the round tables out in the open.

She was perusing the menu, deciding what she wanted to order since she was there by herself and usually ordered a combination of meals to share with Terry, when she was interrupted.

"Miss Erin…?"

She looked up from her menu. "Oh, Dave. Hey, how are you?"

"Good." He looked around. "Are you here by yourself?"

"Yes." Erin hesitated a moment, then motioned to the opposite bench seat. "Do you want to join me?"

"Oh, I don't want to interrupt anything. You look like you wanted some alone time."

"No, it's okay. I'll have plenty of that when I go home tonight." That sounded pretty pathetic. "Well, except for the cat and the rabbit, of course." She laughed. That sounded even more pathetic.

"I thought…" He trailed off and took the seat that she had indicated. Maybe deciding that it was better not to dig into her personal affairs.

"That I would be with Officer Piper?" Erin suggested.

He nodded, getting red around his throat.

"Well, we're not exactly seeing eye to eye right now. So I'm… taking a bit of a break."

"Oh. I'm sorry. Is that because of… the investigation? Brandon Quayle, I mean?"

"Yes. I can't thank the guy enough for dying on my watch. Why did he have to come here and screw everything up for me?"

"Are you getting a lot of flak from the police department? They think you had something to do with it?"

"I don't know. I don't think they believe I did it, but they have to follow the evidence and show that I didn't do it and someone else did. It's very annoying. I want them to be finished with their investigation and not bother me about it anymore. I didn't kill him, and I think it's highly unlikely that anyone would kill a person and then call the police about it. And then hide the body. And then call the police about it again..."

Dave chuckled. "That does seem like a bit of a stretch," he agreed.

"But cops don't like coincidences. They want answers to all of their questions and... I can't give them the answers to everything."

"Yeah. If you could, you probably *would* be the killer. They're the ones who always have the best alibis, aren't they?"

"On TV, maybe. Not in real life. Not in my experience."

And she'd had way too much experience in Bald Eagle Falls. Maybe she should have stayed in Maine and never accepted her inheritance from Clementine. Alton Summers would probably have eventually found Erin's half-sister, Charley, and given it to her instead. If Erin hadn't come to Bald Eagle Falls, she wouldn't have gotten involved in that first murder. She wouldn't have been a suspect. She wouldn't have discovered all of the stuff she did later about her family and what really happened to her parents. She wouldn't have had to worry about drug cartels or kidnappers or cooking contests gone bad. She could have just kept living the way that she had in Maine. Nothing would have changed.

"Do you want to order together?" Dave asked, indicating the menu Erin held in her hands but was not focused on. "It's kind of fun to order a few dishes and have a bit of everything."

"Yeah. That's what we usually do. What do you like?"

Erin managed to bring her focus back to the meal and, for a few minutes, she and Dave were occupied with seeing what they both liked best and wanted to share. After giving their order to the waitress, they both sat back, quiet and trying to think of a conversational topic.

"I was sorry to hear about your break-in today," Dave offered. "Did they catch whoever did it?"

"No." Erin shook her head. "And I doubt they ever will. It isn't like he left fingerprints or DNA all over the place or that the police even care about catching him. Sheriff Wilmot kept saying that I needed to cooperate with his questioning so that they could find my computer and get it back to me, but... I don't think they will put too much effort into trying. It isn't even like it's valuable. I just got the cheapest machine that I could when I was starting off. It isn't fast enough to do anything special. Not like gaming or anything that takes a special graphics card. Or speakers. I don't think it even had speakers."

"Usually they have a built-in speaker, even if you don't have an external sound system."

Erin nodded. "So okay, it probably had sound. But I don't see why anyone would want that computer. Or why they would target me."

"I guess the police have been asking you a lot of questions about Brandon?"

Erin nodded. "But it's been years since I saw the guy; it's not like I knew anything about this tell-all memoir he was working on. Or had a deal for, if you're to believe anything he said to anyone else. And you shouldn't."

Dave laughed. "Not the most honest guy?"

"No. You could never believe anything coming out of Brandon's mouth. He told a lot of whoppers."

"I've known people like that. It can be pretty disconcerting when you realize that none of the stuff they're telling you is the truth."

"Yeah. I kind of start from the position of not trusting anyone, and then if you prove that you are trustworthy, that's great. If not, I'm not disappointed, at least."

"Smart… but maybe a little dysfunctional."

"That's me."

When the waitress brought their order, Dave leaned forward to dish up some of each item onto his plate. "So," he said conspiratorially, "Was Brandon ever involved in anything criminal? Or was he just a liar?"

"Oh…" Erin dished up some General Tso's chicken. "He wasn't just a liar." She thought about the drugs. The abuse. Other things that he did if he thought he could get away with it. There had been run-ins with the police, but Brandon could be very charming and talk his way out of just about anything. He was one of those guys, Erin thought, who would have chatted amiably with a cop while he had a body in the trunk of the car or apparently snoozing in the passenger seat next to him. A guy like Dahmer, who kept escaping by the skin of his teeth because he was so skilled at talking himself out of trouble.

But criminal? He *hadn't* been a serial killer like Dahmer. Just a guy who did whatever he could get away with. Who served himself and his own interests without concern for anyone else.

CHAPTER 31

*E*rin poked at her food, thinking about how much she wanted to tell Dave. She couldn't talk to Terry about anything that had happened back then. He was already upset that she hadn't told him about her previous relationship with Brandon, and he was all mixed up in the investigation. They were barely speaking to each other, aside from a few polite comments as they got breakfast ready or navigated around each other at the house, pretending there wasn't any awkwardness.

She could talk to Vic. Vic even had some relevant experience, with her relationship with Crazy Theresa, and having lived on the street for a short time in Bald Eagle Falls. She understood it better than most people in Bald Eagle Falls. But she also talked to Willie, and Erin wasn't sure she wanted Willie to know about anything. Who knew what kind of reaction he might have to her stories? He *had* gone hunting for Crazy Theresa, even if he wasn't the one who had killed her. It was too late for him to go after Brandon, but who knows what else he might do. And she didn't want him looking at her differently, as Terry now did.

Dave was safe. He had only been in Bald Eagle Falls for a little longer than Erin had been, so he wasn't woven into the fabric of the town like those who had been born and raised there. He wasn't necessarily connected to any of the branches of the grapevine. He had always seemed to her to be a bit of a loner. He didn't hang out with a bunch of other people. Didn't go drinking with the boys after work. He was just a nice guy living a quiet life in quiet little Bald Eagle Falls. He had a steady job at The Book Nook, which was enough to support himself. He was lucky, when she thought about the inadequately housed poor living in and around Bald Eagle Falls. He didn't have half a dozen mouths to feed and have to be constantly worried that he would be kicked out and have to find somewhere new to live. He made enough to rent an apartment somewhere, get internet, and entertain himself with cable or streaming video service.

"How long have you been in Bald Eagle Falls now?" she asked.

Dave slurped a noodle and wiped his face, laughing at himself. "Just over two years. A bit longer than you. I think I'd been here about three months before you moved in."

"And you moved here because of your aunt? Is that right?" Erin tried to remember any details of his arrival and what people had told her about him.

"Aunt Jane. Yes, it's been nice to be able to spend time with her. She's kind of cut off from everyone else."

Erin had heard about his Aunt Jane once or twice, but couldn't remember the woman's last name. She was a bit of a recluse. It was good that he'd been able to move close to her and be allowed into her life. At least she wouldn't be completely alone when she died, with nobody to look after her affairs.

"Where did you come from?"

"I've been all over." He shrugged. "Mostly north."

"Me too." Erin cut up more chicken with the side of her fork. It was a bit tough, and she might need to resort to a knife instead. "Mostly in the north. I tell people Maine because that's where I spent the most time the last few years before moving here, but it wasn't the only place I lived. It's just easier. When you tell people you come from 'all over,' they don't know what to say. How to ask after your people or find out what you were doing when you were living there. There's no reference point."

Dave gave a nod. "People like a reference point. Something to anchor to."

"Yes. Exactly."

She and Dave actually had a lot in common. Both were quiet people, tending toward being alone, arriving in Bald Eagle Falls around the same time, after a semi-nomadic life in the northern states. Working practically next door to each other. It was surprising that she hadn't eaten a meal or had a one-on-one conversation with Dave before. But it was probably because of Terry. It wasn't proper to approach a woman who was seeing someone else. Even for just a casual conversation.

That was the South—lots of rules about what was proper.

Erin took a sip of water, considering how to approach the subject of Brandon and what he had been involved in.

"Brandon took care of me, so I don't want to say anything bad about him. He helped me out when nobody else did."

"I get that. Need can bond people together who wouldn't have normally had anything to do with each other."

"It's true." Erin nodded slowly at the wisdom of this statement. She sometimes wondered how she had gotten involved with some of the people she had over the years. Whether there was something wrong with her. But she had turned to those people because she needed them, or they had needed her. And that had brought them together in solidarity, if not in friendship. "I had lost my job, and it came with board, so when I lost my job, I lost my room too. I hadn't been able to save anything while I was working there. Or not enough, anyway. I couldn't put a down payment on an apartment. Didn't want to go to a shelter. There weren't a lot of other options, other than finding someone who would take me in until I could get back on my feet."

"And you and Brandon got together somehow."

"Yeah. I don't even remember how. We ran into each other at a bar or had friends in common, one of those things. And… he said I could crash on his couch." Erin shrugged.

How long had *that* lasted? A few days? A week? Had it even lasted one night? It was all a bit muddled in Erin's memory. There had been alcohol involved, and she had been stressed out by losing her job. He had been friendly, invited her to crash at his place, comforted her. She knew when she accepted the offer to crash on his couch that she would end up in bed with him. It was inevitable. She didn't have any other way to show her appreciation or earn her keep.

"That was nice of him," Dave said neutrally. How much had he guessed about her relationship with Brandon? Maybe everything. Maybe nothing. Maybe she was reading too much into his carefully smooth, nonjudgmental expression. Maybe he really didn't think that there had been anything else between them.

"It was longer than I thought it would be. It wasn't so easy finding another job. I was always looking, but it isn't easy, as a young woman, to get something stable. Especially in that economy."

"What was he like? Other than what you said—him being a liar."

Erin looked up at the ceiling, thinking back. "He was fun. I thought at first that he was really nice, but he wasn't. I don't mean he was really mean, either, just that… he looked out for himself, and the things that he did, like inviting me to stay with him, or buying a round of drinks, or things like that… were calculated. Things that he did to get what he wanted. I don't know if he thought that's the way the rest of the world operates too or if he knew he was different that way."

"Like a psychopath?"

"No… I don't know. Calculating. Self-centered. What's the word when you do things for money? Mercenary. He'd do you a favor if he thought it would get him something he wanted. Something that was more valuable to him."

"A situation like that could get bad pretty fast."

"Yeah. I guess so. And it did. I was naive in a lot of ways. I was okay having some fun with him. But then I'd find myself at the other end of his fun the next time… the brunt of a joke or his temper. A punching bag because he'd had a bad day or was drunk and couldn't handle himself. I kind of pretended that it wasn't happening. Because what else was I going to do? Where else was I going to go? I was already doing everything I could to find another situation, a job and a place to rent once I had some money. No one else had offered to help me. Any other 'friends' were relieved not to have to. Nice guy Brandon had stepped in and saved the day."

"But he abused you."

Erin shrugged. She didn't want to focus on that. Didn't want to remember or recount the details. "It was a long time ago now. That's all in the past."

"But he did. He wasn't such a nice guy at all."

"Yeah, that's what I found out. But it was too late to back out. I was already there. And I didn't have anywhere else to go. Until I had lined something else up, I was stuck there."

"So, you can see how someone would want to kill him," Dave suggested.

CHAPTER 32

*E*rin's heart thumped harder. She looked at him, studying his face for some sign of what he was going to do about it. Had this whole conversation just been a way of eliciting information that the police wanted from her? She wasn't going to turn herself in to them. She wasn't going to confess to anything she hadn't done. She wasn't going to let them railroad her into anything just because they couldn't find anyone else with a motive.

"There were probably a lot of people who would have wanted to… get back at him other than me," Erin said carefully.

"Because you aren't the only one he treated that way. He took advantage of other people too. Found ways to use them."

"Yeah. I remember one guy…"

Erin stopped short. Dave looked at her, waiting for her to continue. Erin looked away.

"I don't know. I probably shouldn't say. I'm sure he messed up a lot of people. Like you say, he found ways to use people. Especially people dumb enough to think they could trust him."

"Uh-huh."

"He got a call in the middle of the night," Erin said, deciding to go ahead and give him some of the details. Show him what kind of a guy Brandon was, in case he didn't already understand. It wasn't like

Dave would ever know who she was talking about. Erin didn't have to share his identity. And if his story was included in Brandon's tell-all, that wasn't Erin's problem. As she had told the sheriff, she was sure that they would have had to change his name. To protect his publishing house against a liability claim, if nothing else. "This guy… Kyle."

It had been the wee hours of the morning, and Erin hated being dragged out of sleep by something like that. The irritating jangle of Brandon's phone. Him shouting into it to be heard over whatever background noise was going on on the other end. Erin's head hurt and her body hurt, and she just wanted to sleep… knowing that it would start all over the next day. The pointless searching for a job. The claustrophobic feeling of being trapped with Brandon. Whatever demands Brandon put on her for the day.

"Something had happened. Kyle had been driving drunk. Had hit someone. I didn't talk to him directly, so I don't know all of the details. Brandon was shouting at him to settle down. Said that he would take care of things. Kyle didn't need to worry about anything. Go home and settle down, have another drink and just be calm. If anyone came looking for him, Brandon would say that Kyle had been with him. He couldn't have been the one to hit anyone, because the two of them had been together. There would be witnesses. He'd arrange everything, as long as Kyle cleaned up the car and stayed calm."

Dave had forgotten about his dinner, leaning forward with his mouth slightly open, his face a white glow in the dimness of the restaurant.

Erin didn't reveal the whole conversation to Dave. How Erin had lain there and listened to him, her teeth clenched.

"I'll tell them you were here until four. Erin will say whatever I tell her to. Don't you worry about that. We'll all tell the same story, and the cops won't be able to get anything on you. You weren't ever there."

After apparently getting Kyle settled down enough to follow his instructions, Brandon had hung up.

"He laughed about it," Erin told Dave. "He wasn't the least bit concerned for his friend. About what he was going through emotionally or about the person he'd hit. He wasn't worried about seeing that justice was done or that his friend was protected. You know why he said he'd cover for him? What he wanted?"

Dave shook his head wordlessly.

"He said that Kyle would owe him. That from then on, Kyle would do anything he wanted, because if he didn't, Brandon could go to the police and tell them that he knew what had happened that night and that he knew who it was."

"That's… horrible. And you thought he meant it?"

"Of course he meant it. That's the kind of guy he was. He would be more than willing to let Kyle dangle for the rest of his life, doing one favor after another for him. If Kyle ever refused him something, Brandon would remind him, 'You owe me for covering for you. If you don't, I'll go to the cops.' He was delighted to have something to hold over his 'friend.'"

"I wonder how many people he did something like that to."

Erin nodded. She ate a few pieces of her chicken, which was starting to get cold. How many people were there like Kyle, who would be relieved to find out that Brandon was dead and no longer a threat to them? Had one of them followed him to Bald Eagle Falls and killed him? After holding something over Kyle for years, had he threatened to reveal the story of the hit and run to the world in his tell-all memoir? There could be a dozen Kyles out there, each with a motive to kill Brandon and make sure that the memoir never hit the shelves.

The rest of the meeting was somewhat subdued. Erin supposed they were both thinking about Brandon and his false friendship, the people he had used and abused over the years. Erin knew that she should feel sorry that he was dead. He had helped her. He had kept her from whatever fate might have awaited her on the streets. He had made her life more bearable, much of the time. But she wasn't sad for him. She was relieved.

Relieved that he couldn't pop up in her life again. Emailing or messaging her or, worse, walking in the front door at Auntie Clem's. He couldn't ruin her relationships, remind her of what she had been, try to coerce her into doing something else for him. They were done, and she didn't have to worry about him stalking her to Bald Eagle Falls or any other place. She could finally stop holding her breath.

It was while they were each paying their individual portions of the bill that Sheriff Wilmot showed up.

Erin supposed she should have been expecting it. He had told her, after all.

"When you're done here, we would like to talk to you at the office," Wilmot informed her.

Had he been watching her for some time, waiting until she was paying her bill rather than interrupting her dinner? Had he been close enough to listen in on any of their conversation? Had Dave been instructed to see if he could get the story out of her?

She flashed him a look, but he seemed just as surprised as Erin was to see Wilmot there. So maybe it wasn't a setup.

Would Wilmot tell Terry that Erin had been having dinner with Dave? Make something out of it, like it had been a date instead of just a casual discussion between two people who had ended up at the restaurant alone? Erin stood slowly, handing the point-of-sale machine to the waitress, who looked confused by what was going on.

Erin looked once more at Dave. What did she even want to say to him? "Talk to you later"? "See you at the bookstore"?

"This way, please," Wilmot encouraged, nudging Erin's arm.

The other restaurant patrons stared at Erin as she was escorted out of the room by the police. By the time she got to the police department offices, they would already be speculating about what she had done.

CHAPTER 33

"What's going on?" Erin asked as Wilmot opened the door of his squad car for her. He didn't put her in the back seat, pushing down her head so that she wouldn't bump it on the way in. He just allowed her in the passenger side in the front. She could see his onboard computer and equipment and all of the little knobs that she didn't know how to use. "Why do you want me to come in?"

She had a feeling that she already knew. But she didn't want to give anything away. Maybe he didn't have anything more. Maybe it was all just a bluff like they did on TV. If you don't have anything, pretend that you do and make the suspect fall for it.

"We'll go over the details once we get there."

"I'm not sure... I don't really want to go in today. We could arrange to talk sometime tomorrow instead..."

"Are you not working tomorrow?"

"Well... yes, I am."

"Then it's easier for me to just get you while I can today. Otherwise, I won't get you until this time tomorrow, and will have wasted another day of the investigation for nothing."

"I'm not sure that I'm up to any questions right now."

"You seemed fine in the restaurant. At any rate, you've had a little chance to relax, you should be fine for a little longer. We won't keep you up late."

They knew that she went to bed pretty early, so they must not be planning on the questioning taking very long. If Erin insisted on waiting, she would just have another twenty-four hours of worrying and wondering what they had, if anything.

Erin waited, watching out the window. Hopefully, it was just a bluff. She didn't want to end up sleeping in one of the temporary holding rooms in the police department offices, waiting until they could transfer her to the pen.

"Is Terry there?"

"No, I don't believe so. Do you want him there?"

"No… I don't know. Maybe."

"Think about it and let me know. If you want him to be there, I'm sure we can make arrangements. It won't take him long to drive over."

If he even *wanted* to be there for her. But Erin knew that was unfair. Terry wanted to help her. He wanted to support her. He just couldn't stop his cop side from taking over and analyzing the situation, demanding answers. He couldn't seem to control his suspicions about what she was hiding from him. And the fact was, after dealing with a guy like Brandon, it was unlikely Erin would ever share all of her secrets with anyone. It would leave her too vulnerable. And without an escape route if she ever needed to get out of the relationship. If he knew all of her friends and past history, he would know where to look for her. He would be able to track her down.

Of course, as a cop, he could probably track her down whether he knew anything about who her friends outside of Bald Eagle Falls were or not.

Sheriff Wilmot pulled into his reserved spot in the parking lot of the town hall and shut off the engine. "Follow me."

Erin appreciated that he wasn't taking her there in handcuffs, and didn't see the need to keep his hand on her arm to ensure that she followed him in. She didn't feel quite as much like a criminal.

It was after hours, so Clara was not at the reception desk and Melissa was not there doing any filing or other administrative work. The public-facing doors were shut and locked, and it was just official personnel there now. Erin knew Sheriff Wilmot and wasn't particularly worried about being there with him alone. People had seen them leave the restaurant together, after all, so it wasn't like Wilmot could do something to her and then pretend that she had never been there. But she was still relieved to see Stayner working in the office he shared with Terry, tapping away at the computer. He looked up and nodded at Erin as she walked by.

Wilmot escorted Erin to one of the interview rooms and motioned for her to sit down.

"Do you want coffee? No muffins today, I'm afraid."

"I just ate. I don't need any food. But coffee… sure."

He nodded and left the door to the room open while he went to the nearby alcove to pour them each a mug of coffee. He returned and placed Erin's in front of her. He placed his cup slightly to his right and squared a yellow letter-size pad in front of him, lining it up with the edge of the table. He tapped a pen on it and looked at her.

"You haven't been open and honest with us in answering our questions about Brandon Quayle."

"I told you that I don't want to discuss him."

"You said that you haven't been in contact with him."

"I haven't."

"We have recovered a number of emails sent to you from Quayle over the past few weeks."

Erin had been hoping that there was no way they would be able to recover them once they had been deleted from her deleted mail folder. But she knew the axiom. How anything that had been on the internet was still there, somewhere.

"I never wrote to him."

Wilmot sipped his coffee. He put it down and wrote something on the notepad. "You admit that you received emails from him."

Erin shrugged. "I told you that he might have messaged me or tried to reach me."

"You didn't say that you had received emails from him."

"You asked if I was in contact with him. I wasn't. Just because he emailed me, that doesn't mean I had anything to do with him. *Anybody* can email you. Some Prince in Jordan who wants your bank account information. You just junk it and go on."

"Is that what you did?"

"Did you find any emails from me to him?" Erin challenged.

He apparently had not. "Quayle did email you telling you about the memoir he was writing. You acted as if you had no idea he was writing a book."

"I only glanced at the emails long enough to see what they were. I didn't read them through. And if I had, I wouldn't have believed him anyway."

"You wouldn't have believed what?"

"Anything he said. I certainly don't think he ever wrote a book."

"We now have witnesses that confirm that he did."

"They saw it? Read it?"

"Saw it. Read portions of it."

"Do they have copies?"

He shook his head. "It was only shown to them in hard copy format, and he kept the only copy with him. No one has a copy in any format. And we don't know what happened to his printout. I would really like to know what happened to it."

"He probably didn't write a whole book. Probably only enough to make people think there was a full book."

Wilmot grinned suddenly. "You're pretty skeptical, aren't you? You don't believe he could write a book?"

"Not the Brandon I knew."

"From what I understand, he had sobered up. Straightened his life around. Was trying to make things right with the people he had harmed in the past."

Erin shook her head. "I didn't believe it when he said it. I don't believe it from you either."

Remembering the story about Kyle had helped to cement it in her mind. Brandon might look like he was doing the right thing. He might have acted like he was being generous and only wanted the best for his friends. But he was just getting more ammunition. Brandon making sincere amends was the very definition of a leopard changing its spots.

"He told you he was trying to straighten things out with people from his past?"

"He might have. Something along those lines. But how exactly does that align with writing a tell-all book? Isn't he... telling everyone's secrets and worst moments?"

"I think that the point is he is telling all of the things *he* did wrong, not revealing secrets about his friends. Sort of 'all of the stupid stuff I did before I sobered up.'"

"But that would have included stuff he did with friends. Stupid stuff they did or mistakes that they made. People he humiliated. He can't tell about all of the stuff he did when I was living with him and not include me in the story."

"You know that gives you a motive, rather than taking it away."

"If I believed he was going to write something like that. But I don't. And even if he did, it's like I said before. Anyone who knew him would know that he can't tell the truth. And anyone who doesn't know him won't know me."

"So, you had absolutely no reason to want him dead."

No reason to want him dead? Erin wished that he had died years before. But she hadn't been the one who killed him. All she did was leave.

"I didn't kill him."

"Why did you go to Canyon Park?"

Erin had been afraid he would get to that. She looked away from Wilmot. "I told you; I was just out for a walk."

"He told you he would meet you there. At just about the time that you found his body."

"The second time."

He tilted his head slightly. "The second time," he agreed, as if he didn't understand why that part was significant.

"I already knew he was dead. I didn't go there to meet him."

Wilmot sat back in his chair. He pursed his lips and nodded. "Yes. You already knew he was dead. Unless you had any doubts about it. Maybe you thought that since the body disappeared, he had gotten up and walked away. That you were mistaken and he wasn't really dead."

Erin had considered that. But she had known absolutely when she saw him and when she touched him that he was dead. There was no doubt about it. She immediately discarded the idea that he could still be alive after seeing him that first time.

But she had still gone to the park.

"I felt... compelled," she confessed eventually. "I knew he was dead. I knew I wasn't going there to meet him. But I felt like I needed to go there to... close a chapter in my life. I needed to go there and *not* meet him to convince myself that he was dead and would never be coming back into my life again."

"Who put him there?"

"I have no idea. I was... as shocked as could be by him being there. I really was. I have no idea how he got there."

"Were you supposed to meet him there with someone else? His agent? A lawyer?"

"No. Nobody."

"Who else would he have told he was going to meet you there?"

"I don't know. I haven't been in his life for a couple of years. I don't know what happened between then and now."

"Someone knew that you and Quayle were supposed to meet there."

"I don't know who. Did he have a girlfriend? A sponsor? A priest? I don't know who he would tell about any of this. I wasn't supposed to meet anyone else there. Maybe someone hacked my email."

"That's a possibility, I suppose," Wilmot conceded. "Or someone happened to see it while you had it open. Someone shoulder surfing while you were at work or somewhere else? Your computer left on at the bakery with his email on the screen? Your phone put down on the table or counter at home where someone could see it?"

"Do you mean Terry? He never said anything about it. He would have asked me what it was all about."

"Maybe. You have other people in and out of your house too. Vic and Willie. Other friends, family members."

"Vic or Willie? Charley? You don't think that any of those people would have set up a meeting with Brandon in The Book Nook basement and killed him?"

"It seems like a stretch, that's true. Could have been several people in on it, though. You, one of them, one of The Book Nook employees. It could have been a conspiracy."

"A conspiracy. Are you serious? There wasn't any conspiracy to kill Brandon Quayle. If there was, I would not have called the police. We would have just gotten rid of the body our own way, and no one would ever have seen him again."

They kept coming back to that. Why would Erin have called the police if she had been the one to kill Brandon? And if she did, why wouldn't she call it in as self-defense? Say that he had attacked her? What would be the point of making the body disappear between the time she called the police and when they got there?

"I don't think you did this," Wilmot said. "I don't think it was a conspiracy. But I can't make it fit. I can't find any explanation for what happened. And you can't deny anymore that you knew him and lied to me about the fact. You knew from the start who he was and why he was here. You pretended you didn't and waited for us to figure it out on our own. Because you were hoping not to be part of this investigation."

Erin nodded. "That's exactly why."

"Well, it didn't work, did it? I don't know why you would think that it would. Did you really think that you could keep us from finding out who Brandon was or that he had a connection with you? Or that you went to Canyon Park to meet him—or where you had arranged to meet him? You must have known that it would all come out in the end."

"I could hope it wouldn't. Maybe no one would be able to identify him and it would just go away. He would be buried as a John Doe and I wouldn't ever have to think about him again." Erin had known that this was highly unlikely, but such things happened. If there wasn't anything to connect Brandon with his identity in Maine and no one stepped forward, Erin could have gotten lucky.

But she hadn't been lucky.

The police knew who he was. They knew she and Brandon were

connected. And they knew that he had told her to be at Canyon Park, and she had gone, even though she had known that he was dead.

She couldn't explain that. Not because her reasons for going to the park would incriminate her, but because she couldn't even explain them herself. She had felt compelled. So she had gone. She had never imagined that the killer would dump Brandon's body there.

CHAPTER 34

"That's what I don't get," Erin mused, shaking her head. "Why kill him and then make him disappear from The Book Nook? And why dump him in Canyon Park, where he had planned to be? How did whoever killed him know that? And if they made him disappear from The Book Nook, then why dump him there instead of just disposing of the body down a well or in a mining tunnel somewhere? Why make it reappear instead of disappearing forever?"

"To throw suspicion back on you. I think that you are the key here, Erin. I just don't know how."

"How could I be the key?"

"You know something. Maybe you don't even know you know something. Maybe Quayle said something in one of his emails that you didn't even read."

Erin rubbed her forehead. "Then how can I figure it out? Someone must have hacked my emails."

"Or maybe Quayle told them something. Maybe he was in contact with someone else in Bald Eagle Falls. Or near here. And *they* decided that him publishing his memoir was too dangerous for them."

"No one else in Bald Eagle Falls knew him."

"You don't know that."

"He would have said something. Or I would have known them from Maine. If Brandon knew someone here, then he would have known that *I* was here a long time ago."

"He didn't know where you were?"

"I never told him where I was going. I just hopped in my car and left. And I didn't go straight from his place here, either. I had a couple of jobs in between. Different places… different names. I didn't want to leave a trail that he could follow."

Wilmot pondered this. "Then how did he? And when did he?"

Erin shook her head. "I don't know. I guess… I'm on social media now and have a website, and it's all in my real name. The same name that I was using when I was with him. I thought I was safe, being here, in another state, in a small town away from the big cities. I didn't think it would be a problem to use my own name." She shrugged. "I'm not the only Erin Price in the world. Or in the USA."

"He didn't get in contact with you until recently?"

"He didn't *get in contact* at all. He started sending emails. I didn't respond. As far as he knew, I was a totally different Erin Price who didn't know who the heck he was."

"But he persisted, so he must have been pretty sure. You don't have your picture on any of your social media or your website?"

Erin considered this. She had gotten careless over time. Brandon hadn't been a part of her life anymore, and the fear of his tracking her down had faded. She had gone on with her life. She thought that he had gone on with his. That he didn't care where she was anymore. She had probably posted pictures of herself without ever thinking about him, once the danger seemed to be past.

"Maybe, yes. I guess so."

"Then he could know that it was you and not another Erin Price. And he came to Bald Eagle Falls to talk to you. To tell you about his book and that you were in it."

"Why? Why bother telling me I was in it? Why would I care?"

"He must have thought that there was something in there that you *would* care about. If he didn't want to make amends, then maybe he wanted to blackmail you. Or to try to resurrect the old relationship. He doesn't say much in his emails, just that he wants to see you, get together."

"Yeah."

Wilmot sat looking at Erin. "You can't help me out at all."

"I have no idea. I'm sorry, I can't help you. I don't know what's going on any more than you do."

There was a tap at the door, and Erin turned, expecting to see Stayner with a note in his hand to ask Wilmot something. Or maybe Clara back from dinner and checking in to see if he needed anything else before she left for the day. But it wasn't either of them. It was Terry. K9 stood at attention at his side, panting, watching Erin and Terry and waiting for a command.

Terry wasn't smiling. He didn't look happy to be there. Erin supposed he had more questions for her. Why she didn't tell *him* about the emails.

"Sheriff," Terry said gruffly. "I think Erin's ready to go home."

Erin was surprised by this. He'd heard that Wilmot was questioning her and had flown to her side to be her protector now? She expected him to be on the same side as Wilmot, wanting answers from her. The answers that would solve the case.

Wilmot nodded and sighed. "I think we're done here anyway. I wish you had been more forthcoming with me, Miss Price. I think we could have shortcut a lot of this investigation if you had told us who Quayle was and what you knew about him."

Erin stood slowly. "Now that you know... has it gotten you anywhere? Working on your own, you might have found something I couldn't have told you. Something you wouldn't have looked for if you thought it was all about me. I just didn't want to be involved."

Wilmot shook his head slowly. "Take care of yourself, and if you think of anything that might be helpful... please pass it on."

Erin didn't agree or disagree. She went to the doorway to join Terry. He stepped back to give her space to exit, and they walked in silence out to his truck.

Erin climbed up into the seat. She pulled on her seatbelt and buckled it as Terry walked around the vehicle to his side. "Thank you," she told him as he slid behind the wheel.

Terry looked at her for a moment, waiting for her to say something else, but Erin didn't have anything else to say to him.

"You're welcome. It looks like he was ready to wind things up anyway. I'm not sure I saved you anything."

"Still… I appreciate you looking after me."

He started the engine and spent a moment adjusting the airflow to the perfect temperature.

"I do want to help you, Erin. You may not believe that, but I have your best interests at heart. I don't want anything to happen to you. I don't want you to be arrested or even investigated. But sometimes, I am conflicted. I wish I wasn't, but I am. I'm sorry about before… that you felt like I was more interested in being a cop than in protecting you." He hesitated. "Not that you *felt* I was. I don't mean you misinterpreted something or were too sensitive. I *did* make a mistake. I know that you are your own person and you have a hard time sharing. It shouldn't surprise me. And I should wait until you're ready to tell me things and not to share just because I say so."

Erin was quiet, thinking about that for the few minutes it took them to drive to the house.

"You won't ask me to tell you more about Brandon?" she asked before he had cut the engine.

Terry shook his head. "I won't ask you anything else about Brandon."

"Or anyone else I might have had a relationship with?"

"Or anyone else."

"Or anything else I'm not ready to talk about?"

He swallowed and looked at her, trying to meet her eyes and convince her of his sincerity. "I will try not to ask sensitive questions or ask things about the past that you haven't offered to share. But I'm a cop and I care about you, and I might ask something that you aren't ready for. But… you don't have to answer. Just tell me. And I won't make you feel bad for not answering."

It had been a pretty tall order. Erin would have been satisfied if all he would agree to was not to ask her anything else about her life with Brandon Quayle.

"Okay," she said, and popped the truck door open. She heard

Terry scrambling to get out of the truck and catch up with her before she could get to the door. K9 hurried along at his side.

"Okay?" Terry demanded as he and Erin reached the door. "Okay, what?"

"Okay," Erin fit her key into the lock. "I accept your apology."

"You do?"

"Yes."

Erin got the door unlocked and stepped into the house. Terry followed Erin into the house, not stopping to make sure the burglar alarm was disarmed. He was always diligent about arming and disarming it.

"Wait! You do?" Terry's voice was full of relief. Erin intended to beat him to the kitchen, but he was too intent on catching her, and she only got a step or two away from the door before he snatched her up in his arms and whirled her in a wide circle, feet off the ground. Like her father had spun her when she was a little girl. Erin let out a sound that was between a shriek and a whoop. She didn't know how to respond to his enthusiasm.

She didn't have to come up with words, because as Terry bent down to set her feet back on the floor safely, he first kissed her on the forehead, and then grasped her face with both hands and held her still to kiss her again, on the lips this time.

Erin's heart was pounding as she leaned into his embrace. She longed for the closeness and warmth of her partner, a feeling that had been absent for far too long. It had been a lonely week. She didn't like the awkwardness and the solitude, with him spending his time in the spare room instead of with her. She hated the rift and would do anything within her power to heal it. She hated Brandon for being the one to cause trouble between them, even if he was dead. How many times was Brandon going to screw things up for her?

No more. He was out of her life, he was dead, and no matter what happened in the investigation, she and Terry were okay again. For sure.

Terry released her from the kiss when the burglar alarm started to whoop. He swore and dashed over to the panel to shut it off.

"You'd better call the police department to tell them they don't need to respond," Erin advised.

Terry swore again and pulled out his phone to do so. Erin couldn't help laughing at him and at his embarrassment over forgetting to disarm the burglar alarm because he had been too busy with other things.

CHAPTER 35

 $\mathcal{E}$ rin moved into the kitchen to make tea while Terry called the police dispatcher to assure them they didn't need to send someone to deal with the burglar alarm. There was a flurry of noise at the back door, and Erin could see both Vic and Willie trying to get the door open. They had a key, but might have forgotten it when they heard the alarm or hadn't managed to fit it into the lock in their hurry to see what was wrong.

Erin turned the deadbolt to unlock the door and they both pushed their way into the kitchen.

"Is everything okay?" Willie demanded, keeping Vic behind him until he could assess the situation.

"Yes. It's fine. It was an accident. There's no intruder."

Willie pushed past Erin to check the rest of the house to ensure that she was telling the truth and not just saying that because someone was holding a gun on her or something equally terrifying. He heard Terry apologizing to the police dispatcher and quickly checked out the other rooms to make sure there wasn't anyone else there.

Vic moved forward, red-faced with anger or embarrassment at being forced into the secondary position by her boyfriend. She had her gun out, a small handgun she kept in a holster under her bra. She hugged Erin around the shoulders with her free arm.

"Are you okay? Are you sure everything is fine?"

Erin nodded. "Yes. You can put the gun away. I don't want anyone getting hurt by accident."

Vic stayed there, on the alert, ready for any trouble, while she waited for Willie to finish looking around the house and return to confirm that Erin was telling the truth and everything was, in fact, safe and sound. Terry put his phone away, having finished talking with the dispatcher. Erin wondered whether they would send a car by anyway, just to ensure that the call from Terry hadn't been coerced by whoever had set the alarm off, an intruder who could be holding Erin hostage if it weren't for the fact that the house was now filled with protectors.

Erin's phone began to ring, and she knew who it would be before she reached down and found it in her pocket.

"Hi, Mrs. Peach. It's okay; false alarm. Terry and I were just occupied when we came in the door and both forgot to turn it off."

She listened to Mrs. Peach's worried tone, waiting for the words to run out again and leave her space to answer.

"I promise everything is alright. I'll tell you about it later."

She made a few more noises to assuage Mrs. Peach's worries and then hung up the phone.

"You're going to tell her about it later?" Terry repeated, his face already flushed red with embarrassment. "Explain to her why we didn't disarm the alarm?"

"Yes." Erin grinned. She looked at Willie and Vic, who had now both put their guns back in their holsters. "I'm going to explain to her why we were too… busy in conversation to disarm it."

Vic and Willie looked blank at first, but then Vic started grinning. Willie looked at her and then at Terry.

"You were… engaged in conversation?"

"Deeply engaged," Erin agreed. She hadn't thought that Terry could get any redder, but his ears were a brilliant scarlet. His cheek dimpled.

They all started chuckling.

The kettle started to whistle, and Erin motioned everyone to the table as she went to get it. "Everybody sit down and get out of the way," she told them with mock severity.

"I guess that means that the two of you made out," Vic said. "I mean—made up."

Erin giggled loudly and tried to cover it up with a cough. She took the tea things over to the table and gave everyone their favorite mugs. Of course, K9 lay beside Terry to wait for his cookie and Orange Blossom started to yowl. Apparently, Terry hadn't remembered to feed him while Erin had been at the restaurant and then at the police department office.

"Don't you believe a single meow," Terry warned. "He's been fed."

"I'll just give him a little treat, then."

Erin fed K9 one of the gluten-free dog biscuits and skittered several small kitty treats across the floor for Blossom to chase and gobble up. Marshmallow hopped into the kitchen and got a carrot from Erin before she opened the freezer to find some people treats for the rest of them. Some cookies to go with their tea. She sighed as she sat down at the table. Everyone else had already started on their drinks.

"What a day!" Erin declared.

She didn't need to fill everyone in on all of the details. The major points had already made their way around town so that everyone knew that Erin had been questioned by Sheriff Wilmot as part of the ongoing investigation into the murder of Brandon Quayle. They chatted about non-murder-related stuff, keeping the conversation casual and relaxed.

It was amazing to Erin how right everything felt. The four of them around the kitchen table with their tea and cookies. Erin reconciled with Terry. Terry and Willie talking as if they were buddies, despite the way that Willie always seemed to fall under suspicion when some crime had been committed in Bald Eagle Falls. Everything seemed to have fallen back into place. Tonight, she would be able to sleep. Brandon and his death and the repercussions of it would not keep her awake again.

"Oh, that recipe," Willie said, pointing a finger at Erin as he remembered. "You should talk to Jane Pooler."

Erin pulled out her phone to make a note of the name, and any contact information Willie might have. "And who is Jane Pooler?"

"She was a friend of Bertie's and apparently did some cooking and baking for him when his sister was out of town. So she would know all of his allergies and the flours that could be used in his baking."

"Great. Do you have any information on where she lives or her phone number?"

"I gather she is quite protective of her phone number. It is unlisted and no one is supposed to give it out. I think it's a landline. I don't think she even has a cell phone. But I do have her address."

"That will work."

Erin took down the information that Willie gave her.

It was just a little thing, but maybe it was a sign that things were going to change now and flow in her favor instead of landing one catastrophe after another in Erin's lap. If she could find out if the waffle recipe belonged to Jane Pooler and get her permission, she could try it out and see if it would work for her contest entry. She liked the ingredients and, if it turned out like she imagined it... it could be a winning entry.

CHAPTER 36

$\mathcal{E}$rin didn't have to sleep alone that night. Everything was back as it should be. She stayed in Terry's arms for a long time, snuggling back into him if he tried to move away. His arm was probably asleep all night, but Erin wasn't giving up her grip on him.

She felt refreshed and energetic, ready for her morning at Auntie Clem's when her wake-up alarm went off. She was convinced that everything was going to go right for her. No more bodies, no more burglaries, no more mysterious recipes. She would leave the crimes to the police department to solve, and they would. She didn't need to worry about anything except how her baking turned out.

The morning at Auntie Clem's went by quickly. Of course, everyone wanted to know the scoop on Erin having been called in to the police department offices the previous day. Even if they were too polite to ask, they still wanted to listen in on any details they might be able to overhear.

She had arranged for Charley to come in for the afternoon shift—Charley was a night owl, so it was best to schedule her for afternoons —so that Erin could pop over to Jane Pooler's house to find out if the waffle recipe was hers, and then run a few other errands. There were always things to do for a business like the bakery. Something that needed to be fixed or picked up.

Erin put the address into her phone GPS, but it wasn't hard to find. Bald Eagle Falls was a small town laid out on a fairly regular grid. After double-checking the address against what Willie had given her, Erin got out of the car.

She hadn't thought to ask whether Jane worked during the day or if she would be likely to be found at home. She had pictured her as a grandmotherly lady making bread for Bertie Braceling. Bertie had been a contemporary of Erin's mother, so she pictured Jane as being a generation or two older. In her sixties? Her eighties? She would be at home, wouldn't she?

There wasn't any way to find out now except to try. Erin strode up the sidewalk and knocked politely on the door. People in Bald Eagle Falls knocked before ringing the doorbell. She waited, listening for any stirring from within. If Jane was an older lady, she might use a walker or be slow.

Of course, she might also be half deaf and not hear Erin's knock. Erin eventually knocked again, as loudly as she could and, ten seconds after that, rang the doorbell. There was no answer, no stirring from within. Maybe she was out running errands or, despite what Erin had assumed about her age, might be at work. She should have asked Willie what he knew of her schedule.

Erin walked slowly back to her car. As she turned to look back at the house, a movement caught her eye. Not at Jane's house, but next door. A curtain twitched—someone looking out to see who was knocking on Jane's door. Maybe a nosy neighbor who knew Jane's comings and goings and could tell Erin her expected schedule.

After a moment of consideration, Erin walked up the neighbor's sidewalk, mentally composing what she would say about needing information about Jane. By the time she reached the front door, the occupant had opened it. No need for extended knocking and ringing there.

"Who are you?" the woman asked, looking Erin up and down. "Wait... aren't you the baker?"

Erin nodded. "Yes, that's right. I own Auntie Clem's Bakery and do the baking there."

"What are you doing over here? Shouldn't you still be at the bakery?"

"My staff is covering it this afternoon so I can do a bit of visiting and running errands." Erin made a small gesture toward the house she had come from. "Do you know when Jane will be home?"

"She's home."

"Oh, is she? She didn't answer the door. I wondered if maybe she couldn't hear me knock or ring the bell."

"She's not deaf. I'm sure she would have been able to hear you."

"Oh. Then maybe she's out. Maybe she snuck away while you were doing something and didn't notice."

"She doesn't go out a lot. And…" The neighbor hesitated. Erin leaned closer, cocking her head.

"And?"

"I haven't seen her out at all lately. I've been worried that something might be wrong. Because she has to go out *sometimes*."

Erin could hear the concern in her voice. "Do you know when the last time was? Should we call the police? Make sure she's okay?"

"No, she wouldn't like that…"

"If she fell down or anything, she could be hurt and need help."

"I don't think she fell down. She's pretty sprightly. You wouldn't guess she's as old as she is. But it does worry me."

"Does she have a car?" There wasn't one parked at the curb in front of the house. Other than Erin's yellow Volkswagen.

"Yes, but it's in the garage in back."

"Maybe we should make sure it's still there. That she hasn't gone somewhere out of town."

"Well, I suppose so…"

Erin motioned to the side gate of the neighbor's house. "Do you mind if I cut through so I can check?"

"Yes, yes, go ahead. But she hasn't gone out of town. If she goes out of town, she leaves a key with me and tells me where she is going to be. You can't be too careful."

Erin's uneasiness grew at the evidence of the care Jane took to let people know where she was going to be. Would someone like that just ignore the door? What if she *had* fallen?

Erin walked quickly through the neighbor's yard to her back fence and the gate to the alley. Then she moved over a house to try to see in the windows of the garage to see if Jane's car was still parked there as suspected. She couldn't see in the windows on the big garage door because they were too high but, in the yard, she pressed her face to the window to peer in. She could see the dark form of a car parked inside. So, Jane Pooler had not gone anywhere, but was still in her house. Not answering the door.

Erin walked to the back door of the house. She would try one more time and, if she could still not raise any answer from Jane, she would call Terry. Someone who was too nervous to open the door to a stranger might still answer to a uniformed police officer.

She knocked again, hard, trying to be loud enough that Jane would be able to hear it throughout the house. Unlike many houses, Jane's was equipped with a back doorbell, a rare find that Erin took advantage of by immediately pressing it after her initial knock. Not leaving anything to chance, she followed up with another firm knock, ensuring that Jane couldn't possibly miss her arrival. There was no answer. Erin looked at the house on the other side. Maybe the neighbor there would know something. Maybe it was someone Jane talked to more than she did the nosy neighbor? If the neighbor were too intrusive and Jane didn't want to share anything with her, she might go to someone else instead.

Erin stepped down from the doorstep, deciding to go over and check, just to be sure. Then, if the other neighbor didn't know anything either, she would call Terry.

CHAPTER 37

There was a soft click and the door behind her opened. Erin turned back around. She smiled at the older woman peeking out from behind the door. She had gray hair and was dressed in a yellow sundress. The smell of freshly brewed coffee wafted out from the house. She smiled tentatively, wrinkles fanning out around her eyes.

"Hello?"

"Oh, Mrs. Pooler…? You don't know me, but I'm Erin Price, and I—"

"Come inside, come inside," Jane said quickly, opening the door farther and motioning Erin in. "Don't stand out there attracting the attention of the whole neighborhood." After Erin stepped into the house, Jane stuck her head out the door and looked quickly around before shutting it again. Maybe she had been staying inside, out of sight, because of paranoia? It could go along with dementia or even be triggered by something as simple as a bladder infection.

She looked around the house for other signs that the woman might be having mental challenges. The front entryway and the living room were neat and tidy. No growing piles of garbage that she couldn't keep up with or collections that indicated she was hoarding.

Erin got the feeling that the room had just been dusted and the cushions on the furniture shaken out in anticipation of company.

"I don't mean to intrude. If you're expecting someone…"

There was the coffee, too. Jane had just put it on. Was she planning to drink it all herself? Maybe she had a Keurig or similar machine and had only made one cup.

"No, no, dear. Have a seat. I'll get the coffee."

A cozy fireplace and a few chairs made up the living room. The furniture was well-worn but comfortable looking, with a floral printed sofa decorated with colorful throw pillows on one wall and a matching armchair on the other side of the room. A cabinet crammed full of knickknacks and photos sat beside a birch bookshelf lined with Reader's Digest condensed books. A crocheted afghan covered the back of one chair and a basket of yarn and knitting needles sat on the coffee table. The overall effect was homey and welcoming, making Erin feel comfortable and at ease.

She sat on the sofa and waited for Mrs. Pooler to return. There was the sound of clinking dishes in the kitchen and, in a few minutes, the woman was back, carrying a tray. Erin repressed her instinct to jump up and take it from her and serve the coffee herself. She was the guest here and Mrs. Pooler appeared to be perfectly capable of carrying the tray and setting things out herself.

"These are gorgeous," Erin admired the delicate coffee cups with accents of pink roses. "You must love getting them out and having a tea party."

Mrs. Pooler's face crinkled up in a smile. "You know, you're absolutely right. They are an absolute joy to use and take me back to when I was a little girl, playing with my friends or my dolls."

Erin stirred her coffee for a moment before taking a sip. "I work at Auntie Clem's Bakery, and I… well, I found a waffle recipe that someone had left behind, and I've been trying to find out where it came from. I thought I recognized the flour blend; it's similar to what I used when I was doing some baking for Bertie Braceling."

Mrs. Pooler nodded. "Bertie was always a challenge to cook for! And just when you found something that would work, he would start reacting to an ingredient he hadn't before. The buckwheat-arrowroot-psyllium combination was pretty stable for a couple of years, but I always worried about what would happen when he started reacting to buckwheat!"

"He was always so cheerful about it. I couldn't understand how he could be so… accepting of his dietary limitations. Some people can't comply with even one restriction, and he was so limited, but so upbeat about it."

"That was just his nature." Mrs. Pooler shrugged. "I do miss him."

"So… this is your recipe, right?" Erin got out the paper and smoothed it out on her lap. "I can't figure out how it even got into the bakery, because I don't think I've ever seen you there. Did you… drop it? Did someone else have it?"

"Dave had it," the older woman admitted. She was looking down at her coffee rather than at Erin. "He wanted to do something that would distract you from… well, you know, what you found over there, in the bookstore."

Erin felt a warm rush of gratitude toward Dave. He had been worried about what she had seen and how it would affect her, and he had come up with something that would distract her from the nastiness of it. The perfect solution—a mysterious new waffle recipe of unknown origin.

"Well… I would never have guessed that in a million years. How thoughtful of Dave. I guess it worked because I have definitely been engaged in trying to figure out where the recipe came from." She laughed. "I guess the question is, do you need this back? Or do you mind me keeping it? I've been working on a recipe to submit to the waffle contest. You probably know that. If this one works out, would you mind if I submitted it? I don't want to put any pressure on you if it is an old family recipe or something you wouldn't want to be circulated."

Of course, she knew it wasn't an old family recipe. It was a recipe carefully formulated for Bertie Braceling, using only ingredients that he could tolerate. Minus the malt vinegar and the pumpkin spice mix, of course.

"Dave doesn't know anything about gluten-free baking," Mrs. Pooler said, setting her coffee down and finally looking at Erin. She looked childlike. As if she were afraid she was going to be punished for doing something wrong. "He knows that the recipe can't have wheat in it, but that's about all he knows about gluten-free cooking."

Erin nodded. "I would say the same is true of most people. If it's not something you do, then you don't know all of the little tricks, what other ingredients you need to watch for, how someone could have a bad reaction from the smallest bit of gluten exposure."

"But I knew that you do. I knew that you would look at every single ingredient before deciding to make it."

Erin frowned, trying to follow Mrs. Pooler's train of thought. Again, it seemed like the woman was exhibiting symptoms of some kind of dementia.

"Then why would you put malt vinegar and the spice pack in the recipe?" Erin asked. "I know you didn't make it that way for Bertie. And you know that I couldn't bake it that way. Why would you change the recipe to include those ingredients?"

"It was so nice when Dave moved to Bald Eagle Falls," Mrs. Pooler wandered off on a tangent, not answering the question. "Having such a nice young man move in close by. Someone who offered to help, who wanted to do everything he could for me. He was so very sweet and doted on me. He offered to go out and buy my groceries so I didn't have to go to the store, to mow the lawn and do other maintenance around here…"

"Oh! I didn't even put it together." Erin shook her head. Even when Mrs. Pooler had said that it had been Dave who had wanted the recipe to give to Erin, the tumblers had not clicked into place. "You're Dave's Aunt Jane."

"Yes," she agreed. "That's what he calls me. But I'm not really his auntie."

Erin had run into the same situation dozens of times. Younger people were taught to call older relatives aunt or uncle even though they were related another way. First cousins once removed. Second cousins. Married to a relative. They didn't even technically have to be related, though most probably were once they got down to it. Erin had also discovered from Clementine's genealogy files that pretty much everyone in Bald Eagle Falls was related. The old families had intermarried many times. As Mary Lou had once told Erin, "If you're kin to Clementine, you're kin to half the mountain."

"I know how it is with these old Tennessee families," Erin agreed. "Everyone is related somehow."

"He's not from Tennessee."

But he was from a Tennessee family. He had come to Bald Eagle Falls to help care for his aunt. Erin supposed many of the older, established family members would see someone like Dave as an outsider. Sometimes even someone like Willie, who had been raised in Bald Eagle Falls, was seen as an outsider because of how he had decided to live his life.

"I know that," Erin agreed.

"He is from the north."

"Yes, like me."

"From Maine."

Erin nodded. "That's right. That's where I'm from." She was a bit surprised that Mrs. Pooler would know that much about her, but she supposed that even if she was usually at home and didn't come to the bakery, she could still be hooked into the grapevine. And she had one source, in particular, Dave Wolfe, working out of The Book Nook, which Erin was in and out of all the time.

"He does things for me," Mrs. Pooler said, reverting to the previous topic. "Looks after me. Makes sure I have everything I need and don't have to go out."

"That's very nice of him."

"He gets upset if I go out. He wants me to stay here all the time and not to go out and talk to people."

If she had the beginnings of dementia, as Erin supposed she did, then she might not be able to judge who it was safe to talk to and what she could say to them. Dave might have had to be quite stern with her, telling her not to go out or talk to anyone. Erin had seen how frustrated family members and caregivers could become, trying to help their loved ones to live at home for as long as they could, but getting more and more strict about what the family member could do. As they slipped into what had once been called a second childhood, their children became the parents, having to make rules and stay on top of them as they slid further and further out of reach.

Dave was doing a good job. Nothing in that room hinted at any loss of mental faculties. It did not feel institutional or like a prison.

Erin supposed that was why Mrs. Pooler hadn't answered the door right away. Dave had drilled it into her that she wasn't allowed to open the door to strangers. She wasn't allowed to go out or to let anyone in.

"That's why I put those ingredients in the waffles," Mrs. Pooler said, fixing Erin with a bright stare. "So that you would know that something dangerous can be hidden. That something that is apparently so sweet… can kill."

CHAPTER 38

Sheriff Wilmot had been in a meeting for the last couple of hours, dealing with the feds on another case. When he opened his office door, he waved a stack of papers at Terry and motioned for him to come in.

"We need to talk."

Terry followed Wilmot back into his office. K9 kept close at his side. Wilmot sat down behind the desk and settled himself into the chair.

"The background checks didn't all check out," he told Terry. "I got an alert last night about Dave Wolfe's ID and social security number not matching up properly."

Terry raised his brows. "His ID doesn't check out?"

"No. Something is wonky. I'm not sure who he is or why he is using a false name and ID, but we need to get this sorted out."

Terry nodded. "Yes. As soon as possible."

Dave Wolfe worked right next door to Erin. He had casually met her for dinner the night before. He was the one who was supposed to have locked the bookstore the night Brandon Quayle had been killed.

"Have you questioned him?" Terry asked.

Wilmot looked at him over the top of the paper he was holding. "Not yet. I want to see what we can find out first. I've got to get caught back up here. It would help if you could find a way to get his picture to Quayle's family and friends back north. See if anyone recognizes him."

"I'm on it," Terry said, getting up. He paused at the door, having second thoughts about leaving. "Do you think it was him?"

"I don't know. It could just be a coincidence." Wilmot put the paper he was holding down on his desk. "We're not sure yet. We have to be careful."

"Of course." Terry nodded.

"Don't say or do anything that will tip him off. He could bolt, and we have no idea where he would go at this point. Who he really is."

Terry sighed. "I'm on it, but why would someone fake his identity and hide in a town like Bald Eagle Falls?"

"Who knows what he was hiding from." Wilmot shrugged. "I wish I had the answers, but it takes time to follow up on all of the leads."

"I'll get to work on it right away," Terry said.

"Thanks." Wilmot nodded and turned back to his desk.

Terry turned and left the office, distracted.

He'd thought that they had eliminated Dave as a suspect. The man had been so shocked when Terry had described to him how Erin had stumbled upon the body in The Book Nook. The body that had then disappeared before the police could get there. Terry could clearly remember the shocked expression on his face: he had been as white as a ghost, his eyes wide and his mouth hanging open. He didn't see how that reaction could have been faked.

Terry hurried down the hallway and back to his office. He needed to find out just who Dave was.

Erin stared at Mrs. Pooler. She felt like she was losing *her* mind. She'd thought that the older woman was the one who was going senile, but Jane Pooler had just pulled the rug out from under her. Erin was the one who had been stupid, who had not seen what was in front of her own face. She was the one who had been too dense to see what Mrs. Pooler was warning her about.

She hadn't understood the secret language of the recipe. The warning it contained. It had led her to Mrs. Pooler, which was a start, but Erin should have seen that it was more than just an unexpected gift. The red flags were there, but she had chosen not to see them.

She hadn't understood Mrs. Pooler's words as they had begun their conversation.

I'm not really his aunt.

He gets mad if I talk to anyone or go out.

He's from the north. From Maine.

"Who is Dave?" Erin asked in a hoarse whisper, suddenly unable to find her voice.

"I don't know," Mrs. Pooler confided. "He's never told me… his real name or what his story is. I didn't realize what he was doing at first. That he was using me as his cover. Pretending he belonged in Bald Eagle Falls because I was his auntie and he was taking care of me. He was using me to explain why he had just shown up here one day."

Erin heard a car door slam. She and Jane Pooler looked at each other, startled and worried. Erin turned to look out the window and saw that the truck was not in front of Mrs. Pooler's house like Erin's was. It had pulled into the neighbor's driveway. The opposite side of the house from the nosy neighbor.

"It's just the neighbor," Erin said, laughing at them both for being so jumpy.

"No." Mrs. Pooler's eyes were on the window, not reassured as Erin was. "We need to hide."

Erin looked back out at the truck as the driver walked across the driveway and came into view. Dave.

"Don't answer the door," she told Mrs. Pooler.

"He has a key."

Of course he did.

"Come on," Mrs. Pooler insisted. "Hurry."

Erin felt like *she* was the old woman as she struggled to get her body to listen to her. Standing up, hurrying after Mrs. Pooler, feeling like she was pushing her way through concrete. Dave would see Erin's car and know who was there. Maybe he even had a monitoring camera pointed at Mrs. Pooler's house, and that was what had made him return home.

Nice and close. He had met the old lady and helped her, providing her with all of the help she could want before starting to close the net around her. His help gave him a legitimate reason for being there, and she, in turn, had someone to run her errands and mow her lawn, and eventually keep her there, a prisoner in her own home.

Mrs. Pooler had picked up the coffee things and bustled into the kitchen. Erin still had her cup in hand as she entered the homey, breezy kitchen. The curtain over the sink rippled in front of an open window. Mrs. Pooler grabbed Erin's cup from her and quickly rinsed it under the tap and set it on the drying rack. She left her own half-finished cup on the tray.

She looked around, face pale, eyes wide. There wasn't anywhere to hide.

"Do you have a basement or attic?" Erin suggested. "Even… something close by, like a shed."

"The attic," Mrs. Pooler echoed.

She led Erin to the mud room at the back door. Even the mud room was immaculate. There was an enclosed porch or sunroom beside it, and warm sunshine streamed in the windows. Mrs. Pooler pointed up.

A faint rectangle in the ceiling. An eye loop at the edge to pull down. Erin looked around for a stick with a hook on the end to pull it down but couldn't find one. And when they found one, how were they going to get up into the attic? Jump up through the hole? There was no ladder, and Dave was already knocking briskly on the front door, then fitting his key into the lock.

"Here." Mrs. Pooler, rummaging through a slim utility cupboard, managed to find a long broomstick with a hook on the end. Erin reached up with it and tried to fit it through the little eyelet in the ceiling. She failed several times, her hands too shaky, the eyelet too small and too far away. She looked desperately toward the front door.

Dave was going to walk in and find them there. It was time to come up with an excuse. An explanation for being there with Dave's "Aunt Jane."

The best thing would be to tell him the truth, that she was following up on the recipe that he himself had dropped into her lap.

But then what?

He would know from their faces that Aunt Jane had told Erin what she knew and that Erin was no longer distracted by the new waffle recipe.

CHAPTER 39

*P*olice work was so much faster than it used to be. Before Terry's time, fax machines took a long time to transmit a detailed image and it wasn't a great likeness once it got through. And before that, actually having to carry or courier pictures from one place to another. Cops canvassed with hard-copy photos in hand.

So he really couldn't complain about how long it took to find a couple of pictures of Dave Wolfe on social media and to start emailing them out to everyone they had been able to find with connections to Quayle. Even if people didn't like him that much, they were still intrigued by the story and excited to be able to assist in solving a homicide case. The fact that Quayle's body had been discovered, disappeared, and showed up again intrigued people, and they wanted to be a part of the case. It wasn't hard to get people to look at the photos he messaged to them, but it still took time to find anyone who actually knew him and could put a name to the face. Then he started working background on the name that they gave him, trying to figure out why Dave would have left Maine and come to Bald Eagle Falls.

Terry couldn't help but wonder what the connection was. Dave had arrived in Bald Eagle Falls before Erin. Had she followed him there? It wasn't possible. He knew Erin had come to Bald Eagle Falls to receive the inheritance that her Aunt Clementine had left her. She hadn't come looking for Dave. And if the two of them had wanted to run away together, they could have sold the properties and taken off whenever they wanted to.

If Erin had not come to Bald Eagle Falls because of Dave, then had he come because of her? That didn't make sense either because his arrival preceded hers by several months.

Terry rubbed his forehead, trying to loosen the knot of muscles and relax. He needed someone to brainstorm with. To try to come up with the connections that they were missing. Who was Dave Wolfe? Did he have a friend in Bald Eagle Falls that he had come to visit, and then decided to stay there? Had he been on the run?

It would be a while for the name he had input into the computer to come up with anything. There were a lot of databases to search through, and not-Dave could show up in any of them.

"Terry?"

Terry pulled his hand away from his head and focused on the form in the doorway. Clara, looking tentative. "Sorry, I don't mean to interrupt you, but…"

"No, it's okay. I'm trying to figure everything out here, but I'm not getting far. I could use an interruption about now."

"Well… it's Naomi from The Book Nook. She wondered if she could see you."

"Of course I'll see her." Terry glanced around his office. It wasn't messy, exactly, but it was… busy. His desk was piled high with files, reports, and mail. "Uh, just hand me that stack of files." He indicated the chair. Clara picked them up and Terry put them on the credenza behind him. He held his hand over them for a moment, making sure they weren't going to immediately slide to the floor, taking everything else with them in an avalanche. He turned back around to face Clara. "Okay. Show her in."

Clara nodded and withdrew. She was back a minute later with Naomi. Naomi swept back her straight, blonde hair and sat in the chair when Terry indicated it. She had a stack of papers in her hands and, by the time they were finished with small talk, he was burning to find out what they were.

"What have you got there?"

Naomi looked down at the thick bundle of papers. "I found this… in a box in the basement."

Terry's heart quickened in excitement. He kept his voice even and his face as expressionless as he could manage, trying not to influence her answer.

"It wasn't there before. I ordered in some books that the freshman English class needs in the fall, so they were just set to the side. I didn't look at them again until today."

Terry nodded his understanding.

"I guess… well, it isn't anything that *I* put there. I think… it must have been put there by Brandon Quayle." She swallowed and licked her lips, clearly dry from talking to him. "His name is on the front page." She lifted the bundle and turned it away from her so that he could see the front page.

It certainly looked genuine. He'd never held a manuscript in his hands before, but it looked like he would have expected a manuscript to look like. A thick stack held together by a black fold-back clip. Somewhat dog-eared, with sticky notes protruding here and there. It looked like it had been read and re-read several times.

"Let's see." He held out his hand for the papers. Naomi handed them over. Terry placed the manuscript squarely on the desk in front of him. He opened it to a random page halfway through.

It was blank.

Terry turned it over and looked at the next. It was also blank. He thumbed his way through several at once. There were a few random photocopies. Like Brandon had emptied the recycling bin at the library and just thrown a bunch of completely disparate topics together. Terry picked a few of the pages with flags or sticky notes at the edge to see if the notes made any more sense than the random pages he had picked out. Several of them were blank. Others were random topics, again.

Terry looked at Naomi. "This is supposed to be his manuscript? But what would he do when he had to show it to someone?"

"I don't know. Maybe there are a few actual pages from his

memoir in there… Or maybe he would email them something, and this was only a prop."

Terry fanned the pages a few times, looking for anything that was not so random.

No luck. Terry pushed it away. He looked at Naomi. "When Dave came to work for you, did you check references?"

"Uh…" Naomi took off her black-framed glasses and considered the question. "I always do, so I must have."

"But you don't remember?"

"I'm sure I called his references. I don't remember any specifics."

"Nothing out of the ordinary? Just what you were expecting?"

"I guess so, yes. If there had been something wrong, I wouldn't have hired him. He's been an excellent employee. Never late. Learned the systems quickly. Was diligent in his job."

"Didn't murder anyone in the basement until now," Terry contributed.

Naomi's mouth dropped open. "You don't think Dave had anything to do with the murder!"

"We know that he didn't close and lock the store like he was supposed to."

"But that doesn't mean he had anything to do with the murder. That was just an oversight."

"Which happened the exact day of the murder. You said he was diligent. He'd never forgotten anything like that before?"

"No. It was just a one-time mistake."

"On the day of a murder."

Naomi shook her head. "It doesn't have anything to do with the murder. You know that. He was just as shocked as anyone."

"You never had any issues with his social security number?"

"Why would I?"

"Because Dave Wolfe isn't his real name."

Naomi frowned. "But it was… that was the name I used when I talked to his references. They all knew him. There weren't any issues."

"There weren't any issues because the references didn't actually exist. They were set up. People telling you what Dave had told them to tell you."

"I can't believe that. He's been such a good employee. I've never had any trouble with him."

"He had to keep his head down and stay out of trouble if he didn't want to be caught."

"No," Naomi continued to shake her head. "I can't believe that."

Terry's phone rang. He looked at the number on the caller ID. "Do you mind if I take this?"

"Sure, of course." Naomi looked around. "I should go. Give you some privacy. I guess…" She motioned to the faux manuscript, "You'll keep that."

"Yes, thank you for bringing it in," Terry told her, reaching for his phone before the call could go to voicemail. "It was enlightening."

Naomi nodded and left the office as Terry picked up the phone.

"Piper here."

"Officer Piper." The voice on the other end of the call was low and gravelly, sounding like the owner of it had stayed up half the night drinking and wasn't quite ready for the day, even though it was mid-afternoon. "Detective Percival Jones here."

The caller ID already told Terry what police force Jones was calling from, and Jones didn't bother to supplement or repeat that information, driving straight to the topic of his call. "You are looking for information on a subject surnamed Pinckney."

"Yes. That's the name I was given. It may be an alias. I'm not sure yet; this is very early stages."

"We are also looking for information on Pinckney. Am I to understand that you know where he is?"

Terry's heart started to beat harder in anticipation. "He's a murder suspect in Tennessee."

"So he's there? You know where he is?"

"Yes. Do you have an active warrant on him?"

"He is wanted for questioning in connection with a felony murder. Owner of a convenience store who was shot during a hold-up."

"And wanted for questioning means he is your prime suspect?" Terry double-checked.

"Our investigation led us back to Pinckney but, by the time we had identified him, he had disappeared. In fact, it would appear that the hold-up was part of his departure from Maine. He was on the road at the time. Needed money. By the time we had identified him, any trace of where he had gone from there was gone. Though indications are," Jones paused for effect, "that he was headed south at the time."

Terry thought about that. "Just over two years ago?"

"Yes."

"Sounds like he came straight here."

"If you're investigating him for murder, chances are you're on the money. You'll want to keep eyes on him until you have enough to arrest. Make sure he doesn't slip through your fingers like he slipped through ours."

"Do you have enough for an arrest?"

"We have fingerprint and DNA evidence, but they need to be verified as being his. If you happen to have either on file, that would be most helpful."

"No. But I'll see what I can do about getting them to you."

"If they are his, we have enough for an arrest. The rest of what we have is circumstantial. Surveillance videos are grainy and he doesn't look directly at the camera. Eyewitnesses were shaky and aren't likely to have gotten any better with a two-year hiatus. But fingerprints and DNA would confirm his presence at the scene."

"Okay. I'll see what I can do. If we can make an arrest based on your evidence, then we can hold him while we pursue the investigation here. See if we can get him for both."

"Good. Anything else you need from me?"

"Anything you have on file that you would like to share. Contacts who knew him before he changed his identity. I've managed to track down a couple through a mutual acquaintance but, the more we can get, the easier it will be to make our case."

"I'll go through the file. Pull up any family or friends."

"Great. Appreciate that. I'll be in touch."

After Terry hung up, he stared at the phone for a few minutes, not seeing it, just working through everything in his head. It was hard to see Dave as a possible murderer instead of the polite and earnest young man who had worked at the bookstore for two years, respectful and hardworking, never causing any trouble. Most criminals gave themselves away eventually. Went to the bar and started a fight or got talking too much. Couldn't resist pulling a scam that they had done before. Did something to attract attention to themselves.

But Dave had been good. He had been very good.

CHAPTER 40

Terry drove to Dave's place of residence, but parked around the corner where the man would not be able to see his police truck when he looked out the window or door. Best to keep it all on the lowdown until they had a way to get a sample of Dave's fingerprints or DNA. A garbage search was the obvious route. Dave was unlikely to be wiping everything down before he threw it out. Even if he'd thought to do that two years ago, the chances that he would still be doing it two years later were pretty low.

But Terry wanted to get the lay of the land before moving in. He had called Naomi to ask what Dave's work schedule was, but hadn't been able to get through to her and had to be content with leaving a message. Terry checked out the back of the house first, peeking in the garbage bin to see if there was anything he could grab. Unfortunately, garbage pick-up day had been just a couple of days before, and Dave hadn't thrown anything out since then. Or else he burned his garbage or buried it somewhere out in the woods. Some people did that, but it was too much trouble for most. Since Bald Eagle Falls had started a municipal garbage collection program, all but the oldsters who were too set in their ways to change had adopted it.

In a few days, he would come by again and, if there were a fresh bag of garbage, he would throw it into the back of his truck and search through it in the parking lot behind the town hall.

K9 sniffed with interest around the base of the bin, and Terry let him for a few minutes, then gave his collar a little tug and ordered him to heel. K9 fell into place and they walked around the block to the front of the house.

Terry stopped and stared at the yellow VW bug in front of the house next door. Erin could not have driven anything much more recognizable. Her bright yellow bug stood out like a sore thumb wherever she parked it. He looked along the street for any sign of her. Had she come over to see Dave about something? Had Dave decided that she was too much of a liability and he needed to get her out of the way? Erin had been right in the thick of things from the time she had discovered Brandon Quayle's body. Dave couldn't let that go on forever.

Terry ducked back as a truck pulled into Dave's driveway. It was moving quickly, and he was worried at first that he might have tripped a burglar alarm or some other kind of early warning system that Dave had in place to let him know if someone started nosing around his property. But he saw Dave hop out of the truck and cross in front of his house to the neighbor's house.

The one Erin's car was parked in front of.

Terry hesitated, hanging back to see what Dave would do and whether there was any reason to interfere. Dave might have a completely innocent reason for visiting his neighbor at the same time as Erin. Dave might, for that matter, be completely innocent and have nothing to do with Brandon's murder or the robbery case gone bad.

But where there was smoke, there was fire. The chances that Dave was involved increased dramatically with every crime that he was suspected of.

Dave went to the door and pounded on it several times. There was no answer. He was already jangling a ring of keys and, in a moment, fitting one key into the lock.

There were a lot of reasons that Dave might be visiting his neighbor. The fact that he had keys and would go in the front door in broad daylight suggested that he had a legitimate reason to be there. A reason that did not involve Erin.

K9 whined at his side. Terry should have been reassured by the fact that Dave had keys to the house, but he was not. It didn't matter to him that Dave's neighbor trusted him.

They had all trusted him.

Naomi, Erin, Terry.

They all thought that he was a nice young man, an upright citizen, a nice guy working at the bookstore, not getting in any trouble.

But he thought K9's instincts were right. There was still reason to be concerned about what was going on. Why was Dave going into the house? Why hadn't the homeowner answered the door? He would have assumed that the house was empty or Dave was house-sitting while his neighbor was away, except for Erin's car parked in front of the house and the fact that Dave had knocked on the door.

Erin could be visiting with another neighbor on the block. She could be across the street and just hadn't turned around to park on the correct side. The odds that she and Dave would just be in the same place coincidentally was about as likely as the chances that Erin had randomly stumbled across Brandon Quayle's body after he had died.

Twice.

He waited until Dave stepped into the house and then followed, moving quickly, wishing his shoes were quieter when they clicked on the concrete sidewalk blocks. He slowed down when he reached the doorstep, unsnapped his holster, and eased his gun out. Somewhere in the house were Erin and the homeowner. And a suspected killer. A man who may have killed multiple times.

He moved silently, K9 at his side, on high alert.

~

"Jane?"

Erin heard Dave's voice. He was inside the house already. She wished she'd had more time to piece the clues together and figure out what was going on, but it was too late now. He was there and there was no time to call the police or bluff. Atheist though she was, Erin begged the universe that Dave wouldn't discover their hiding place. He could come in, look around, and then decide that Aunt Jane had just gone out for a walk or something equally innocuous. Erin had not left any sign of her presence.

Except, of course, there was the bright yellow bug parked in front of the house. Erin swore in her head. He was too close for her even to whisper it aloud.

"Aunt Jane, it's Dave. Where are you?" There was a pause as he looked around, taking the time to check each of the bedrooms as he walked by them. It would have made sense to hide in one of them. In the closet or behind the door, and then when he made his initial pass, jump out and run away.

"Is there someone here? A visitor?" Dave asked. "I thought I saw Erin Price's car out front."

His voice was calm and conversational—no reason for Jane and Erin not to show their faces.

Except that they knew he was a killer.

Dave made his way steadily toward them, his feet progressing quietly down the hall as he checked each room on the way to the back of the house.

"Jane, Erin, where are you hiding?" Dave asked in a pleasant, good-humored voice. "What kind of game is this?"

Neither of them moved. Neither breathed more than they had to. Dave came out of the hallway. He checked the kitchen and then the mud room.

The long red broomstick handle with the hook on the end was still leaning against the wall, not put away in the broom closet where it had been. Dave stepped over to it and picked it up. She could hear the gears turning in his head. Though she couldn't see him, she imagined him looking up at the rectangular patch in the ceiling. He was taller than either of the women and would find it easier to reach the attic door.

It only took him one try to get the hook through the eyelet. He gave the trapdoor a little tug, and the hatch opened slowly and noiselessly. The ladder unfolded and touched down right in front of Dave's feet.

Erin's heart was racing so fast she could barely breathe. But she suppressed the urge to gasp or draw in any more air than usual. If he couldn't see or hear her, maybe he would just give up and go home.

"In the attic?" Dave asked as he mounted the steps. "What are you ladies doing hiding in the attic? Did you really think that I wouldn't find you up here?"

Erin listened to him climb the ladder, step by step. She pictured his head and shoulders protruding into the attic and squeezed her eyes shut tightly, trying not to give their position away.

"Hold it right there, Dave."

CHAPTER 41

*E*rin swallowed a gasp. She knew that voice! Terry!

She did nothing that would distract him from his task at hand. Screaming and attracting attention to herself would not do any of them any good. She stayed still, though a shiver ran through her body that had nothing to do with how warm or cold she was.

"Who's that?" Dave demanded.

"I said to hold it there. Don't move. Drop the gun, Dave."

A gun? Dave had come after them with a gun? His dear old Aunt Jane?

"Officer Piper?"

"Yes. Let's see the gun. Just drop it through the hatch to the floor."

"I'm afraid it might go off if I do that," Dave said, wheedling, looking for a way to put himself back on the same level as Terry, to get an advantage over him.

Normally, the high ground won out as the best position. But with his head above the ceiling, Dave couldn't see Terry, but Terry could see him.

"I'll take that chance," Terry countered. "I said drop it. I'm not going to tell you again."

Still, Dave hesitated. Erin swallowed. Her eyes were still tightly shut as if Dave wouldn't be able to see her if she couldn't see him.

Then Erin heard the clunk of Dave's gun hitting the floor. Another noise that sounded like Terry had slid it along the floor. Away from Dave, Erin supposed, so that Dave wouldn't be able to get it again, like the criminals did so often on TV dramas.

"Come down slowly. Keep your back to me. Put your hands behind your head before you take the last step down."

She could hear Dave moving slowly and carefully, looking for a way out of the situation as he came down to Terry's level.

"What's this all about, Officer Piper? I was just looking for an intruder…"

"You're under arrest for breaking and entering," Terry told him firmly, handcuffing him and then feeling his pockets for any other weapons.

"Breaking and entering?" Dave laughed. "I have a key."

"When I hear that you had permission to come in here with a gun to check for intruders, then I will reconsider. Sit down cross-legged."

Erin could hear Terry lowering Dave to the floor. K9's collar jangled.

"Erin? Are you here?" Terry called.

For a moment, Erin couldn't respond. She had been doing everything she could to keep quiet, and her brain and her body didn't want to release and take the chance that something could happen to her if she were discovered. She forced her eyes open and tried to take deeper breaths.

"Erin?"

"We're here."

As Erin emerged, she saw Terry looking around in confusion. He looked up at the attic hatch and then at Erin and Mrs. Pooler.

"What?"

Erin giggled as she stepped out from the coat she had been hiding behind in the mudroom. She stepped out of the boots that had been hiding her feet and legs below the coat. Mrs. Pooler did the same, straightening the coat neatly on the peg and stepping out of a pair of gardening boots.

"I thought…" Terry looked up at the attic.

Erin shook her head. "I couldn't get it open. We didn't have enough time."

He chuckled and looked over at Dave, sitting on the floor. Dave's face was red, embarrassed that he had fallen for their trick, that he hadn't seen them standing right there in front of him. Not that it would have made any difference with Terry coming in right behind him.

"Erin, I think you know Kyle Pinckney," Terry said, looking down at Dave.

Erin felt like she'd been slapped in the face. "What? Kyle?"

"That's not my name," Dave protested. "I'm Dave Wolfe."

"You're not," Terry said firmly. "You have been identified as Kyle Pinckney. Who, by the way, is a person of interest in at least one other criminal investigation at this time."

"Kyle," Erin repeated breathlessly.

Terry looked at her curiously.

Dave's—Kyle's—eyes were dark and angry as he stared at Erin, threatening her without words. Warning her that he would come after her if she opened her mouth and spilled what she knew.

"I know Kyle," Erin explained. "That is… I know his name. I never knew his last name or met him. I just… heard him on the phone one night. Heard Brandon talking to him."

Dave tried to jump to his feet, but Terry knocked him down again easily and didn't let him get up. "You want me to shackle your ankles too?"

"I don't know what she's talking about. I didn't have anything to do with… Brandon. I never met him. She's the one who killed him. She's the one who kept saying that she'd just *happened* to find him. You really believe that? She's the one who knew him; of course it was her!"

Terry stared at Dave for a moment, then shrugged. "It probably doesn't make any difference what Erin says at this point. Detective Jones in Maine wants you for felony murder. We'll get enough evidence to prove that you killed Brandon when he confronted you with his fake manuscript. Anything else is icing on the cake."

"Fake manuscript?" Dave repeated, blood draining from his face.

Terry nodded. "The one he had with him when he met with you was fake, anyway. I don't know if that means there is no real manuscript or he just had the sense not to bring it with him."

"I told you he didn't really write a memoir," Erin pointed out, feeling vindicated.

"He might still have written one. We just don't have a copy of it. People in Maine said that he had written one."

"But no one ever read it," Erin suggested.

Terry nodded. "No one ever read it."

"That's what I figured."

"So, what exactly did you know about Kyle?" Terry asked curiously. He looked at Dave to ensure he stayed down and didn't try to attack anyone.

"He called Brandon one night. He'd hit someone while driving drunk. Brandon covered for him, gave him an alibi." A wave of nausea washed over Erin as she remembered how she had told Dave the story at dinner the night before. It was no wonder he'd been so pale. If Sheriff Wilmot hadn't come to get Erin when he did, and it had been up to Dave to walk her out to her car... alone, in the dark parking lot...

Dave didn't volunteer that Brandon had told him that Erin would cover for him too, would do whatever Brandon told her to. He had no way of knowing whether Erin had ever been faced with making that decision.

Terry looked at Mrs. Pooler. "And... I apologize for intruding in your house, Mrs...."

"Jane Pooler," she introduced herself with a bright smile. "And I think I can forgive the intrusion this once."

"This is Dave's 'Aunt Jane,'" Erin explained. "Only, they're not really related. Dave kind of... adopted her."

"More like took me hostage," Mrs. Pooler said. "Maybe now I can start going out again. If it's not too dangerous out there. Dave always told me..."

"It's safe. Officer Piper and the others keep Bald Eagle Falls safe," Erin assured her, putting aside any thoughts of the murders and violence she had been exposed to since moving to Bald Eagle Falls.

That was an anomaly.

Mrs. Pooler would be safe leaving her house to go to the grocery store, church, or bakery. She didn't need to live like the recluse Dave had forced her to be.

CHAPTER 42

"*I* don't really understand what happened," Vic said, shaking her head. "I mean… I thought that Dave had been eliminated as a suspect. How could he have had anything to do with Brandon's death? And how did he end up here, of all places? How could he and Erin both have ended up in the same small town by coincidence?"

"It wasn't a coincidence," Terry said. He'd explained it to Erin once already. Well, maybe twice. It was taking a lot of time and effort to unwind Dave's story, which was pretty convoluted. "Brandon Quayle *sent* Kyle Pinckney here to keep an eye on Erin. He held this hit-and-run accident over him and used it to blackmail him, to get him to do whatever Quayle wanted. It was a serious threat—Pinckney had killed a child in that accident. So he's been… *observing* Erin ever since she arrived in Bald Eagle Falls."

Erin shuddered. "Working at The Book Nook, watching me coming and going… I can't believe that none of us knew what kind of a guy he really was. That he was a criminal. He must have never let down his guard, never let anyone see him doing something out of character. It must have been really hard."

"Maybe he got to play at being the kind of guy he wanted to be," Vic suggested. "Not some egomaniac spy, I don't mean that, but… a nice guy. Always pleasant, helping out the old lady next door. Just an honest, straitlaced, quiet kind of guy."

"Maybe." Erin shook her head. "I don't know." She sipped her tea, thinking about it. What she knew about him or had learned from Terry's investigation. Someone who wanted to be good and enjoyed playing that role? Or someone who hated it and had exploded when Brandon showed his face in Bald Eagle Falls, letting out all of the built-up pressure from the last two years.

"But Dave—or Kyle—came to Bald Eagle Falls before Erin," Willie pointed out. "How did he swing that?"

"Even *I* didn't know I was coming to Bald Eagle Falls yet," Erin agreed. She could almost believe that he had psychic powers, like Reg pretended to. She'd seen some things when Reg had been around. Strange, inexplicable stuff. But she had never believed Reg was psychic.

"How did you find out about your inheritance?" Terry prompted with a smile. "When did you learn that Clementine had left you her tea shop?"

"Right before I came here. From Alton Summers."

"A private investigator."

"Yes."

"Who had been tracking you from one place to another and asking questions about you."

"Yes! Oh…" It became blindingly obvious to Erin. "He found Brandon. He asked about me after I had left Brandon, telling him about Clementine leaving me the house and the shop."

So Brandon had installed Kyle in Bald Eagle Falls to keep an eye on Erin and report back on what she was doing. Had Brandon known about her relationship with Terry? How the bakery was doing? For two years, he hadn't come to Bald Eagle Falls. He hadn't tried to take her away from Terry or to get in on the success of the bakery. He hadn't decided that he wanted to live in Bald Eagle Falls or that she should come back home to him.

And then, two years later, the emails. The claims of recovery from alcoholism. A memoir being published. A date to meet her in the park.

"Was he really sober?" she asked Terry. "When you talked to people back home… did he really give up drinking? Was he trying to make amends? Or was this just some big conspiracy to get me back? I don't understand what this was all about."

"According to friends back in Maine, yes. He had stopped drinking. As for the rest of it, I don't know. I think… saying he was going to publish a tell-all book and showing up to talk to Dave… that sounds like more blackmail. Not amends."

"Did Dave say what happened? That Brandon confronted him…?"

"He has a story. I can't get into the details of an ongoing investigation. And of course, his story is designed to make himself look good. He says he was… protecting others from Brandon's predatory behavior."

"Me?" Erin squeaked.

Terry shrugged. It was as good as acknowledging that was Dave's story.

Had Dave tried to protect her? Or just to protect himself and his own reputation? The life that he had built in Bald Eagle Falls while he had been following Brandon's directions. She wasn't sure she believed it had anything to do with her.

"The thing I want to know…" Vic put her teacup down on the table and leaned forward. "Is how and why did he move the body? How did he make it disappear so fast?"

Erin had been thinking about that. She had worked through several different scenarios, trying to find one that fit. Knowing that the killer had been Dave, who knew his way around the bookstore, helped. He hadn't had to carry the body up the stairs, past Erin or following her up when she had fled.

She'd heard noises when she had stepped into the building. She had thought that Naomi was downstairs because she'd heard movements.

"I think… he cleared boxes out of the elevator or loading dock and then went downstairs to get Brandon's body. Maybe he was even in the elevator when I saw Brandon. I couldn't do anything for him or get a cellphone signal, so I left. Dave got off the elevator and used it to take Brandon's body upstairs. Used a dolly, took him right out from the loading dock to his truck and was out of there when he heard the sirens."

"At that point," Terry chimed in, nodding his agreement, "he had no idea that Erin had been in the store, gone to the basement, and seen the body while he was getting ready to move it. He thought he was alone the whole time. So, the shock he showed when we told him that Erin had found a body in the basement of The Book Nook and then it had disappeared was real. He had no idea anyone else had been there and seen the body."

"And in the meantime, he'd already dumped it in Canyon Park because that was where Erin was supposed to meet Brandon? So it would make her look guilty if the police ever got access to her email," Vic suggested.

It was strange how clear it seemed once they knew Dave's relationship with Brandon.

"But how did he know that Brandon had emailed me to meet him there?" Erin asked.

"Brandon told him," Vic said. "Or emailed him about it too. Maybe it was supposed to be all three of you. But first, Brandon wanted to meet with Dave for some kind of debriefing."

"It's just all so bizarre." Erin shook her head. "I thought I had left all of this back in Maine when I moved to Bald Eagle Falls. That life was behind me. But all the time, Dave was watching me. Brandon knew exactly where I was and what I was doing. Sheriff Wilmot said that he thought I was the key to solving Brandon's murder. I thought he was way off base. But..."

"But there you were, right in the center of it," Terry finished.

Now that Brandon was gone and they knew who Dave was and he had been sent to the penitentiary pending trial, maybe now Erin's life could finally get back to normal. She could just be a baker and not worry about the past catching up with her.

Vic put her hand on Erin's shoulder and squeezed it lightly. She didn't say anything.

CHAPTER 43

*E*rin took the platter filled with waffles, cut into small wedge-shaped pieces and condiment cups of real maple syrup for dipping out to the front of the bakery, filled with the usual morning crowd.

"Okay! Here they are!"

"Are those the waffles you are going to enter in the contest?" little Peter Foster asked, his eyes wide.

"Yup. This is the big day. I want to see what people think of them before I enter the recipe into the contest."

"And you win a big waffle iron."

"Well, I'd sure like to. I don't know if I will or not! I'd have to have a pretty big ego to be sure that I could win it. But I've won some other contests, and I think these are really good. They have a chance, anyway."

"How big are the waffles that the big waffle iron makes?"

"Just regular sized," Erin made a circle with her hands to demonstrate. "But you can cook twenty waffles at once!"

"Oh, wow."

Erin passed the platter around to her customers, encouraging them to have a piece or two of the waffles and see what they thought. There were full mouths and *mmmm*'s of pleasure and nods that it was a good recipe. Erin stopped in front of Mrs. Pooler and held the platter before her. "These are 'Aunt Jane's Waffles,'" she said, "I hope they live up to their name."

"They look lovely. I'm sure they taste just as good as any I ever made," Mrs. Pooler said as she took a wedge of waffle and cup of maple syrup to test it herself.

Joshua had come with Mary Lou to the bakery, which was unusual. Roger was not with them, so Erin assumed that the care worker who visited twice a day was probably still with him. They each took a piece of waffle. Mary Lou did not help herself to the maple syrup, but took a bite of the plain waffle. She watched her diet very carefully, which Erin suspected was why she was so slim when most of the other women in Bald Eagle Falls of her age were thickening around the middle.

Joshua took both the waffle and the syrup. "I was wondering if we could get together, Miss Erin," he said politely. "So I could talk to you about Brandon Quayle and Dave Wolfe."

So that he could include her thoughts and background in whatever story he would be submitting to the Bald Eagle Falls weekly newspaper. Erin grimaced and looked around. "I'm pretty busy with things right now, the contest and everything. And getting ready for the next book club meeting. I don't really... I don't really want to talk about Brandon and our history."

"People will want to know. And maybe if it's in the paper, they won't have to come around here to bug you about it," Joshua coaxed.

"No. I don't think... I really don't want to, Josh. I'm sorry."

Mary Lou looked at Joshua and raised one brow, looking stern. Joshua shrugged. "Okay. I guess if you don't want to talk about it, you don't want to talk about it."

Mary Lou nodded her agreement.

"Cookie!" Traci Foster's high toddler voice rose over the chatter of the bakery customers. "Want cookie! Dat one!"

"It isn't cookie day," Mrs. Foster tried to explain to her. "We're here to try out Miss Erin's waffles. Come have a piece of waffle."

"No!" Traci shrieked and pounded on the glass of the display case. "Cookie!"

"If the kids don't want a waffle, they can have a cookie," Erin was quick to offer. She directed her words at Vic. "Go ahead and give her a cookie, if that's what she wants."

Vic nodded and followed Traci's directions to the exact cookie that she had to have.

"Dat one… dat one… no! Dat one! Yes!" She started to jump up and down. Vic handed the cookie over the counter to Mrs. Foster. "And the rest of you? Do you want a cookie or a waffle?"

Jodi also wanted a cookie, but Karen went with a waffle, like the grown-ups. Peter looked worried, trying to decide which he wanted.

"You don't really like pumpkin spice," Erin told him, remembering his reaction to pumpkin pie and gingerbread the previous Christmas. "So maybe you want to pick a cookie like the girls instead."

Peter looked around at the adults, shaking his head. He clearly didn't want to be one of the little kids. He wanted to do what the adults were doing. "I'll try a waffle."

"Are you sure? You don't have to. You can pick out something else."

"No, I'll try."

Erin lowered the platter so that he could reach it. He took a wedge of waffle and cup of maple syrup, and carefully dunked the corner of the waffle into the syrup. He bit off the corner he had dunked, and chewed and swallowed. Erin waited for his verdict. "I like it!"

"You do? Wow! I really do have to enter it into the contest."

Peter nodded. "You'll win. I know you will."

"Well, thank you for your confidence!"

The bells over the door jingled, and Erin looked over to see who it was. It was Naomi, looking somewhat harried, even though The Book Nook was not due to open for a couple more hours. She pushed a stray lock of hair back over her ear.

"I just had to come over to try your new recipe."

"That's so sweet! You look like you're pretty busy over there at the bookstore."

"Yes! It's kind of crazy with Dave being gone. I thought we would have plenty of staff to cover his shifts for a while, but I didn't realize how much time he was putting in. I'll need to fill his position soon, because I can't cover it all without him."

Erin nodded. She looked over at Mrs. Foster. "Is Mr. Foster still looking for something? Maybe he could put in an application."

"Well, yes. He is," Mrs. Foster agreed, bouncing baby Allan in his sling. She looked over at Naomi. "Do you think that you would consider him? He doesn't have any experience in a bookstore."

"I can train, if he is willing to learn."

"Okay! I'll tell him to bring his resume by."

Naomi nodded her agreement. "I need someone in there pretty quickly, so the sooner, the better!"

Naomi only stayed long enough to try a piece of waffle and render her opinion that, as Peter had said, the waffles should be entered into the contest. Then she headed back over to her own store.

Peter had a huge, Cheshire cat grin, and he helped his mother to get the girls rounded up. Erin laughed at his expression. "What's that about?"

"If Dad worked at the bookstore, he'd be able to come over to the bakery all the time," Peter observed.

Erin laughed. Mrs. Foster ruffled Peter's hair. "Your father is *not* spending his entire paycheck on gluten-free cookies!"

Peter just smiled. "And waffles."

Did you enjoy this book? Reviews and recommendations are vital to making a book successful.

Please leave a review at your favorite book store or review site and share it with your friends.

Don't miss the following bonus material:
Sign up for mailing list to get a free ebook
Read a sneak preview chapter
Other books by P.D. Workman
Learn more about the author

Sign up for my mailing list at pdworkman.com and get
Gluten-Free Murder for free!

Download a sweet mystery for free

PREVIEW OF MURDER MERINGUE PIE

CHAPTER 1

$\mathcal{I}$t was Sunday morning, so Erin was having a relaxed breakfast with Terry rather than having to be at the bakery in the wee hours of the morning to bake bread and get everything ready for the day.

When she had first moved to Bald Eagle Falls, she had been surprised and taken aback by the insistence of the women in the community that the bakery could not be open on Sunday, because that would be breaking the Sabbath. It didn't matter that Erin was an atheist—that was a whole other problem—she was still expected to comply with the unofficial town by-law on the matter.

But that wasn't the most confusing part. They had been excited when she inherited the storefront from her Aunt Clementine, who had run it as a tea shop until her health began to fail. They hoped Erin would reinstate the ladies' tea after church services. She couldn't open the bakery to sell her gluten-free goods that day, but she was expected to open for a couple of hours and supply tea and treats for the church ladies.

She'd been not only confused, but a little resentful of the idea to begin with. But now, a couple of years in, she enjoyed the tradition. It meant that she did not have to get up early on Sunday, even on the days she took the Sunday shift, and she enjoyed meeting with the ladies of the community in something other than a baker/customer relationship.

Today, Bella was taking the shift for the ladies' tea, so Erin and Vic did not have to be there. And it was one of those rare days when Erin and Terry were both home all day—or could go out and could spend the whole day together.

"Do you want to go into the city?" Terry asked. "We could go to a movie, dinner, run some errands…?"

Erin was trying to run her errands during the week so that she could have Sunday to relax instead of chasing after bakery supplies and getting caught up on grocery shopping and anything else she needed to do, ending up more exhausted by the end of her "day of rest" than if she had gone to work.

But a movie and dinner with her "Officer Handsome" sounded nice.

"Maybe," she agreed. "But no shopping."

"That's fine with me," Terry agreed with a smile that brought out the dimple on his stubbly cheek. He washed his toast down with a sip of coffee. "I'm quite happy to avoid malls and line-ups."

Erin and Terry heard a bang from the backyard and, looking out the kitchen window, saw Willie storming down the steps from Vic's loft apartment over the garage. Without another word, he hopped into his truck, slammed the door shut, and drove away with his tires spinning in the gravel. Erin watched with concern as he left.

"Uh-oh. That doesn't look good," Terry observed.

Erin looked away from the window, embarrassed. She didn't want to pry into Vic's private life. She didn't want to be that nosy neighbor who was always craning her neck to see what was happening.

"None of our business."

Terry gave a nod of agreement. As a law enforcement officer in Bald Eagle Falls, he knew which relationships were most likely to be volatile. He'd never been called to Vic's or Willie's residences to deal with a domestic dispute. They might shout, argue, or slam doors, but it had never escalated to violence as far as Erin knew. She'd never seen any indication of physical abuse in the relationship. They were just two very passionate people who didn't hold anything back.

The door to Vic's apartment opened again, and this time it was Vic's tall, willowy figure. She let Nilla out and locked the door behind her, then came down the stairs at a more sedate pace than Willie had. She let Nilla into the dog run to do his business, and then joined Erin and Terry in the kitchen.

"Mornin' ya'll."

"Good morning." Erin scratched Nilla's ears and chin when the fluffy white dog ran over to her. K9, Terry's partner, heard the little dog running around the kitchen and came to investigate. The shepherd and the small dog sniffed each other and ran to the back door to be let out. Vic let them out to play. She sighed and sat down at the table. She ran a hand through her long blond hair, hanging loose instead of in a bun like she wore it when baking at Auntie Clem's. It was the opposite of Erin's short, dark hair that never stayed in place like it was supposed to. Erin poured hot water from the teapot into Vic's cup and Vic chose a teabag from the selection on the table.

"That man." She shook her head. "I love him dearly, but he does have a temper."

"Mmm." Erin didn't ask for the details of their argument.

"What's going on?" Terry apparently didn't have the same compunctions. And Erin supposed that if Vic didn't want to talk about it, she wouldn't have brought it up or would just tell Terry it was none of his business.

"I don't rightly know. He's been on edge all weekend. But it isn't anything to do with us. It's just… probably work, I guess. The mines would be my best guess. But he hasn't said. He doesn't want to talk about it, but then he gets a call or text and just goes off like that." She motioned toward the backyard.

So it wasn't an argument. It was something different, an outside irritant. "Well, I hope he doesn't take it out on you. I always feel like slamming doors are aimed at me, even if they aren't. It's hard not to take your partner's anger personally."

Vic nodded. "It gets my back up," she admitted. "I get it; I know he's mad at something else, but I'm the only one there to hear him complaining or slamming doors. So I can't help feeling like he's aiming the gun in the wrong direction."

"You don't know what's going on with work that's bothering him?"

"He doesn't share that stuff. Never has. The closest I get to his mining operations is when we go spelunking together."

Erin's transgender employee was far more adventurous than Erin was. Caves and tunnels underground were *not* Erin's thing. She wouldn't have expected Vic to still be interested in spelunking after being caught in a tunnel collapse, but Vic and Willie had been right back at it as soon as they had their casts off. It wasn't like it had been a natural collapse. But the fact that there were people out there who would intentionally set explosives to trap or kill someone else did not reassure Erin. That was just one more good reason to stay away from caves. It had been a long time before she could even look into a cave, let alone walk a few steps into one. And a tunnel or shaft where she would have to crawl... no way. No, thank you.

"Well, whatever bee Willie has got in his bonnet, I hope he deals with it soon," she told Vic.

"Me too, sister." Vic sipped her tea. "Me too."

Monday afternoon, Vic and Charley, Erin's half-sister, helped Erin carefully pack several pies for a catering order.

"Lemon meringue does not travel well," Vic worried. "All you need to do is go over one bump, and the tops will all be sticking to the boxes."

"I'll go slowly," Charley promised. "No potholes."

Erin had seen Charley drive before. She wasn't sure the woman knew the meaning of "slowly" or "carefully." She could just see Charley unloading the boxes at their destination and finding that all of the meringues were pasted to the tops of the boxes.

"I really don't want these to be wrecked when you get there," she fussed. "I should have told them no. Made them go with apple pie or something with a top crust that would travel better."

"I'll get them there in one piece," Charley assured her. "You don't have to worry about it. Clive William Fontainebleau III shall have his pies."

"If he's happy with the results, he could be a profitable client. I don't know how many of these fancy parties he holds, but if we can supply him with desserts regularly, it could be lucrative."

"Don't pin your hopes on it," Charley warned. "I know guys like this. They're not loyal to one supplier. He'll go wherever he can get the best deal. And he'll keep asking for a lower price until you're not making anything."

Erin frowned. She hoped it wasn't true. But she hadn't heard many good things about Mr. Fontainebleau, so she couldn't argue with Charley's assessment.

"So you don't think it will be worth it?"

"I'll tell you what you do," Charley said. "You raise your prices next time. Tell him that they are *artisanal* pies. That he won't get quality product like that from anyone else. Especially not gluten-free. If he wants high-quality, gluten-free pies, you are the only game in town. Anywhere in the state, in fact."

Erin's cheeks warmed. "I couldn't do that."

"That's what you've got to do. Make him respect you. Make him want pies from Auntie Clem's Bakery and nowhere else, because no one else even compares. Why do you think guys like him buy Rolexes and Cartiers? It isn't because they tell the time better than any department store wristwatch. He wants people to see that he is willing to pay for the very best."

"I don't know." Erin slowly boxed another pie. "I'll think about it."

"Whatever you do, *don't* lower your prices. No matter where he says he is going to go instead."

Erin pressed her lips together, thinking about it. Charley was probably right. Charley was the one who had experience in dealing with bigshots like Fontainebleau. She should take Charley's advice.

"You do your part and get them there in one piece. Then… maybe I'll get you to help with any negotiations too. I'm not sure I can stand up to a guy like that. Or his office manager, since I never talked to Mr. Fontainebleau directly."

"I'll take care of it," Charley agreed. "You can count on me."

~

Peter Foster showed up at Auntie Clem's Bakery after school had let out, without his mother and siblings. Erin had rarely seen him by himself, though she knew that he had sometimes been allowed to go to the store to pick up something his mother needed when she had been pregnant and on bed rest. The young boy looked at the cookies in the display case, standing tall and looking important.

"Hi, Peter. How's it going?"

He smiled, showing off the gaps in his teeth. "Good."

"Are you here for a Kid's Club cookie, or are you buying something? I have something in the back for you if you need it…"

The Foster family didn't normally take advantage of Erin's offer of free day-old bread. But they'd been struggling lately, and Erin hoped they would take what they needed.

"I'm just looking," Peter told her archly. "I'm going to visit my dad at the bookstore."

"Oh, I see. How is he enjoying working there?"

"He says that Mrs. Naomi is a good boss. And mom is glad that he *finally* has something stable since they cut back his hours at the other job."

"I'm sure it's a big relief for her. Especially since she wanted to be able to stay home with the little ones."

Peter nodded his agreement. "It's a good thing that you told Mrs. Naomi that Dad was looking for something. You're a good friend."

"Thank you. I'm glad I could help. Are you sure you don't want your kid's club cookie?"

"No. I'll get mine one day when I bring the girls."

"Oh, okay. That sounds good, then. Can I walk with you over to The Book Nook?"

"I don't need you to. I know where it is."

"I know, but I need to talk to Naomi about the book club."

Peter shrugged. "Okay. You can come over with me."

Erin trailed Peter down the street to The Book Nook and followed him in. The bells over the door jingled to announce their arrival. Both Naomi and Mr. Foster looked up from shelving books to greet them.

"Well, there's my son," Mrs. Foster said, smiling. "School's out already?"

"Yes. You know I wouldn't skip!"

"That's what they all say. And Miss Erin. How are you?"

"Good. Peter just stopped to say hello to me at Auntie Clem's, and I needed to talk to Naomi about the book club, so we came over together."

Mr. Foster nodded, looking calm and relaxed about this. Erin was glad she hadn't gotten Peter into trouble, but she wanted to ensure that his parents knew where he was and were okay with it. They were strict about some things and lenient about others, and Erin hadn't quite figured out where the line was. She didn't want to be accused of encouraging Peter to do anything he wasn't supposed to.

Erin felt her phone vibrating, so the next time she went into the kitchen to take a tray of cookies out of the oven, she pulled her phone out and looked at it. Charley had texted her. Opening the text, Erin saw the pies that she had sent over for the party all laid out on a black granite counter, with Charley's comment that they had gotten there safe and sound, with no breakage or meringue stuck to the top of the boxes they had transported them in. The golden peaks on the white meringue looked picture-perfect.

Mr. Fontainebleau can eat pie to his heart's content

Erin was relieved. She texted Charley a heartfelt thank you and returned to the front of the shop to let Vic know they had arrived safely.

"See?" Vic said. "All that worry for nothing. Everything went smoothly. He's sure to call you back for another job."

Murder Meringue Pie, Book 21 of the Auntie Clem's Bakery series by P.D. Workman can be purchased at pdworkman.com

ABOUT THE AUTHOR

P.D. Workman is a USA Today Bestselling author, winner of several awards from Library Services for Youth in Custody and the InD'tale Magazine's Crowned Heart award, and has published over 100 mystery/suspense/thriller and young adult books, including stand alones and these series: Auntie Clem's Bakery cozy mysteries, Reg Rawlins Psychic Investigator paranormal mysteries, Zachary Goldman Mysteries (PI), Kenzie Kirsch Medical Thrillers, Parks Pat Mysteries (police procedural), and YA series: Tamara's Teardrops, Between the Cracks, and Breaking the Pattern.

Workman loves writing about the underdog, who the reader may love or hate. She has been praised for her realistic details, deep characterization, and sensitive handling of the serious social issues that appear in all of her stories, from light cozy mysteries through to darker, grittier young adult and mystery/suspense books.

P. D. Workman, does not shy from probing the deep psychological scars of childhood trauma, mental illness, and addiction. Also characteristic of this author, these extremely sensitive issues are explored with extensive empathy, described with incredible clarity, and portrayed with profound insight.

— —KIM, GOODREADS REVIEWER

Some of Workman's titles have been translated into Spanish, French, Portuguese, German, and Italian.

Workman began writing at an early age and is a prolific reader as well as writer. She is also passionate about teaching and learning, expresses her creativity through art and cooking, and loves exploring the Calgary parks and green spaces where the Parks Pat Mysteries are set. She was a legal assistant for many years and has done extensive charitable work.

Workman was born and raised in Alberta, Canada, and is married with one adult son.

Please visit P.D. Workman at pdworkman.com to see what else she is working on, to join her mailing list, and to link to her social networks.

If you enjoyed this book, please take the time to recommend it to other purchasers with a review or star rating and share it with your friends!

tiktok.com/@pdworkmanauthor

facebook.com/pdworkmanauthor

twitter.com/pdworkmanauthor

instagram.com/pdworkmanauthor

amazon.com/author/pdworkman

bookbub.com/authors/p-d-workman

goodreads.com/pdworkman

linkedin.com/in/pdworkman

pinterest.com/pdworkmanauthor

youtube.com/pdworkman

Find P.D. Workman's books at

PDWORKMAN.COM

Scan the QR code below

www.ingramcontent.com/pod-product-compliance
Lightning Source LLC
Chambersburg PA
CBHW050757080726
47590CB00020B/410